MURDER ON THE
MINNEAPOLIS

Flora Maguire, a young governess, is on her way home on the SS *Minneapolis* after the wedding of her employer's daughter. She meets the charming Bunny Harrington on deck on the first night and is conscious of her status among the first-class passengers. Flora finds the body of a man at the bottom of a companionway and when his death is pronounced as an accident, she is not convinced and is driven to find out the truth. Following a near drowning during a storm and a second murder, the hunt is on for the killer. Will Flora be able to protect Edward, her charge, as well as herself?

MURDER ON THE MINNEAPOLIS

by

Anita Davison

Magna Large Print Books
Long Preston, North Yorkshire,
BD23 4ND, England.

British Library Cataloguing in Publication Data.

Davison, Anita
    Murder on the Minneapolis.

    A catalogue record of this book is
    available from the British Library

    ISBN   978-0-7505-4325-5

First published in Great Britain 2015 by Buried River,
an imprint of Robert Hale Ltd.

Published in Large Print 2016 by arrangement with
Robert Hale Limited

Magna Large Print is an imprint of Library Magna Books Ltd.

Printed and bound in Great Britain by
T.J. (International) Ltd., Cornwall, PL28 8RW

Chapter 1

Day One – Saturday

On Pier 39, well-wishers stood four deep beneath a sea of colourful hats wide as sailboats, waving handkerchiefs or crying into them. Beside the bottom of the gangplank, an enthusiastic conductor on a podium led a brass band in *The Washington Post March*. Porters strained behind trolleys while couples strolled the decks, issuing braying instructions for the disposition of their luggage.

'It's huge!' Flora said, her foot tapping in time to the music. She had seen ocean-going steamers before, even travelled on one, yet there was something awe-inspiring about the SS *Minneapolis*, with her gleaming black hull, bright red smoke stack and taut metal winch lines draped with bunting.

'Six hundred feet long, and 13,400 tonnes,' Eddy read from the brochure that had been his constant companion for the past week. 'She's a first class only steamship, carrying a smaller than usual complement of passengers this trip.' He swiped a hand across eyes that looked suspiciously wet as he tucked the booklet back into his pocket.

'Eddy.' Flora's hand hovered above his shoulder without making contact. 'I'm sorry your parents didn't stay to say goodbye. They had a train to catch.'

'They didn't even bother to get out of the carriage.' Eddy sniffed, his morose glare trained on the clamour of emotional farewells on the quayside. Tall and handsome for a boy of thirteen, Edward, Viscount Trent was still very much a child.

'You're very important to your father, Eddy, you're his heir, remember.'

'I would sooner be just his son.' He turned and pounded up the gangplank, headed for the metal companionway that led up to the promenade deck.

Flora kept her eyes on his sandy hair as it bobbed amongst the mass of passengers crowding the deck. Following, she eased through the press of bodies, murmuring repeated 'excuse me's'.

She tried to imagine how she would feel, if at thirteen, her parents had packed her off home while they toured the Eastern states. The question was moot, for her mother had died when she was young and, as Lord Vaughn's head butler, her father didn't possess the resources to send her anywhere.

Flora had resigned herself long ago to viewing the peripatetic lives of the English aristocracy from the sidelines.

When she reached the top of the companionway, her attention snagged on a woman of about her own age in a claret wool travelling coat with mutton leg sleeves beneath the deck canopy who appeared to be arguing with a man.

Her arrestingly pretty features hardened, her fists clenched at her sides in barely restrained anger. The object of her fury was older, with olive

6

skin and thick eyebrows that met in the middle. He accepted her tirade in silence, repeatedly easing his collar away from his throat with a finger.

Her message delivered, the lady shot him a final hard glare, swivelled on her heel and stalked away. The man raised a lit cheroot he held behind his back, inhaled deeply then shot the smoke in a straight upward stream. He turned and leaned both forearms on the rail, shoulders down and his eyes closed as if the encounter had drained him.

His yellow-stained fingers and badly cut hair made Flora wonder what he could have to say to the immaculate girl in her expensive clothes.

'Come on, Flora,' Eddy called, his sullenness forgotten. 'Our suite is over here!' His last words were drowned by the ship's horn sounding a long, plaintive note. Flora felt a shiver of excitement at the renewed burst of cheers from the quayside, accompanied by a cacophony of horns, hooters and whistles.

They were leaving.

The boards beneath her feet vibrated, while far below, the twin screw steam engines thrummed into pulsing, whirring life as the vast ship eased away from the pier and swung into mid-river.

'There's the pilot boat!' Eddy pointed when she reached him.

She followed his gaze to where a tiny vessel ran fast and straight towards the bow, disappearing out of sight beneath the hull. A flotilla of other small vessels jostled like minnows round a whale, and with an arm raised in perpetual salute, the Statue of Liberty slid by on Bedloe Island while lights blinked on in the receding city as dusk approached.

'Goodbye, New York,' Flora said on a sigh.

'Goodbye, Meely,' Eddy whispered, using his childish nickname for his favourite sister.

'You'll see her again one day,' Flora said. 'Perhaps once you have finished school, or Lady Amelia and her husband will come to England?'

'That won't be for ages.' Eddy snorted.

'I've had a wonderful time on this trip. I'm thrilled your parents invited me.' Flora lightened her tone, aware another platitude would simply annoy him. 'I would never have had the opportunity to see America otherwise.'

Invited was a somewhat generous term, for Lady Vaughn had included Flora as a temporary lady's maid for her bride-to-be daughter. With Lady Amelia now safely married, Flora had been charged with escorting Eddy home.

'Why do I have to go back to rainy old England, and school?' Eddy shoved a hand through his untidy hair.

'School is a fact of life.' She slipped an arm round his shoulders in a one-armed hug; the only sort he allowed these days. 'Which suite is ours?'

He cocked his chin at the line of white doors behind them. 'That one.'

Flora's gaze took in a hand-written label in a brass frame attached to the nearest door, the words, *Edward, Viscount Trent and Miss Flora Maguire,* in cursive script, set above a brass doorbell.

In the cream and white panelled sitting room, a maid bustled between their open steamer trunks and the bedrooms, tutting good-naturedly when

8

Eddy got in her way in his bid to try out the beds, open drawers and peer into cupboards. Two windows overlooked the covered promenade deck, while doors at either side of the room led to two compact bedrooms, each with a tiny bathroom with polished brass taps and gleaming mirrors.

Discarding her hat onto her bed, Flora smiled as she ran a hand across the soft white coverlet with its pattern of red bud roses. This luxurious new suite was to be her home for the next eight days, when she would be at no one's beck and call but Eddy's.

'Did you know there's a wireless telegraphy room on board, Flora?' Eddy leaned against the door frame. 'The "Minne" class ships are among the first to have one. Do you think they'll let me see how it works?'

'I don't see why not. We could ask the purser.' Flora closed the door behind her and dropped a swift kiss on his cheek just as trumpets sounded from outside. 'Goodness, what was that noise?'

'Dinner!' Eddy scrubbed at his cheek with a fist as if removing her kiss. 'I'm starving. Good job no one dresses on the first night.'

He slicked down his hair with both hands then gave her a swift up and down look. 'Hurry up and change, Flora, or we'll be late.'

The creeping worry that had plagued her all day found a voice as Flora caught sight of her reflection in the mirror above the mantle. Her cinched-waist grey jacket above a matching straight skirt conveyed an image of a new century professional woman, though nothing like the lady passengers in their pastel-coloured silk moiré gowns and furs.

'I'm not very hungry. You go along on your own.' She hoped her stomach wouldn't growl, making her a liar.

'Are you sure?' Eddy peered at the printed menu card on the mantle. 'It's roast lamb, and Charlotte Russe.'

'It's been such a busy day what with all the packing.' She feigned a yawn. 'I'll ask the stewardess to bring me something here.'

'If you're sure.' Eddy frowned, his hand already on the door handle. Not much kept him from a meal. 'I'll see you later, then.'

The door closed behind him at the same second the stewardess appeared from Eddy's bedroom. 'I've finished now, miss. Is there anything else?'

'Might I have a tray sent in for supper?' Flora asked. 'Something light, perhaps?'

'Of course, miss, I'll arrange it straight away.' She pronounced it 'awee', revealing her Celtic origins.

Left alone, Flora chastised herself. Her excuse to Eddy seemed feeble now, combined with the guilt at having left him to face a room full of strangers on his own. Not that such a prospect would bother Viscount Trent, who took social occasions in his stride. In one sense she was proud of his confidence, even took credit for it, but it only served to emphasize the differences in their worlds.

The *Minneapolis* was a first class only ship, thus Flora couldn't simply disappear into a third class dining room like she had done on the outward voyage.

In what seemed like no time at all, the stewardess returned with a fluffy omelette on a plate, a selection of tiny biscuits, fruit and cheese together with a pot of aromatic coffee on a tray, all of which Flora demolished in half the time it took to arrive.

Anticipating a solitary stroll on deck before Eddy returned, she let herself out of the suite into the internal corridor that ran the length of the ship. At the stern end, she pushed through a glazed door into a staircase hall grand enough for a London hotel.

A crewman saluted her as she emerged onto the boat deck, the rhythmic whoosh of the ocean below the only indication the vessel was moving. Muted strains of orchestra music came from the stern dining room. A soft glow of yellow light from the long windows reflected on the water.

Flora shivered as a gust of cold air lifted the hair at her temples. Glad of her shawl, she headed for the aft deck, where land was no more than a blur on the horizon beneath the purple and navy of a darkening sky.

Apart from steamer chairs and lifeboats, the boat deck stood empty but for a square, bulky shape under canvas, fastened down with thick ropes.

Flora recalled from Eddy's lecture that the SS *Minneapolis* was designed to carry livestock, but sailed in ballast this trip, used to keep the vessel upright and discarded when unloaded.

A few inches taller than herself, the object stood several feet wide and distinctly square, but with vague shapes protruding from the front; that

11

it was ballast seemed unlikely.

With a swift backwards glance to ensure she was not observed, Flora eased into a gap between the swaddled shape and a stack of fenders piled into the space beneath the companionway. The oiled canvas proved heavier than she imagined, but a determined tug revealed a rubber wheel more than two inches thick beneath a curve of black-painted metal. Smaller than a cartwheel, the wooden section was also painted, in cream with thick spokes picked out in brown; some sort of wheeled cart, but much sturdier.

'Magnificent, isn't it?' a male voice said at her shoulder.

Flora jumped back, her head colliding with the metal support that sent a sharp pain through the crown of her head. She raised her hand to the sore spot, turning to where a young man stood, his feet splayed and both hands tucked into the pockets of a dinner suit. His tie lay undone, collar open on his throat and his fair hair in disarray from the evening breeze. Penetrating brown eyes behind a pair of rimless spectacles regarded her with unnerving intensity.

And he was laughing.

A reprimand rose to her lips, suppressed when he removed his hand from his pocket and held it out, whether to draw her from beneath the metal support, or to shake hers, she wasn't sure.

'I cannot tell,' Flora snapped, taking small revenge by ignoring his hand. 'Whatever it might be is covered by this canvas sheet.'

'Quite right. And I shouldn't laugh, should I?

I've simply never seen someone look so guilty, and yet so angry at the same time.'

'Next time,' Flora said carefully, 'I would appreciate some sort of warning.'

'Next time?' His lips twitched. 'By that should I assume you make a habit of skulking round ships in search of treasure? Because if so, you do know that makes you a pirate?'

'I beg your pardon?' Flora tucked in her chin, frowning. Either her throbbing head was making her dizzy, or he was deranged.

'I've never met a pirate,' he chattered on. 'But as I always say, life is an adventure.' He thrust out his hand again. 'Bunny Harrington, pleased to meet you.'

Gingerly, she accepted his hand, startled at how firm and warm his grip was in hers. Her pulse raced uncomfortably, and she snatched back her hand.

'Actually it's a nickname,' he said in response to her surprised start. 'My real one is worse.' He eased her from beneath the overhang with one hand, his other at her waist. 'Do you have a particular interest in motor cars?'

'Is that what this is? One of those horseless carriages?' Her thoughts flowed again, though with less clarity than normal, hampered by her throbbing scalp.

'Indeed, yes. Would you like to see her?'

Before she could answer he had hauled the canvas aside, revealing what resembled a scaled-down hansom cab, but on four wheels as opposed to two, with a fifth wheel on a pole behind a sheet of glass where the driver should be. Instead of traces for a horse, sat a rectangular metal box with rounded corners.

'It's, um – quite impressive.' Flora stared, fascinated. 'This is yours?'

'She's a Panhard-Levassor Landaulet. Isn't she magnificent?' He ran a hand gently over the fender in a caress.

'They make these in America?' Flora asked, no longer afraid a furious passenger was about to accost them. Following his example, she stroked the caramel paintwork, surprised to find it was smooth as glass beneath her fingers.

'This particular masterpiece is French.' He adjusted his glasses by a sidebar. 'Had her shipped over in the autumn to show to the Duryea Motor Wagon Company.'

'And it really goes all by itself?' Flora had seen pictures in the *London Illustrated News* of motor cars, but she had never seen one.

'Not exactly.' His bemused frown made him look even more attractive. 'She's powered by a front-mounted engine with rear wheel drive, a sliding-gear transmission–' His mouth closed with a snap. 'Well, never mind all that, I'm sure it's of no interest to you.' He pushed a hand through his hair, revealing a well-defined brow and arched eyebrows. 'Besides, I still don't know your name.'

'Um – it's Flora. Flora Maguire,' she stammered, disarmed by the intensity of his stare.

'Delighted to meet you, Miss Maguire.'

'What are you going to do with the horseless carriage once you are back in England?'

'I plan to manufacture similar vehicles. Not the first to do so, you understand. The Daimler

14

Company beat me to that particular accolade. At present, I'm seeking partners to provide the engineering expertise, while I–' He checked himself again with a self-conscious cough. 'I do apologize, but when I get started, there's no stopping me.'

'I'm fascinated, but this is all quite new to me, I'm afraid.' Flora bent to study the front mounted lamps that looked like eyes peering back at her. 'It looks as if it has a personality.'

'Splendid!' His face lit up like a schoolboy's. 'I'm so glad you see it too. Most people think it's ridiculous that I should attribute a character to a pile of metal, wood and rubber.' He leaned towards her, his breath warm on her cheek, 'I've named her Matilda.'

'That's not so outrageous.' Flora closed her eyes briefly, enjoying his closeness, though he was a stranger. 'After all, they call boats "she" and give them feminine names.'

'Exactly.'

'There you are, Flora.' Eddy's rapid footsteps clattered across the boards. 'I've been searching for you everywhere. I thought you'd fallen overboard.'

'There's no need for melodrama, Eddy.' Flora's governess tone emerged by habit. 'I was merely taking a walk when I happened to meet Mr Harrington here.'

Eddy wasn't listening. 'Golly, it's a motor car.' He eased between them, his feet trampling the canvas to get to the vehicle.

'A Panhard-Leva-um,' Flora began, failing miserably in her attempt to display her knowledge.

'Panhard-Levassor Landaulet,' Bunny corrected, following Eddy's progress round to the rear.

'Mr Harrington plans to open a factory in England making them,' Flora said, wondering when, if ever, she would be able to call him Bunny. Then remembered he hadn't asked her to.

'Well, perhaps not these,' Bunny said. 'I hope to make one from a design of my own.'

Eddy's head appeared above the rear canopy. 'Do you have your designs with you?'

'I do as a matter of fact. I would be happy to show them to you sometime.'

'Oh, yes please.' Eddy ran a hand along the bodywork as he circled the motor car, firing rapid questions, while Bunny responded with enthusiasm.

Flora stepped back, an observer to these two males, who, though physically dissimilar, their confident air of knowing their own place in the world marked them as from the same mould.

She began to feel invisible; rarely remembered and easily replaced. Lord Vaughn called the housemaid who made up the fires Molly, despite the fact Molly had left two years before and her post had been held by several others since.

The night air had grown colder and goose bumps erupted on Flora's arms beneath her shawl. She cleared her throat. 'Eddy, I think we should leave Mr Harrington in peace. Perhaps, he will allow you to see the motor car another time?'

'Of-of course. Any time he wishes.' Bunny opened his mouth as if on the verge of saying something, but changed his mind and closed it again.

'Come along, Eddy.' Flora strode away, aware of Bunny's perplexed stare boring into her back.

'What did you think of Mr Harrington?' Eddy caught up with her on the metal steps up to the promenade deck.

'He seems pleasant enough.'

'I think he's a really good chap.' His voice held disappointment at her lack of enthusiasm.

'Because he has a motor car?'

'No. I had a long talk with him at dinner.' Eddy opened the door of their suite, standing aside to let her enter. 'He's seated at our table.'

Chapter 2

Over cups of hot cocoa delivered by the stewardess, Flora anticipated her next encounter with Bunny Harrington would be at breakfast. He would have concluded by now she wasn't simply another passenger, and secretly hoped it would make no difference.

Eddy hovered at her shoulder, shuffling his feet, a well-known precursor to a confession.

'Isn't it time you got ready for bed, Eddy?'

'In a minute, I wanted to ask you something first. There's this grand chap on our table at dinner tonight. His name is Ozymandias.'

'Really?' Flora raised her brows. 'Does his mother have a fondness for Shelley by any chance?'

'What?' Eddy frowned.

'Don't say, "what" Eddy. Say "pardon".' She gathered their empty cups onto a tray. '"I met a traveller from an antique land,"' she quoted.

'I don't like poetry. It's sissy.' He wrinkled his nose. 'Besides, he likes to be called Ozzy. It was that old lady's suggestion. Mrs Penry-Jones.'

'What was?' Flora looked up at him and frowned. 'Calling him Ozzy?'

'No, not that.' He rolled his eyes. 'She said Ozzy and me ought to take meals with the other young people on board and not in the main dining room.'

Flora whipped round to face him. 'This Mrs Penry-something said that? How presumptuous of her. I've a good mind to–'

'No, Flora, really.' Eddy bounced on his heels. 'Mrs Gilmore, that's Ozzy's mother, was annoyed too, but Ozzy said there'll be other boys our age there. They eat an hour earlier than the other passengers.'

An image of a woman with a thrusting bosom and chicken-lipped mouth puckered like a schoolteacher filled Flora's head.

'I'd rather eat with the other boys, Flora, honestly,' Eddy went on. 'The old people are stuffy and spent the entire time at dinner discussing whether or not McKinley will be re-elected as President. I'll have more fun with Ozzy. He's a trump.'

'I'm glad you've found a friend of whom you think so highly.' Flora placed the tray on the bureau by the door ready for the stewardess to collect. 'Incidentally, did this Mrs Penry-Jones happen to have an opinion about where gover-

18

nesses should eat?'

'That's an odd question.' Eddy tucked in his chin and regarded her with his head on one side. 'Papa bought you a ticket. You've every right to eat with the other passengers.'

'Sorry, I didn't mean to whine.' She smoothed his hair where it stuck up at the back. 'If that's what you prefer, then it's fine with me. Now go to bed, it's after ten o'clock.'

'Gosh, thanks, Flora. Goodnight.'

She released a sigh as his bedroom door banged shut. Now she would have to face all those stuffy people on her own.

Flora woke with a start, then lay still in the darkness, relieved only by a thin beam of light beneath the door from a lamp left on in the sitting room.

The thump that had woken her came again, as if something had been thrown against the bulkhead above her head. Pushing her hair away from her face, she flicked on the bedside light and peered at the hands on her travelling clock.

Twenty minutes past midnight.

Sighing, she flopped back against the pillows, when a man's voice came clearly through the bedroom wall.

'Things change...'

'...I thought we agreed...' a high, female voice said.

Flora drew her knees up into a crouch and pressed her ear to the bulkhead. A brief surge of shame ran through her, immediately suppressed. Anyone vociferous enough to wake her in the middle of the night must expect eavesdropping.

19

In a lower, more menacing timbre, the man next door spoke again, although Flora couldn't make out the words.

Then a door slammed, followed by silence. No rapid footsteps, or enraged sobbing, just the tick of the mantle clock that now read 12.26.

Muttering to herself about the selfishness of others, Flora turned over, and slapped the pillows into submission in an effort to settle back to sleep.

Raised voices were a common occurrence at Cleeve Abbey, where Lord and Lady Vaughn's arguments were legendary. Apart from a stifled giggle or two amongst the younger housemaids, nothing was said about the pieces of broken china or glass left on floors.

The night passed slowly, alternating with periods of wakeful restlessness, accompanied by the persistent low thrum of the engines below.

When she woke, her cabin was bathed in weak daylight, although still unsociably early. With no pressing need to rise, she relaxed, enjoying the comfort of the soft mattress and crisp linen.

A vague recollection of shouts from the cabin next door came back to her. Had she dreamed it? What she did recall with clarity was the charming young man with the uninhibited laugh she had met on deck, whose eyes had a way of looking right into her soul.

A warm flush spread through her when she recalled her abruptness towards him when Eddy arrived. Annoyed, but resigned, she threw off the bedclothes and padded to the bathroom. She had simply saved him the embarrassment of having flirted with a governess.

He would thank her later.

Day Two – Sunday

After the luxury of a hot bath where the water geyser didn't splutter and bang like her one at home, Flora dressed, then eased open the door of Eddy's room. He lay spread-eagled among rumpled covers, snoring gently.

The stewardess wouldn't arrive with morning tea for almost an hour, so throwing a shawl around her shoulders, Flora let herself out onto the promenade deck, where a sprinkling of white-flecked waves below a milky blue sky augured the beginning of a calm day.

She paused beside the door next to hers, where the label read *Miss E Lane*.

Flora chewed her lip. A woman travelling alone? Then who was the man she had argued with the night before? Another passenger, or a member of the crew?

A voice called from somewhere above, followed by a slammed door, but no one appeared, so she continued along the deck, staggering a little against the gentle rise and fall of the ship.

An outside companionway, surrounded on three sides by a rail above a set of narrow metal steps, dropped steeply to the boat deck below, with what appeared to be a bundle of clothes at the bottom. A closer look revealed the figure of a man lying prone on the boards.

Flora clattered down the step, her boots ringing on the metal treads and the words, 'Are you hurt?' dying on her lips.

The man lay unnaturally still, eyes open and sightless; and quite dead.

His features, though slack and colourless, were recognizable as the worried-looking man she had seen talking to the lady in the claret coat when they boarded.

Was he here alone? Would anyone be looking for him? Whom should she call?

She swept the deck on both sides with a frantic gaze, but nothing moved; the only sounds the wind and a distant engine noise as the ship glided over a calm ocean.

Horror turned to curiosity. She crept closer, taking in his black dinner suit and scuffed shoes. A large purple bruise had formed on his right cheek. Her gaze slid to a three-inch long gash at the base of his skull. She winced, then looked again as something struck her as wrong. The open edges gaped a deep liverish red, but apart from a dried smear of red-brown on his shirt collar, there was no sign of blood. The boards beneath him looked clean, if damp.

'Are you all right, miss?' a male voice said, making her jump.

Flora looked up into the frowning features of a man in naval officer's uniform, a much younger crewman at his shoulder. Without waiting for her to respond, he bent to the figure on the deck.

'Has the gentleman had a fall?' the first man enquired.

'I-I don't know,' she addressed the crouching officer's back. 'I simply found him like this. I think he's dead.'

'Blimey!' the younger sailor muttered, his eyes wide.

'Fetch Dr Fletcher immediately,' the officer cocked his chin at the younger man.

'Aye, sir.' The sailor backed away, turned and pounded down the deck.

The officer rose to his full height and touched a hand to his cap. 'Second Officer Martin, at your service, miss...?'

'Maguire. Flora Maguire.'

He blinked, distracted, as if making a mental search of the sailor's manual but couldn't find the part about dead bodies. Then he appeared to make up his mind and straightened, taking her arm. 'Perhaps you should step away, Miss Maguire.'

'I'm fine, truly.' Flora rolled her shoulder out of his grasp. She was staying where she was for now. The sound of running feet signalled the return of the young crewman in the company of a man Flora assumed was the doctor, confirmed when he rested a finger on the man's neck and then his wrist.

'I'm Dr Fletcher,' he announced once his examination was complete. 'Did you see the gentleman fall, miss?' His gaze slid over Flora as if trying to assess what part she had played in the incident. His nut-brown hair was short, well cut, but untidy, as if he'd just got out of bed.

Two more sailors and a steward appeared from somewhere and hovered a few feet away.

'I didn't see it happen, no, but...' Flora lowered her voice, adding, 'Are you sure he fell?'

The doctor's eyes narrowed. 'Why do you say

that?' He swallowed, his Adam's apple bobbing like a fishing float.

'Well,' Flora began, 'if he fell forwards, the way he's lying now, how did he get that wound on the back of his head?'

'He most probably hit the handrail on the way down.' Dr Fletcher turned away, dismissing her.

'Maybe. But if so, wouldn't he have tried to save himself? His arms are by his sides as if–'

'You've clearly had a shock, Miss Maguire.' Officer Martin stepped in front of her, blocking her view. 'I suggest you return to your suite while we deal with this.'

Flora bridled, but resisted. 'Why do you keep trying to get rid of me? I'm not hysterical, and I asked a perfectly reasonable question.' She directed a look of enquiry at the crewmen, each of whom studied her with varying degrees of scepticism.

Heavy footsteps approached. Flora braced herself for yet more censure, but the startled, 'Good grief, what's happened?' came in a voice both familiar and reassuring.

'Mr Harrington, thank goodness.' Flora grabbed hold of his sleeve, urging him forwards. 'I found this man on the deck.' She lowered her voice to a whisper. 'He's dead, and not only will the crew not answer my questions, they keep trying to make me leave.'

'Did you see it happen?' Bunny slid an arm around her waist, though she was in no danger of falling. She left it there, his touch comforting, and safe.

'No, he was just lying here,' Flora said. 'The

doctor thinks he fell down the steps, but I'm not so sure.'

'The lady is a trifle distraught, Mr, er–' Officer Martin took her arm again with one hand and saluted Bunny with the other, a brow raised in enquiry.

'Harrington.'

'Mr Harrington. Coming upon a body like that could upset anyone, especially a young lady.'

'I am not upset!' Flora glared at him.

Officer Martin removed his hand from her arm as if burned. 'It appears to be a simple, but regrettable accident, sir. Easily done when one isn't used to the motions of the ship. Added to which, the companionway is quite steep.'

'Do fatal accidents occur often on board ships?' Bunny's penetrating gaze made him flinch.

'Not at all!' Officer Martin's voice held affront. 'Falls do, especially in rough seas, but I cannot say we have many deaths. This gentleman must have been extremely unlucky.'

Flora frowned. Was his bland reassurance an attempt to shield the other passengers? Or to allay blame that the companionways weren't safe? A metal rail ran around three sides of the hole, but the steps were thin and metal, thus quite slippery. They had also been washed recently, judging by the sheen of water that clung to the treads.

'Do either of you recognize him?' the doctor asked, fastening his jacket.

Flora hesitated. 'N-no, I don't know him.' Her attempt to eavesdrop on his conversation with the lady in the red coat hardly counted as an acquaintance. Nor was she certain the argument

25

she had heard was with the same one who occupied the stateroom next door to hers.

'His name is Parnell,' Bunny interjected. 'Frank, I think.'

'You knew him, Mr Harrington?' Officer Martin's expression hardened to suspicion.

'We met for the first time at dinner last evening,' Bunny said. 'He was travelling in the company of a young lady. An actress, I believe.'

Flora frowned. The woman in the claret coat didn't strike her as being an actress. Not that she knew any.

'I see, now if you would excuse me, sir.' Dr Fletcher beckoned two members of the crew who proceeded to maneuver the dead man onto a sheet of tarpaulin.

'Shouldn't the captain see the body before it's moved?' Flora whispered to Bunny.

He shrugged. 'I don't know what the procedure is. I assume they know what they are doing.' He addressed the nearest sailor. 'Where are you taking him?'

'To my office for the time being,' Dr Fletcher said over his shoulder before following.

'The matter is out of our hands now,' Bunny said with a sigh, turning back to Flora. 'Won't you allow me to escort you back to your suite?'

'But–' she halted and exhaled, resigned. After all, she hadn't known the dead man, and whatever had happened to him was none of her concern. 'All right, if you insist. I mean – thank you.' She accepted his proffered arm, and started to climb the steps, pausing halfway up, her gaze roving the metal treads.

'Are you looking for something?' He halted beside her, followed her gaze, one arm of his spectacles gripped by the edges between a thumb and forefinger.

'There's no blood on these steps,' Flora said slowly. 'Or on the deck. In fact there's not a drop anywhere.'

'Perhaps one of the sailors cleaned it up. Can't leave it there for the passengers to see.'

'No one came near us with anything resembling a mop,' Flora murmured as she resumed her climb. 'Besides, there was none to remove.'

Her confusion made the walk along the deck a silent one. Why did no one else wonder about the absence of blood on steps that had inflicted a wound deep enough to kill a man?

If indeed that's what killed him.

Chapter 3

By the time Flora arrived back at her suite, she was overcome by a belated wave of nausea.

The wound on the man's head had stirred a recurring memory from her past that was unnervingly similar. An image that ambushed her at odd times, leaving her with more questions than she could answer.

Fighting dizziness, she inserted herself between Bunny and the door. 'Thank you for escorting me back, Mr Harrington, I shall be perfectly all right now.'

'Most probably.' Bunny pushed the door open and indicated she should enter ahead of him. 'However, you look decidedly shaky if I may say so. I wouldn't be a gentleman if I abandoned you now.'

Discouraging him was too much of an effort. Instead, Flora sank into the nearest wicker chair, leaving him to close the door.

'It must have been a dreadful shock finding a body like that,' Bunny said.

'Not at first, but when I saw that gash on his head, I...' She motioned him into the chair opposite. 'I imagine it must have been worse for you.' She thrust her hands in the folds of her skirt to still their shaking. 'You knew him.'

'Not really.' He tugged up his trousers and sat, dwarfing the chair. 'After dinner, those at our table repaired to the saloon for drinks. I only remember him because he instigated a game of poker.'

A light knock came at the door, and Flora half-rose, glad of a reason to break eye contact. The intensity of his stare made her uncomfortable. 'That will be my morning tea.'

'I'll go.' Bunny halted her with an upraised hand, leaving her with little choice but to relax back into her seat.

She squeezed her eyes shut to banish the image of the man on deck, which mingled with that of a woman from another time, though the first disturbed her far worse than the second. That the lady was her mother was deeply ingrained, though the circumstances remained indistinct. 'Steward thought he had come to the wrong suite.' Bunny's

28

cheerful voice cut short the memory. 'But I soon put him straight. Shall I pour?' He hovered above the loaded tray he had placed on the table between them, from which the comforting smell of tea wafted into the room, reminding her of the Cleeve Abbey nursery in the afternoons.

'The steward told me word has already begun circulating about that poor chap.' Bunny's evident unfamiliarity with china caused him to misjudge the arc of hot water and he slopped some into a saucer. 'What were you saying about the blood?' he asked, dabbing at the wet tray clumsily with a napkin.

Flora attempted a smile. 'There was none. Not on the companionway, the deck or the handrail. Do you believe it was an accident?'

He adjusted his glasses, as if taking time to think. 'I didn't have time to form much of an opinion, what with those sailors in such a hurry to take him away.' He handed her a full cup, a finger pointed to the sugar bowl.

Flora declined. 'I thought it was odd, that's all.'

He stirred his tea slowly. 'The doctor didn't agree though, did he?'

'He didn't consider anything *I* had to say. But then I suppose the last thing the crew would want on the first day at sea is a murder. That would certainly upset the passengers.'

'Murder?' His eyes glinted with surprise, magnified by his spectacles. 'Why would you think that?'

Flora's confidence waned. 'I-I don't know. Maybe Dr Fletcher was right, and he did fall.' She met his gaze over the top of her teacup. 'Incidentally, what were you doing up so early?'

'I was on my way to check on Matilda.' His mouth tilted up slightly at one side. 'Why? Did you think I was out pushing card sharps down steps?'

'No, of course not,' she said, mildly exasperated. 'Unless you lost money to him.'

His brows lifted. 'I work too hard to risk my money on games of chance.'

Flora smiled at this, pleased with the fact he was a man of high moral principle. 'What was the late Mr Parnell like?'

Bunny thought for a moment. 'Early thirties, dark, heavy-featured with thick black hair.'

Flora had gathered that much for herself. 'I meant his personality. Aggressive, self-effacing, unassuming?'

'Well, not the last two. He spoke with a Brooklyn accent, but claimed to know London. That didn't seem likely to me, though I have no reason to disbelieve him.'

'Hmm, what about this lady you told the officer he was with?' The hot tea helped her relax and she began to enjoy the exchange.

'Ah yes, the actress. A petite, dark-haired girl with pretty blue eyes. Clearly more intelligent than him, so I was surprised they were together.'

This description sounded nothing like the lady Flora had seen talking to Parnell.

'Was it a high stakes game?' She poured herself more tea and held the pot up in enquiry.

He nodded, his cup held out for a refill. 'Depends what you mean by high. Man named Gilmore lost $1,000.'

'A thousand?' The handle of the teapot slipped from Flora's fingers, though she managed to catch it before it hit the table.

'He didn't seem particularly upset by it. Quite well-heeled, I imagine.'

'That could be ocean liner talk.' In response to his sideways look she continued, 'My employers warned me that when separated from our ordinary lives, one's history can often be embellished.'

'Not Gilmore. His wife's diamonds were real.'

'Isn't it bad taste to wear one's jewels at sea?' Flora recalled Lady Vaughn's discourse that sea air spoiled the stones' lustre.

'Maybe so,' Bunny said, laughing.

'Had you met them before this trip?'

'I don't know anyone on this voyage. Except you, of course.' His smile caused her stomach to perform a strange, lurching flip. She dipped her nose to her teacup to hide the sudden heat that flooded her face.

'I say, I hope you don't mind my hanging about, treating you like an old friend?' He eased forwards, resting his forearms on his thighs. 'Actually, I wondered about how you left me so abruptly last night. I imagined we were getting along famously. Did I say something to offend you?'

'No, not at all.' She dropped her gaze to her lap. 'It's just that, well, Eddy–'

'Ah, yes, I see. Eddy.' He nodded slowly. 'I understand. You're his governess, aren't you?'

'Yes. The *Minneapolis* was the first ship with accommodation available when my employer booked passage.' Flora did not add that she had felt more comfortable in her third class cabin on the *Oceanic* during the outward voyage.

'I don't see why that would send you rushing away like you did. I have very happy memories of my governess.' He produced a handkerchief from somewhere, removed his spectacles and proceeded to polish the lenses.

Flora bit back a retort and focused on the tiny red mark the metal bridge had caused on his nose and had to resist the urge to stroke it away. Then she imagined what Lady Vaughn would say about entertaining young men in her suite, reigniting the slow burn in her cheeks.

'Tell me about the other passengers.' She offered him the plate of biscuits, hoping he hadn't noticed her discomfort.

'If you hadn't avoided the dining room last night.' He took one, pointing it at her. 'You would have met them yourself.'

'Well, I didn't, so I must rely on you to paint me a picture.'

'Let's see.' He took a bite of the biscuit and chewed. 'The Gilmores are an English couple with a son about Eddy's age. Nice lad, if young for his age. He got on well with your young charge at dinner, actually.'

'I know.' A surge of guilt welled at her having abandoned Eddy to a room full of strangers.

'The Cavendishes are our on-board honeymoon couple. Standard requirement on sea voyages, so they get lots of attention.'

Flora dipped her head to her cup while she summoned images of these people in her head. 'Tell me about them.'

'You sound as if you're trying to root out

possible suspects.'

'Isn't that what the sleuths do in the best crime novels; discover all they can about those involved?'

'Are you an Arthur Conan Doyle fan, by any chance?'

'Isn't everyone? However, during my stay in New York, I read *Marked Personal* by Anna Katharine Green. Her father was a lawyer, I believe, so she gets the legal aspects spot on, and–' she broke off, embarrassed. 'Sorry, you were about to describe the honeymooners.'

'So I was. Max Cavendish is in his early thirties I would say, affluent English businessman.' He stared off for a second. 'Puts me in mind of a bulldog puppy, no grace, but plenty of enthusiasm.'

'Very descriptive, which means I shall be hard put not to smile when we meet, and thus will completely baffle him.' She dragged her gaze back to her cup. 'What's his bride like?'

'Cynthia? She's a stunner. Slim with reddish hair and startling cerulean eyes. Extremely wealthy, if her wardrobe is anything to go by, with an aloof, disdainful air about her. In fact,' he waved his teaspoon in the air, 'all the chaps I went to school with had sisters just like her.'

Flora nodded slowly. He had described the lady she had seen talking to the dead man.

The rattle of the doorknob announced the arrival of Eddy, who stumbled into the room, still fumbling with the cord of his blue and red chequered dressing gown.

'Why is everyone up so early?' he demanded in a voice heavy with sleep. 'There are people running along the deck past my window. Is the ship on fire? Oh, hello, Mr Harrington. What are you doing here?' He perched on the edge of the third armchair and peered at the tea tray, frowning.

'I'm afraid Mr Harrington used your cup,' Flora said. 'You'll have to wait until breakfast.'

'I don't mind.' Eddy shrugged, pragmatic as ever.

'One of the gentlemen at your table last night has met with an accident,' Flora said. 'A Mr Parnell.'

'The one with the eyebrows that meet in the middle?' Eddy plucked a biscuit from the tray and nibbled at it, one knee looped over the arm of his chair. 'What sort of accident?'

'He suffered a fall on the companionway steps,' she replied carefully.

'Will he die?' Eddy whispered round a mouthful of crumbs, his eyes round.

'Already dead,' Bunny replied, ignoring Flora's frantic hand signal.

'Spiffing!' Eddy dropped his unfinished biscuit on the tray and headed for his room. 'Must get dressed and find Ozzy. He'll want to hear about this.'

'You can tell him Flora found the body,' Bunny called after him.

'Excellent!' Eddy's delighted yell came from behind his closed door.

'Why on earth did you say that?' Flora said, aghast.

'Don't look so disapproving.' Bunny smiled. 'Shipboard gossip will have filled in the details anyway.' Not at all abashed, he swept another biscuit from the plate. 'Besides, it will give Eddy some kudos amongst the other boys. These things matter, you know.'

'Hmm.' Flora narrowed her eyes. 'Slightly morbid if you ask me.'

Dismissing the strange proclivities of young boys, and older ones, Flora checked the time. The breakfast bugle would go soon. The thought of a roomful of strangers speculating on what part she had played in the death of a passenger did not appeal. She would be the talk of the ship by luncheon.

Flora toyed with the thought of skipping breakfast altogether, and was about to float the idea with Bunny when Eddy reappeared, having apparently thrown on whatever came to hand.

'Did you really find the body, Flora?' At her nod he went on. 'Was there much blood?'

'Not enough,' Flora said under her breath, then more loudly, 'never mind that. I rather think a yellow sweater with red socks is a little–'

'No time.' Without glancing at either of them, he left, banging the door behind him

Almost immediately, the doorbell rang, and sighing, Flora rose and flung it open. 'What have you forgotten, Eddy?' The words froze on her tongue at the sight of the two uniformed men who filled the doorframe.

'Miss Flora Maguire?' asked an older man, the four gold rings on his sleeves announcing him as the captain.

Her mouth dried but she gathered herself enough to nod.

'Captain Gates, how do you do.' Of medium

35

height and a stocky build without being fat, his eyes glinted with amusement in a face that Flora expected to break into a laugh at any second. An aroma of old tobacco hung about him, echoed by the polished walnut pipe poking out of his breast pocket. 'Would you mind answering a few questions about this morning's ah, unfortunate mishap?'

'No, of course not.' She stepped aside to allow them to enter, her attention caught by the sight of a crewman in front of a cabin two doors down. A diminutive maid stood, feet planted apart in front of him, a pile of white towels hugged to her chest.

'You had no cause to throw me out,' she said. 'I have to clean, or I'll lose my job.'

'I can't help that,' the crewman snapped, unmoved. 'Mr Parnell's cabin must not be touched. Captain's orders.'

'Then just you be sure to tell the housekeeper those things are missing, and it wasn't me who took 'em.' With a final sniff at the unbending sailor, she stomped off along the deck.

The crewman mouthed something at the girl's back before locking the door of the cabin, then pocketed the key before striding off in the other direction.

Flora closed the door slowly. So Mr Parnell had occupied the cabin on the other side of Miss Lane's. Not that it mattered now. He wouldn't be using it.

'Is there something wrong?' Bunny asked, while the two sailors regarded her with identical looks of puzzled enquiry.

'No, no not at all,' Flora resumed her seat.

The two crewmen tucked their caps neatly beneath their arms as Flora directed them to the remaining chairs.

'Should I leave you alone?' Bunny inclined his head towards the door, though his expression indicated he would do so reluctantly.

'Actually, Mr Harrington.' Officer Martin produced a notebook from his pocket. 'We hoped you would remain.'

Bunny took up a position beside Flora's chair, a gesture she found both protective and reassuring.

'What was the first thing you saw this morning, Miss Maguire?' Officer Martin's pen hovered above a page.

Flora frowned. 'You know what I saw. You were there too.'

'I'm sorry.' He exchanged a look with Captain Gates, who nodded. 'This needs to be kept formal as an official record.'

'I see.' Flora took a deep breath. 'I was about to descend the companionway to the boat deck, when I spotted something at the bottom.'

'You didn't use the internal staircase lobby to get to the lower deck?' the captain interrupted.

'Well, no. I wanted some air and it was a lovely morning.' Flora flinched. 'At least, it was one before...'

'I see.' He instilled a world of speculation in the words. 'Do go on.'

'I-I thought it was a bundle of clothing at first, but a closer look told me it was a man. A dead one.' She nodded to Officer Martin. 'That's when you arrived.'

'That's true, sir.' Officer Martin addressed the captain. 'When I got there, the young lady was bent over the body.'

'Of course it's true.' Flora tensed, at which Bunny's hand came down on her shoulder in warning. 'I apologize, I don't mean to be sharp.' She bit her lip. 'It must be the shock.'

Not that she was in the least upset any more, but as an excuse, it would do.

'Did you see the man fall?' Captain Gates asked.

'No. In fact the blood on his head had congealed, so it must have happened some time before I discovered him. Hours possibly.'

'We don't think that was the case.' Captain Gates twisted his cap repeatedly between his splayed knees. 'The decks are washed every morning at six. None of the crew reported a body in that location then.'

'What did Dr Fletcher say?' Flora glanced at Bunny, who shrugged.

'As far as I know, nothing. He didn't appear to regard the fact as important.'

Flora gave him a hard look and Officer Martin cleared his throat. 'You must understand, the doctor can only give the body a cursory examination, the post-mortem will have to wait until we reach England.' His gaze shifted from her to Bunny. 'Were either of you acquainted with the deceased?'

The deceased. Flora shivered. How quickly death consigned the man to non-existence.

'I met him for the first time last night at dinner.' Bunny's hand squeezed Flora's shoulder, reminding her he had not removed it. 'Miss Maguire ate dinner here in her suite, so they never met.'

'I believe Mr Parnell won a good deal of money in a card game last evening?' Captain Gates fell into the role of questioner.

'Um, yes.' Bunny replied. 'Gilmore took it in his stride, while Crowe was more put out at his losses.'

'Put out?' Officer Martin posed it as a question.

'Parnell goaded him and Crowe appeared rattled.'

'You didn't join this game, Mr Harrington?' Again that accusatory tone.

'I did not.'

'Are either of you acquainted with,' Officer Martin paused and squinted at his notebook, 'a Miss Eloise Lane?'

Flora shook her head. Raised voices heard through bulwarks didn't count, surely?

'Again,' Bunny said, 'I met her for the first time last night.'

'In your opinion, Mr Harrington,' Officer Martin asked, 'did Mr Parnell and Miss Lane appear amiable towards one another?'

'I got the impression their association was a business arrangement.' The vibration of Bunny's shrug went through Flora's shoulder. 'One where the lady's expectations outweighed Parnell's promises.'

'In what way?'

'Miss Lane intimated Parnell had got her a part in a London production of *School for Scandal* at the Theatre Royal. He claimed acquaintance with Cyril Maude, the producer.'

'Did Mr Parnell endorse this at any time?' Captain Gates asked, shifting the interview to a three way discussion, with Flora relegated to that of spectator.

'He appeared embarrassed, actually,' Bunny said as if the thought had just that moment occurred to him. 'He tried to dismiss it.'

'What was the lady's reaction to that? Disappointment? Anger?'

'Petulance.' Bunny shrugged again, the movement felt by Flora rather seen. 'She insisted Parnell had guaranteed the part was hers.'

'Did anything out of the ordinary occur in the saloon last night?' Captain Gates asked. 'An argument perhaps or harsh words?'

'Nothing other than I've already mentioned.'

'And you and Miss Maguire, sir?' Officer Martin's pen moved between each of them. 'The two of you had not met before yesterday?'

'That's right,' Bunny said, and Flora gave a curt nod, irritated at being ignored and questions answered for her.

A loaded look passed between the two crewmen, then Captain Gates cleared his throat and rose. 'I think that's all we need for the moment, sir. Miss.' He waited until his companion had pocketed his notebook, then cocked his chin as a signal for them to leave.

'What do you think happened to Mr Parnell?' Flora blurted.

Captain Gates turned back at the door, his expression bland. 'We have no reason to believe the gentleman's death was anything other than an unfortunate accident.'

Flora slumped back in her chair, disappointed but not surprised. After all, people died all the time from falls. Maybe the most obvious explanation was correct. Then an image of the body on the deck intruded and her disquiet surged again. They were wrong.

'I hope this incident doesn't spoil the rest of your voyage,' the captain went on. 'If there is anything you need – either of you – do feel free to call upon myself or one of my crew.'

Bunny saw them both out, while Flora remained seated, her teeth gripped so hard her jaw ached.

Chapter 4

'It's evident they believe the man fell,' Bunny said, when he returned from seeing the crewmen out.

'They weren't prepared to discuss the alternative either, were they, for instance–' she broke off, wincing at the strident note of a bugle from outside. 'I'm never ready for that sound.'

'It does take a little getting used to.' Bunny laughed. 'It's been a long morning already, and it's only breakfast time. Shall we go in together, or do you want to wait for your young charge?'

'Eddy has elected to attend the young persons' mealtimes, so I shall have to do without his company from now on. I hope he hasn't been upset by this incident. Despite his mischievous nature, he's a sensitive boy.'

She had almost said killing, but to persist with her suspicions would make her look foolish.

'He didn't look too upset when he ran out of here earlier.' Bunny retrieved Flora's shawl.

'No, he didn't, did he?' She stood passive as he draped the soft wool over her shoulders. 'Will Captain Gates make an announcement during divine service about what happened?'

'Probably.' He shot her a mischievous sideways look as they stepped onto the deck. 'I doubt he'll mention you, though. Women on board are considered bad luck. Sailors are superstitious that way.'

'You aren't making me feel any better about this at all, Mr Harrington.' She cast him an oblique look as she moved past him and stepped onto the deck.

'Sorry, just my perverse sense of humour. And I wish you'd call me Bunny.'

She was considering this request as they drew level with a door further along the deck, where a young woman in a cream and white gown exited a suite into their path, her head turned to address someone behind her.

'Oh, do hurry up, Max, I want my breakfast.'

'Good morning, Mrs Cavendish,' Bunny said, bringing Flora to a halt beside him.

The woman turned to face them, a bright smile on her face. 'Good morning to you, Mr Harrington. How nice to see you again.'

Flora recognized the lady she had seen arguing

with the man who now lay lifeless in the doctor's office.

'How did you sleep on your first night aboard?' Bunny asked.

Her wide, grey gaze slid over Flora before returning to Bunny. 'Perfectly fine, thank you, until the entire crew stampeded past our window at some ridiculously early hour. I've a good mind to complain to the captain.'

Flora now knew how a sparrow must feel in the company of a kingfisher. Clumsy, brown and invisible.

'Forgive me,' Bunny said with a start. 'Allow me to introduce Miss Flora Maguire.'

'Do call me Cynthia,' the lady gushed in a clipped Home Counties accent, her delicate hand limply extended.

'I'm afraid there was an accident, which explains all the activity,' Bunny said. 'One of the passengers fell down a companionway.'

'Really? How inconvenient.' Cynthia fussed with her scarf. 'Anyone we know?'

'That Parnell chap from last night.'

'How awful!' Cynthia froze in the act of tugging on a white glove. 'W-was he badly hurt?'

'He's dead,' Flora said, watching her closely.

The blood drained from Cynthia's face, her hand stilled in mid-air. 'He can't be!'

'I know it's hard to believe,' Bunny said. 'Seems he hit his head as he fell. Shocked all of us, especially Flora here, who was unfortunate enough to have found the body.'

'I'm sorry if we've upset you,' Flora said. 'Did you know him? The dead man?'

Cynthia's eyes rounded in an innocence that Flora didn't find convincing. 'No, not at all, we met for the first time at dinner last night.'

'Really?' Aware of Bunny's puzzled frown directed at her profile, Flora couldn't resist. 'Only, I'm sure I saw you arguing with him when we boarded yesterday.'

'Oh, was that the same man?' Her gasp of surprise was too contrived to be genuine. 'He bumped me with his suitcase. I gave him quite a set down, I can tell you.'

'We're on our way to breakfast, won't you join us?' Bunny asked.

Cynthia smoothed her gloves over each wrist in turn, as if giving herself time to think. 'Er no, I have to wait for Max. We'll be along in a moment.' She backed hurriedly through the suite door and closed it firmly behind her.

'That was one half of our honeymoon couple,' Bunny said as they reached the door to the interior lobby.

'So I gathered.' It was on the tip of Flora's tongue to ask him if he thought Cynthia was pretty, but changed her mind. He had already described her as stunning, so it would be like probing a sore tooth to check it still hurt.

'Did you really see her arguing with Parnell yesterday?' Bunny asked, frowning as they descended the staircase to the lower deck.

'That's what it looked like. I didn't see any suitcase, either.'

'But she said she didn't know him.'

'She did, didn't she?'

44

The dining room door flapped open at Bunny's touch, releasing a low murmur of voices. Panelled in light oak with a domed, stained-glass ceiling that rose through two storeys, a blaze of jewel-tinted light flooded the scene below.

Long maple wood tables filled the room, arranged like a school dormitory; while wide windows gave onto the glistening ocean on one side, and tall gilt mirrors made the room appear twice its size.

Heads swivelled in their direction as Bunny guided Flora across the room to their table. One or two whispered something to a companion, who watched them pass.

Flora fought the urge to turn tail and run, but Bunny's grip on her arm prevented her. 'Keep walking. It won't be nearly as bad as you imagine.'

She didn't believe him.

'There you are, Harrington.' A broad-shouldered man unfurled from his chair as they reached the table, enveloping Flora's hand in both of his. 'Is this the young lady who eschewed our company last night?' He raised her hand briefly to his lips. 'Gerald Gilmore. Lovely to meet you, my dear.'

A wing of silver graced one temple in his black hair; a hereditary trait more than a sign of age, as Flora judged him to be no more than forty.

'This is my wife, Monica,' he indicated a lady in a dove grey silk gown which did little for her pale skin and unremarkable features.

'How do you do.' She offered Flora her hand as if conveying a blessing. 'I'm Ozzy's mother,' she added unnecessarily. 'This awful business about

Mr Parnell is all over the ship.'

'Ah yes, the finder of our unfortunate dinner companion,' a middle-aged man with salt-and-pepper hair said with a slight Germanic accent. 'Carl Hersch,' he said, taking Flora's hand in a firm, dry grip; a contact that lasted longer than politeness required, though was not unpleasant.

'It's nice to meet you, Mr Hersch. I'm afraid so.' Flora retrieved her hand and took the chair Bunny held out. 'A fact which I hope won't be held against me.'

'Nothing to fret about.' Gerald's clipped manner appeared to be his normal mode of speech. 'Storm in a teacup. Forgotten by tomorrow.'

Flora doubted it.

'It could have been worse,' Monica said. 'I mean, no one actually knew the man, did they?' she added with a wry little smile.

'Miss Lane did,' Mr Hersch said, taking his seat. 'They were travelling together.' Though no one reacted to this comment.

'Have you met Miss Ames, our resident author, Miss Maguire?' Monica indicated a grey-haired lady beside her as if she were a personal pet. Flora imagined she had either dressed in the dark or simply desired to be noticed in her purple-frilled blouse coupled with a bright orange skirt.

'Mary Ames, how nice to meet you,' the lady said in a voice as loud as her clothes.

Flora released her hand, just as a young man of around twenty-five with untidy dark hair in need of a barber approached their table.

'Morning, everyone.' He threw himself into an empty chair, sending Mr Hersch's napkin flutter-

46

ing onto the floor. 'I'm Gus Crowe.' His lingering gaze slid over Flora in a way that made her want to shake it off. 'Nice to see another attractive face.' Then in the same breath he addressed the table. 'I say, has everyone heard about that Parnell chap?'

A steward rushed forwards to replace the fallen napkin, while Mr Hersch flicked an exasperated look at Mr Crowe.

'He's quite dead, y'know,' Crowe continued, oblivious of the combined looks of censure from the rest of the company.

'We're very aware of the situation, Mr Crowe.' Monica glared at him. 'The poor man fell down a companionway. They ought to put warning notices on those things.'

'They do, Monica,' her husband said. 'You need to wear your glasses more often.'

'Is that all we know? That he sustained a fall?' Miss Ames asked.

'What's to know? He bashed his head and copped it.' Crowe spread butter liberally on a slice of toast, took a bite and chewed.

Flora bit her bottom lip, resisting the urge to offer her own opinion.

'Is this all of us?' she asked Bunny, indicating the five empty places.

'That's odd.' Bunny glanced at the door. 'I distinctly heard Cynthia say she wanted her breakfast when we ran into her this morning. Yet neither she nor Max have turned up.'

'That's honeymooners for you,' Gerald said, sawing vigorously at a sausage. 'Most likely they had a tray sent to their suite.'

Bunny frowned. 'Mrs Penry-Jones isn't here

47

either, nor is Miss Lane.'

'I'm not surprised the actress isn't here,' Monica said. 'She's probably too distressed after hearing what happened.'

'Doesn't explain the old lady, though,' Gerald said, thoughtful. 'Struck me as an up-at-the-crack-of-dawn sort of person.'

'The captain is still interviewing everyone, which may explain their absence.' Mr Hersch reached for the last bread roll from a basket, which Gus Crowe snatched from beneath his fingers, grinning like a schoolboy.

Hersch sighed and pushed his plate away.

'We've already been interviewed by the captain.' Bunny included Flora in his response.

'What sort of questions did he ask?' Miss Ames produced a moleskin-covered notebook and pen from her handbag.

'Only what I saw, which was very little,' Flora replied, then before she could stop herself, said, 'when I pointed out there should have been more blood on the deck, he didn't agree.'

Bunny's eyes narrowed and he gave a tiny shake of his head which Flora pretended not to see.

'How interesting.' Miss Ames unsheathed her pen and began writing. 'Do share your theory, Miss Maguire. I love a good mystery.'

'I don't have a theory, as such. I simply thought it odd, that's all.' She refrained from mentioning the gash on his head, or what the maid had said.

Bunny's sigh sent a rush of defiance into her tongue. 'Actually, I also wondered how he came to be on an outside companionway at six in the morning in a dinner suit.'

Flora jumped as Bunny's shoe connected with her shin.

'You mean he was there all night?' Monica asked, her eyes round.

'Not according to the captain.' Flora exchanged a look with Bunny, who rolled his eyes but stayed silent.

'How curious.' Miss Ames held each of their gazes in turn.

Gerald gave a half amused snort. 'Something for your next book, Miss Ames? Fiction is more interesting than fact, after all.'

Flora didn't agree.

Flora excused herself at the end of the meal with vague promises of catching up with Bunny later. His disapproval of her thoughts on Mr Parnell had annoyed her, though on her walk back to her suite, she had to admit no solid evidence existed to disprove the accident theory.

Despite that, her head buzzed with unanswered questions. Had the argument she had heard through the bulkhead turned into a lover's quarrel, followed by a crack on the head? If so, how did Parnell end up at the bottom of a staircase hours later?

Preoccupied, she collided with another female passenger, the impact sending her sideways into a steamer chair.

'I'm so sorry!' Flora righted herself and made a leap for a clutch bag that had skittered across the deck. 'I wasn't looking where I was going.'

'That's quite all right,' the young woman replied in a soft, lilting voice. Her cloud of black curls contrasted sharply with porcelain skin and a heavy layer of blood-red lipstick.

'I'm Flora, Flora Maguire. I don't think we've met.'

'How do you do. I'm Est–' her bag dropped onto the deck again, and she dipped to retrieve it before extending her hand. 'Oh, I'm so clumsy this morning. Eloise, Eloise Lane.'

Flora accepted the hand as if in a daze, staring at the occupant of the suite next to hers. The actress travelling with Mr Parnell.

'You're the lady who found Frank's body, aren't you?' Eloise blurted.

'What?' Flora broke off from staring. 'Oh, yes, I'm afraid I did.'

Eloise offered a weak smile as if she could think of nothing more to add, then wandered towards the ship's rail and leaned against it, her scarf whipping behind her in the wind.

'You were missed at breakfast.' Flora joined her in the hope of instigating a conversation, though Eloise appeared in no hurry to leave.

'Was I?' Her cornflower blue eyes beneath thick lashes widened, then sharpened. 'By whom, exactly?'

Flora thought quickly. 'The gentlemen, naturally.'

'I'll wager their wives didn't.' Eloise placed an elbow on the rail and dropped her chin into her hand; a gesture Flora guessed she practised in front of a mirror. 'I had no appetite after I heard Frank had–' she broke off and bit her lip.

'It must have been such a shock to hear he had died,' Flora said carefully.

'It was. Awful. I've just spent the most ghastly hour with the captain. He wanted to know everything. How long I had known Frank? How did we meet? How close were we?' She ran the end of her scarf repeatedly through her fingers. 'Such impertinent questions. All because the silly man fell down a set of stairs.'

'They're only doing their job. I doubt they think you had anything to do with it,' Flora said, her question as to whether Eloise was romantically involved with Mr Parnell answered.

'Of course I didn't!' Her cheeks coloured, eyes flashing in an outrage that struck Flora as genuine. But then, Flora reminded herself, she was an actress.

'How am I going to present myself to Mr Cyril Maude without Frank?' She stared morosely out at the ocean, apparently not expecting an answer.

Flora tried to think of something profound to keep the conversation going, finally settling on flattery. 'Perhaps you don't need his influence to get you the part. I mean, I imagine you could impress this Mr Maude by your acting ability alone.'

At first, Flora thought she had overdone it, but Eloise gave an acknowledging nod and puffed out her boyish chest. 'You're right. I don't need Frank. I'll attend that audition and prove to him what a wonderful Lady Teazle I'll make.' A beatific smile softened her expression as she consigned Mr Parnell to the past.

Flora smiled back, though as she far as she remembered, Lady Teazle did not speak with a Southern accent.

'I only wish I'd realized that before, I–' Eloise broke off as gust of wind unravelled the knot in her scarf.

'Before what?' Flora watched her as she caught the billowing end.

Eloise's eyes hardened. 'It's nothing. I didn't mean anything by it.'

Flora wasn't going to let that go. 'Even if you were most probably the last person to see him alive?'

Her head whipped round, pinning Flora with a direct stare. 'What are you talking about?'

Flora hesitated. To challenge her directly was a gamble, but this verbal dance was getting her nowhere. 'I don't mean to imply anything, but I heard you arguing with him last night.' She broke eye contact and pretended to study a group of children playing hopscotch on the deck below.

'Oh, I remember now.' Eloise's feigned memory lapse indicated she had been caught out. 'Frank arrived at some ungodly hour last night wanting to talk. He smelled of whisky, so after a few sharp words I sent him away. That's what you must have heard.'

Flora was about to probe further, but Eloise had already turned away. 'I think I'll go and lie down. It's been a stressful morning and this wind is giving me a headache. Maybe we'll see each other later.'

'I expect so.' Flora watched her go, unsure whether to believe her or not. Thoughtful, she pushed away from the rail, turned and came up short.

A woman whom Flora judged to be a few years

older than herself stood several feet away, apparently studying the horizon with fierce intensity.

In a drab grey dress that clung to her ample curves, and a shapeless hat that hid her hair, Flora couldn't recall having seen her before. Briefly she wondered if the woman had overheard her conversation with Eloise? But then, why would she?

Flora raised a hand in greeting, but instead of acknowledging her, the woman turned abruptly away and marched off down the deck.

Dismissing her as the nosy, but unfriendly sort, Flora let herself into the suite.

Chapter 5

Flora unearthed her copy of *Northanger Abbey* and descended to the steamer chairs stood lined up facing the rail, and located the one with her name attached. When Lady Vaughn had suggested she pay the eight shillings for two chairs, Flora had ventured this unnecessary as Eddy was unlikely to use one. Lady Vaughn had insisted, suggesting Flora might find someone congenial to sit with in the afternoons; though she doubted Bunny Harrington had featured in her ladyship's calculations.

She settled down to read and having reached the part where Catherine had endured Mr Tilney's indignant tirade for trespassing in a private area of the house, Flora slapped the book face down in her lap with a sigh.

'I would have gone looking too,' she murmured, her sympathies lodged firmly with the misunderstood heroine.

'Talking to yourself?' a voice asked.

Flora flung a hand over her eyes to where Bunny stood, the sun at his back.

'Sort of. Won't you join me?'

'Hmm, better not occupy someone else's seat, or I'll be in disgrace for the rest of the voyage.'

'Borrow Eddy's, I doubt he'll notice. He's at divine service with the Gilmores.'

Bunny dragged the nearest chair closer, tugged up his trousers and sat.

'I suppose everyone is still talking about this morning's drama?' Flora said darkly, having studiously ignored several curious looks from passers-by.

'Does that surprise you?' Bunny plucked a cushion from a pile beside his chair and tucked it behind his neck, his head tilted back to receive the morning sun.

'No, I suppose not,' she said, distracted by a savoury aroma that drifted towards her on the wind. 'What's that wonderful smell?' She sniffed appreciatively.

'Bouillon.' Bunny indicated to where a steward moved along the line of chairs, pausing at each one. 'Would you like some?'

Without waiting for an answer, he beckoned the man over and requested two cups. Handing one to Flora, he tossed a coin onto the tray.

The steward examined the coin so closely, Flora half expected him to bite it.

'Thank you very much, sir!' Pocketing it with a

flourish, the steward withdrew.

'I see you're a generous tipper.' Flora wrapped both hands round the cup, allowing the steam to drift over her face.

'The work is demanding for the Southampton boys. Long hours for derisory pay, so they tend to rely on passenger's tips.'

'The housemaids at Cleeve Abbey work equally hard, but they never get more than a day-old cake or cut of left-over pork to take to their mothers on a Sunday.' She looked up from her cup and took in his expression. 'Oh dear, that sounds bitter, doesn't it?'

'Not really. I'm impressed you consider those less fortunate than yourself with some charity. So many people don't.'

'The same applies to yourself, I think. Anyway, don't stewards have to hand their tips in to the steamship treasury?' Flora repeated what Lord Vaughn had used as an excuse for a measly gratuity on the outward voyage. 'It's not all added to their wages, either.'

'Really? I didn't know that.' He adjusted his spectacles with a disgruntled sniff. 'I'd like to think good tips keep them honest. The temptation to cheat must be irresistible amongst all this luxury.'

Flora spotted Gus Crowe at the other end of the deck in conversation with a prosperous looking man in a fur coat.

'Talking of cheating,' she began, changing the subject, 'you told the captain Mr Crowe was angry when he lost at cards. Is it possible he suspected Parnell of double-dealing?'

'Ah, we're back to that, are we?'

'I don't like mysteries,' Flora said, mildly disgruntled at being dismissed by yet another man, however politely.

Bunny shook his head. 'I doubt Parnell employed sleight of hand. He was just lucky. Biscuit?' He held up one of the flat beige roundels, twirling it like a conjurer.

Flora took it eagerly, surprised at how hungry she was, despite her breakfast.

'What did the ladies do while the men played poker last night?' She bit into the still warm, floury biscuit, following it with a mouthful of hot, salty bouillon that slid warmly into her stomach.

'The old lady from Baltimore loudly disapproved of card games played for money.'

'The old lady who didn't make an appearance at breakfast?' Flora asked round a mouthful of crumbs.

'Mrs Penry-Jones. That's right. Claims to be one of the four hundred.'

'Forgive my ignorance, but what's the four hundred?'

'Fascinating American idiosyncrasy.' Bunny chewed his biscuit and swallowed. 'Four hundred was the number of guests who could fit into Mrs William Backhouse Astor Junior's ballroom. Thus the number of New York society considered the elite.'

'Really.' Flora silently resolved to avoid Mrs Penry-Jones, then remembered that she was seated at the same dining table.

Bunny grinned at Flora over the rim of his cup. 'Perhaps she tripped Parnell with her cane and sent him to the bottom of the stairs because she objected to gambling.'

'I shan't rise to that, Mr Harrington.' Flora narrowed her eyes. 'And you? What did you do all evening?'

'Me?' He blinked, then thought for a moment. 'I chatted to Cynthia for a while, and then Mr Hersch joined us.'

'An interesting man, I thought. He's German, isn't he?'

Bunny swallowed a mouthful of bouillon, nodding. 'Originally. He's been a resident in New York this past twenty years, or so he said. Affable chap, but, well, buttoned-up is a good description.'

'Did he play cards last night?' Flora asked, not sure of the relevance of this card game. But it was somewhere to begin.

'For a while, but folded early on. He was winning too, which struck me as odd. I asked him what he did for a living at one point, but he was vague. It wasn't until later I realized he hadn't answered my question.' Bunny shrugged. 'I suppose he only agreed to play to be sociable. Not like Parnell.'

'What about Parnell?'

'Hah! He played as if his life depended on it.' He caught her eye and winced. 'Sorry, bit inappropriate in the circumstances. Ah, here's young Eddy.' He looked pointedly at his watch.

'What are you doing here, Eddy?' Flora asked, her ear cocked to the strains of 'Eternal Father Strong to Save' drifting from the deck above. 'Divine Service hasn't finished yet.'

'Um.' Eddy shuffled his feet, rubbing both

57

hands down the side of his trousers. 'Me and Ozzy didn't go.' He indicated a boy with blunt-cut straight blond hair and mouse-brown eyes beside him. 'We played shuffleboard instead.'

'I see.' A reprimand died on her lips. She could hardly chastise Eddy when she had not attended service herself. 'I'll forgive you this once, though you'll be expected to display more conspicuous devotion at Marlborough.'

Eddy's shoulders slumped in relief. 'Oh, I will, I promise.'

Bunny mouthed the words 'conspicuous devotion' behind the boy's back with a mock-horrified expression that made Flora clamp her lips together to prevent herself laughing.

'Did you really find the body, Miss Maguire?' Ozzy could evidently not hold in the question a second longer.

'I did. However, I trust neither of you have discussed the gentleman's demise with the other boys. It's disrespectful.'

'How would he know if we talked about him or not?' Eddy demanded, with all the straight-forwardness of youth. 'He's dead.'

Bunny chortled and Flora sighed.

'Captain Gates told my father that card sharps might be on board.' Ozzy peered at her myopically. 'Perhaps Mr Parnell was a professional gambler.'

'It was simply an accident,' Flora insisted, despite her own thoughts on the subject.

'They'll bury him at sea, you know,' Ozzy announced with dispassionate authority. 'Wrap his body in a sail and sew it up like a parcel with the last stitch right through his nose.'

'Really?' Eddy's eyes widened. 'Straight through the bony bit, or just the soft end?'

'Eddy!' Flora spluttered on her bouillon.

Bunny's shoulders shook with ill-concealed mirth, at which Flora threw him a 'don't just sit there' look.

'How would you boys like an ice cream?' Bunny withdrew a dollar note from his wallet and waved it in front of them.

'Jolly decent of you, Mr Harrington.' Eddy palmed the note with the speed of an illusionist. 'See you at luncheon then.'

The boys were halfway along the deck before Flora spoke. 'You do know ice cream on this ship is complimentary?'

'Is it really? I had no idea.' Bunny's lips twitched as he dipped his nose into his cup, then immediately held it at arm's length, grimacing. 'Dash it, my bouillon has gone cold.'

Flora spent more time than usual selecting what to wear for luncheon, finally settling on a sage green blouse in soft cotton with pale grey trim over a grey skirt. While fastening a gold and garnet brooch left to her by her mother, a gentle rap came at the door.

Assuming it was the stewardess with clean linen, Flora's welcoming smile froze in place at the sight of Bunny Harrington in a dark blazer and buff slacks, one arm braced above his head against the door frame.

'I thought I would offer my services as your escort to luncheon.' His smile betrayed he was not totally confident of his welcome.

'That's most kind of you.' Her voice came out surprisingly calm, considering how his slow, appraising gaze unsettled her. Flora pulled the suite door closed behind her and fell into step beside him. His rimless glasses made him seem less studious than the horn-rimmed ones. 'How many pairs of glasses do you own, exactly?'

He slid them off his nose, peering at them as he walked as if he had never seen them before. 'Several. They're an indulgence of mine.' He replaced them on his nose, then reached past her to push open the door that led into the staircase lobby.

'Actually, I have a small confession to make,' he said as they descended the oak staircase side by side. 'I ran into young Eddy earlier, who suggested I call on you.'

'I see.' Her stomach did a tiny dip of disappointment, suspecting Eddy did so to assuage his guilt at preferring Ozzy's company to hers.

'Although I imagine every unattached man on board will be lining up to be your escort soon,' he went on. 'I simply thought to steal a march on them.' He stood to one side at the dining room doors to allow a line of passengers to pass them.

'Well recovered,' she murmured, acknowledging Officer Martin as they passed him on their way to the table. The sailor's benign smile reminded Flora of something she had meant to ask Bunny, and by the time he had settled her into her chair, the thought had solidified.

'Bunny? When Officer Martin asked about last night's card game, you looked about to say something, but changed your mind.'

'What? Ah, yes, that.' He grimaced. 'Thought better of it. A chap shouldn't gossip if it's likely to stir things up for anyone.'

'For whom exactly?'

'Max Cavendish. He said something to Parnell, I didn't hear what, but for a moment I thought Parnell was about to punch him.'

'Why didn't you mention that to the captain?'

'Don't know really, but why spoil the man's honeymoon by suggesting he held a grudge against a dead man?'

His exaggerated shrug was reminiscent of Eddy when caught out in a misdemeanour.

Flora was about to suggest he had implied exactly that, when a voice sounded at her elbow.

'Miss Maguire.' Dr Fletcher paused beside her. 'I'm glad to see you have recovered from our little upset this morning.'

'Not much recovering was necessary.' Flora regarded him steadily, pleased when he looked away first. 'I had never met Mr Parnell.'

'Quite so. Though some of the other ladies on board don't possess your constitution. I've been handing out sedatives all morning.' He gave a curt nod and then strode in the direction of the captain's table, pausing to talk to passengers on the way.

'What are you thinking?' Bunny asked, his head tilted toward her.

'That he's a handsome, amenable man with good manners. I'm simply not convinced of his professional ability.'

'Because he dismissed your question about the

blood on the deck?'

'Lack of blood.'

She looked to where Monica Gilmore approached and greeted them both like old friends, with planted kisses on cheeks and pressed hands. Having noisily persuaded her husband to re-arrange the seats, her attention shifted past Flora's shoulder.

'Here's someone you haven't yet met, Flora. Mrs Penry-Jones and that odd companion of hers.'

Flora turned to where an angular elderly lady limped towards them, leaning heavily on a black cane, a large black bag hooked over her other arm. Three rows of pearls the size of hazelnuts encased her wrinkled neck above a forest green taffeta gown in the style of some ten years previously.

'Assist me, won't you, Hester?' she demanded of the woman who followed close behind. 'Take my bag and place my cane where I can reach it.'

Flora recognised the companion who rushed to obey as the same woman who had been listening to her conversation with Eloise on deck. Her mousy brown hair was scraped back from her round face into a severe chignon which gave her eyes a cat-like tilt.

In response to Monica's introduction, the old lady pressed the ends of Flora's fingertips, muttering, 'Adele Penry-Jones,' in a tone which intimated Flora should have heard of her. 'My companion, Hester Smith.' She directed a backwards wave at the woman beside her without looking at her.

'Maguire,' Mrs Penry-Jones turned the word over on her tongue, then added, 'Irish?'

'Somewhere in my ancestry perhaps,' Flora replied. Scottish grandfathers notwithstanding.

'Every hansom driver and waitress we came across in New York was Irish,' Monica said.

Flora groaned inwardly. Already the odds were stacked against her. Wait until they found out she was a governess.

A heavy-set young man with floppy hair and slightly bulging eyes weaved between tables towards them, his face brightening when Bunny introduced him to Flora.

'Max Cavendish.' He pumped her hand with enthusiasm, his gaze constantly searching the room. 'I'm travelling with my wife, but she appears somewhat tardy.'

Flora blinked, having expected the exquisite Cynthia to be married to someone more physically impressive than this well-fed puppy of a man.

'I run Beaufort's department store,' Max said, pausing when Flora hesitated. 'I can see you've not heard of it, but we're opening a branch in London this year.'

'I'll be sure to pay a visit when I'm next in the city,' Flora said, suspecting her salary was unlikely to run to such extravagance.

Amongst the ensuing clink of crockery and low hum of conversation, the doors opened again to admit Cynthia, who entered with the measured walk of a woman seemingly oblivious of her surroundings but who was aware she commanded attention. At the table she bent slowly and dropped a lingering kiss on her husband's head before taking her seat.

'Steady on, old girl, everyone's watching.' Max flushed and ducked his head.

'Give the busybodies something to talk about,' Cynthia murmured, her eyes narrowed in response to Mrs Penry-Jones's critical tut.

The companion, Hester, ignored the new arrivals, and nibbled at a bread roll as if the dining room was the last place she wished to be. Flora idly wondered if her red-rimmed eyes were her normal appearance, or her employer's treatment had been a cause of her tears.

'It was the Scotch with us,' Mrs Penry-Jones drawled, continuing a thread already abandoned. 'I believe Queen Victoria insists all her servants are Scotch.'

'I think you'll find the inhabitants of that country are called Scots or Scottish, Mrs Penry-Jones,' Mr Hersch said slowly. 'Scotch is whisky.'

'Indeed?' The old lady sniffed and narrowed her eyes at him, which made him smile.

Flora's hunger was back in full force when a waiter slid a plate of lemon sole in lobster sauce in front of her. She began loading her fork when she became aware of Mrs Penry-Jones peering at her.

'Didn't Lord Vaughn's eldest girl marry one of the Astor boys last month?' She dabbed puckered lips with a napkin. 'You must be one of the sisters.'

Flora's fork hovered enticingly an inch below her lips before she laid it down carefully, steadying herself for the moment she had dreaded since boarding.

'Actually, Viscount Trent is my charge. I'm escorting him home so he can start at Marlborough next term.'

'Charge? You mean you're his gov-er-ness?' She gave the word three syllables, her upper lip curled in disdain. 'How unconventional! When did it become acceptable for such persons to eat in first class dining rooms?'

'When they have a ticket?' Flora replied, emboldened by Bunny's arm pressing against hers.

'Bravo, Miss Maguire.' Mr Hersch hid a knowing smile behind his napkin. 'We have entered a new millennium. These are modern times, and we must all learn to adapt.'

'Not to my mind.' Mrs Penry-Jones's tone implied she ought to have been consulted on the matter. 'Being forced to share a table with those of another class is most galling.'

'I quite like it,' Gerald said. 'I've made some extremely good scrapers on board steamships.'

'What, may I ask, is a "scraper"?' Miss Ames reached for her notebook that sat beside her plate.

'It's what they call shipboard friendships.' Gerald ignored Mrs Penry-Jones' sour look. 'On board, everyone is what they appear to be.'

'Or pretend to be,' Flora said under her breath, her thoughts still on the late Mr Parnell.

'Has anyone seen Miss Lane this morning?' Monica asked, giving the room a sweeping glance. 'I should imagine she was distraught to hear of Mr Parnell's accident.'

Mrs Penry-Jones mumbled something incoherent, while beside her, Hester flushed a deep red. Flora didn't hear what was said, but assumed

65

Hester was being reprimanded.

Miss Ames leaned forward, her pen still poised. 'Miss Maguire doesn't think it was an accident at all. Do you, Miss Maguire?'

'Really?' Max's ever-present smile congealed. 'What do you think happened?'

Flora caught Bunny's 'you are on your own' look and sighed. 'I have no sound reason or any proof. Merely an impression.'

'Trusting your instincts is a creed of which I always approve.' Miss Ames underlined something in her notebook with a flourish. 'The man may very well have been murdered.'

Hester stopped chewing and inhaled a noisy breath, her face suffused with red. She began to cough, but before it could turn into a full-blown crisis, Mr Hersch delivered a single, hard slap between her shoulder blades.

Thanking him, she patted her upper chest, blushing furiously.

'I'm quite all right now.'

'What exactly are you suggesting?' Ignoring Hester, Mrs Penry-Jones glared at Flora.

'I didn't mean to suggest anything.' Flora bit her lip, aware all eyes had turned towards her. 'I'm sorry, I shouldn't have spoken.'

'I heard a rumour he was a professional gambler. Perhaps he cheated at cards,' Monica said.

'One can't accuse the man of being a broadsman without proof, Monica,' Gerald snapped.

Hester fumbled her water glass, which tipped half its contents across the table. 'I-I'm so sorry, Mrs Penry-Jones,' she stammered, oblivious to the fact it was Max who was forced to leap out of the way to avoid his trousers being soaked.

'Clumsy!' Mrs Penry-Jones's thin lips twisted into a sneer.

The companion dabbed at the spillage with her napkin, but her feeble efforts seemed to annoy the old lady more.

'Oh, do stop that. Hester, you're making it worse. Summon a steward.'

Gus Crowe watched the small drama with a self-satisfied smirk. Flora had seen his type before. He would never begin an argument, but provided ammunition for others to do so.

'I don't believe this speculation about Parnell helps matters.' Mr Hersch topped up his wine glass before ostentatiously offering the bottle to the rest of the table. 'Starting rumours will only make the situation worse.'

Cynthia toyed with the pendant at her throat, pulling the jewel along its gold chain. 'I agree. This voyage is going to be unutterably boring if that man's demise is the only topic of conversation.'

'One cannot stop people talking, my dear.' Miss Ames spoke with the relish of someone who was glad of the fact. 'We're all captive on this ship for another week.'

'If it's not inconvenient, Mrs Penry-Jones, may I return to the suite?' Hester discarded her plate and rose. 'The movement of the ship is making me queasy.'

'Oh, if you must.' The old lady sighed, and turned away.

'Poor Miss Smith, she's such a timid little thing,' Monica whispered, her gaze on Hester as she manhandled the cumbersome bag between waiters and passengers on her way out. 'She made a dreadful fuss about tipping over a water glass.'

Flora nodded but stayed silent, her gaze on Hester's retreating back. It wasn't the falling glass that had upset her, but something that was said earlier. Flora wished she could recall what it was.

Chapter 6

'I went straight back to my stateroom after dinner last night, so missed all the excitement.' Miss Ames slid into Hester's vacated chair.

'There was none,' Gerald said. 'When Parnell left the bar he was in perfect health.'

'Oh well, anyway, I had this idea for a novel you see, and simply had to write it down.'

'Do share it with us,' Monica gushed. 'We could do with a distraction from this horrible business, couldn't we, Gerald?'

'Can't wait.' Gerald's lip curled. He cast a re-signed look at Max, who rolled his eyes in sympathy.

The dining room had begun to clear. Bunny made his move to leave and Flora rose, though her contrived excuse to take her leave proved unnecessary. Mr Hersch and the Cavendishes had already left, and Miss Ames gave her no more than a distracted wave, returning immediately to an enraptured Monica and a clearly bored Gerald.

Bunny joined her at the rail on the boat deck, where a warm breeze lifted the loose hair at Flora's temples. The sea was like glass, and the only sounds above the thrum of the engines below them was the whoosh of the waves as the vast ship cut through the ocean beneath a clear sky.

'How about a game of poker?' Gus Crowe appeared at Bunny's shoulder, nudging him hard.

'Good idea.' Max came into view, rubbing his hands together. 'Cynthia's busy writing letters this afternoon.'

'Thank you, no.' Bunny clutched his arm, a weak smile directed at the two men. 'Though I'm sure Gilmore will be happy to join you.' He nodded to where Gerald had emerged onto the deck.

'Is that right, Gerald?' Max asked. 'Are you game for a hand or two?'

'Long as Monica doesn't find out.' Gerald gave the door behind him a swift furtive glance. 'Let's repair to the smoking room before she finds something for me to do.'

'Ah well, see you later then, Harrington, Miss Maguire,' Crowe drawled, as the three of them sloped away like schoolboys intent on mischief.

'Please don't feel you need to miss the game on my account,' Flora said.

'I'm not a card player, and those three play for very high stakes.' Bunny twisted toward her. 'I see you are sticking to your theory that Parnell was murdered.'

'For all the good it will do me.' She fell into step

beside him as he set off along the deck, her face turned into the wind, dislodging strands of hair that blew into her eyes. 'Besides, Mr Hersch was right about idle speculation. I should be more careful what I say until I have some proof.'

'You're probably wise. By the way,' he asked in a change of subject she suspected was deliberate. 'Did I hear you mention Eddy was enrolled at Marlborough?'

Flora nodded. 'I hope he'll be all right, he's never been away from home on his own before. He's a sensitive boy.' When she had ventured her misgivings to Lord Vaughn, he had dismissed her with talk of family tradition.

'I'm sure Eddy will cope beautifully.' He leaned his back against the aft rail, both forearms balanced behind him while the wind tugged his hair into disarray. 'I'm an old Marlburian myself.'

Flora blinked, surprised, though there was no reason why she should have been.

'My father claimed it was because Charterhouse wouldn't take me. Which I suspect was a ploy aimed to keep me on my toes.'

'Did it work?'

His face cleared and his lop-sided smile appeared. 'Oh yes. Top marks all the way through to Oxford, and then a first.'

'Impressive. Shall I see you in the Commons, your speeches quoted verbatim in *The Times?*'

'Definitely not.' His snort of derision spoke volumes. He angled his head toward her. 'What's that look for? My motor car isn't simply an indulgence, you know. It's how I intend making my living.'

'I just thought–' Her gaze slid over his immaculate dark blue blazer, the diamond pin that held his tie in place, then down to the hand-made shoes of soft leather.

'Appearances mean little,' he said, following her look. 'Granted, I benefitted from a privileged upbringing, but after my father died and the debts were paid, all that was left was a crumbling mansion and an annuity.'

'You have no other family?'

'Only my mother.' His change of tone reflected his devotion to his lone parent. 'She sold the crumbling pile, and we now share a charming eight-bedroom house on the Thames in Richmond and an annuity. I've had to apply my expensive education to earn my living.'

Flora hid a smile, bemused that his idea of reduced circumstances was a house with eight bedrooms and a private income. She doubted Bunny Harrington had ever woken to a winter's dawn in an attic bedroom with a quarter inch of ice inside the glass.

'May I take you in to dinner this evening?' Bunny asked, suddenly.

She turned her face into the wind in order to hide the sudden warmth that flooded her face.

'I appreciate the offer, but I don't expect you to escort me to every meal.' His face fell and she rushed on, 'I'll look forward to your company, though. After all, we occupy the same table.'

His unsmiling nod told her this was poor consolation. The next few moments passed in mildly embarrassed silence, until he indicated a man in an overcoat who stood between two lifeboats smoking a cigar.

'That chap over there asked to see my designs, so if you don't mind, I–'

'Of course not, please go ahead.'

Flora watched him go, surprised at the depth of her attachment to him, when twenty-four hours ago she had never heard the name Bunny Harrington. He didn't seem to mind she was a governess, but then why would he? To him she was most likely a temporary amusement with whom to pass a few days aboard ship. Or was she denying herself the chance of getting to know a perfectly nice man who seemed genuinely interested in spending time with her?

A dilemma for her to ponder, and almost as mysterious as who might have killed Mr Parnell.

Flora pushed open the double doors of the library, where tapestry upholstered sofas formed horseshoe arrangements set round low tables in a room divided into alcoves, marked by supporting pillars. Like the dining room, a glass lantern ceiling flooded the space with light, while rows of polished walnut bookshelves lined the walls from floor to ceiling; every one entirely empty.

'Where are all the books?' she enquired of a passing steward.

'They were pledged as a gift by the City of Minneapolis in recognition of the ship bearing the same name,' the freckle-faced young man she had accosted informed her with the air of a tour guide. 'Though, unfortunately they didn't reach New York before we sailed.'

'What a shame.' Flora had intended to give

Eddy some work in preparation for school.

'We do, however have a few magazines to accompany afternoon tea perhaps?' He handed her a copy of *London Illustrated News*. 'It's two months old, though I could find more if you wish.'

'This one is perfect, thank you.'

So engrossed in an article about Ramsay MacDonald's new Labour Party, only Mr Hersch's distinctive timbre from a nearby table told Flora she wasn't alone.

'You're certain as to the cause of that head wound?' he asked someone else.

Flora straightened, confident the white painted pillar she sat behind shielded her from sight, but could just made out Dr Fletcher's profile on the sofa to her right.

'I cannot be sure,' he replied. 'However, the signs indicate a fall.'

'Might it have been administered by something heavy?' Hersch persisted. 'An ashtray, perhaps?'

Flora smiled. Of course. The square brass ashtrays were a feature of every cabin, and would be the perfect weapon. Eddy had knocked theirs off the table onto his foot, his subsequent yell attesting to its considerable weight.

'That's somewhat specific,' the doctor said. 'What made you mention that?'

'A maid reported the one in Parnell's cabin went missing after he was found. Poor girl was worried she would be made to pay for it.'

'The housekeeping staff have their wages docked for breakages, most of which never happen,' Dr Fletcher said. 'Harsh, maybe, but company policy.'

'When the crew were questioned, they said the

deck was washed before Parnell's body was discovered, but insisted there was no blood on the steps, or beneath the body.'

'I found that somewhat unusual, but fear it's destined to be one of life's mysteries.'

'What about the lividity on his face?'

'What about it?' The doctor's voice took on a sharp edge.

'Can you explain it?'

'I am qualified, you know,' Dr Fletcher snapped. 'I suppose you could say it was odd if he had only lain there a short while, but hardly conclusive.'

Flora hunched against the pillar, taking small bites of a shortbread biscuit, her excitement growing at the knowledge she wasn't the only one who believed Parnell may have been dead for hours, not minutes.

'Could he have been killed elsewhere?' Hersch asked. 'And his body left on the steps to make it appear as if he had fallen?'

'Steady on.' The doctor dropped his voice to a fierce whisper Flora struggled to hear. 'You could damage my reputation with such talk.'

'What is more significant, is that it would mean there's a murderer on board.' Hersch appeared to be losing patience with the good doctor.

'Quiet, man! You don't want to go spreading rumours like that.'

Flora imagined the doctor giving the room a swift, nervous glance to see if they had been heard.

'What do you expect me to do about it?' he continued in a fierce whisper.

'Nothing, for the moment,' Hersch said, unfailingly calm. 'However, I suggest you ensure your record-keeping is flawless, or this could come back to haunt you.'

'I hope you're wrong, Hersch.' The creak of leather signalled the doctor was about to leave. 'Anyway, I must be off, I've a patient due with a boil that needs lancing. One of the few ailments I can charge for as it didn't occur on board.'

His footsteps tapped across the polished floor, followed by his cheery greeting to someone on his way out. The room fell silent, the clink of china and the slap of the door the only sounds as stewards and passengers came and went.

'He didn't appear particularly interested in my theory, did he, Miss Maguire?'

Flora froze. Aware it would be pointless to pretend she hadn't heard, she peeked around the pillar to where Carl Hersch stirred his tea, the silver spoon dwarfed by his manicured hands. His immaculate nails were the first thing she had noticed about him.

'Did you know I was here all the time?' She rose and eased round the pillar whilst bidding a mental farewell to the last remnants of her reputation. As if tripping over dead bodies wasn't enough, she had now been caught blatantly eavesdropping.

'I doubt you wear perfume, my dear, but your soap is distinctive. Jasmine, I think.' He gave a low chuckle, indicating the seat the surgeon had vacated. 'Would you care to join me?'

Flora sat. 'Is it my imagination, or did Dr Fletcher seem nervous?'

'You noticed that, did you?' Hersch lifted the teapot in invitation. 'You don't suffer fools gladly, do you, Miss Maguire?'

'He's not a fool, but I think he's lazy.' Flora declined his offer of tea, but his compliment gave her confidence. 'Do I understand you saw Mr Parnell's body after it was taken to the doctor's office?'

'How did you know that?' He took a slow sip from his cup before returning it to the table.

'You mentioned the purple bruise on Parnell's cheek, which you wouldn't have known about had you not seen it for yourself.'

'Very astute of you.' His eyes crinkled at the corners as his probing gaze met hers.

Flora stiffened, suspecting she was being teased. 'It's not merely idle curiosity. I have responsibility for a young boy whose safety is my chief concern.'

'I apologize, Miss Maguire. I don't mean to be flippant.' He leaned back in his chair as if settling in for a long talk.

'Tell me, what were your impressions when you first came upon the body?'

'Well.' Flora cast her mind back to her initial horror at discovering the pile of clothes was in fact a dead man. 'He lay face down with a gash on the back of his head that had already congealed. I couldn't see blood anywhere else. Not on the steps or the handrail.' Hersch looked about to ask a question, but she rushed on, 'I have no medical training, but on a large country estate, injuries occur quite often from farm equipment and horses. I can tell an old wound from a fresh one.'

'All this told you what?' He steepled his fingers

76

below his chin.

'That if Mr Parnell fell down those steps, he did not do so in the half hour before I got there.' When he did not correct her she asked, 'Is lividity what that purple mark was? It covered half his face.'

Hersch's mouth twitched, but did not expand into a smile. 'Indeed yes. It's what happens when the heart stops pumping. The blood in the veins pools at the lowest points, causing that purplish blue colour. It doesn't appear for at least half an hour after death. Parnell's injury would have rendered him either dead or unconscious, so I doubt he could have moved on his own.'

'There was a small amount of dried blood on his shirt collar,' Flora ventured.

'Dried, you say?' His brows drew together, his glance drifting to the ceiling. 'The body had already been stripped when I saw him, but that puts the time of death into dispute as well.'

'There's something else.' Her enthusiasm grew at the fact she was being taken seriously at last. 'Why was he still wearing his dinner suit at six in the morning?'

'A good point.' He stroked a thumb and forefinger down his clean shaven chin.

'Mr Hersch? Is it possible Mr Parnell died much earlier and his body was thrown down those steps to make it look like an accident?'

'I'll reserve judgement until more information comes to light.' He leaned towards her, lowering his voice. 'But between you and me, Miss Maguire, I'm not happy about the circumstances of this man's death. It doesn't look right.'

A rush of excitement fizzed through her veins that she wasn't alone in her opinion. Though as he said, they needed more proof. In which case, she would have to find some.

Chapter 7

Eddy emerged from his bedroom already half way into a conversation. 'Some of the chaps want to listen to music after dinner,' he said, his tongue protruding as he fumbled with his tie.

'There's a piano in the smoking room and one of the crew has offered to play for us. You don't mind if I join them, do you, Flora? I promise to be back by 9.30.'

'What sort of music?' Flora completed the knot for him. Sometimes, she had to remind herself he wasn't yet fourteen, but at times behaved as if he were much older.

'It's not boring stuff. Tin Pan Alley mostly.' He stood passive while she tweaked his collar and smoothed his hair.

'I doubt your parents would object. Your father often hummed the one about the bank if I recall.'

'"The Man Who Broke the Bank at Monte Carlo"?' he hummed in perfect tune. 'I like it too.'

'9.30 at the latest then.' Flora dismissed him with a gentle push. 'And remember, it's Sunday, so decorum is called for. Oh,' she added in mock seriousness. 'No smoking, either!'

'Flora!' He snorted in mock disgust. 'In any

case, they chuck us out before the grown-ups come in.'

Flora dressed in a gown of primrose yellow lawn with a fine lace overskirt; a lacy shawl over her exposed shoulders quite inadequate for evening sea breezes, but far too pretty not to wear.

When the meal bugle sounded, she went along to the dining room on the deck below.

Through the filigree gold etchings on the glass in the dining room doors, Flora spotted Bunny seated at the table. Cynthia sat opposite him, one elbow propped on the table, her chin in her hand and staring into his eyes as if he conveyed the meaning of life.

Despite Flora reminding herself Cynthia was a married woman, her confidence dwindled. She was the type of woman Bunny was destined to be with; not a shy girl who hovered in a doorway trying to summon the courage to go in.

A group of diners approached, all talking at the top of their voices; a trait characteristic of the upper classes. Flora stepped behind a pillar as they passed, just as a voice sounded in her ear.

'Don't turn around.'

Flora froze, though she was more confused than alarmed. A blast of hot breath enveloped the back of her neck as the voice came again in a sort of breathless croak.

'Leave well alone, Miss Maguire. People disappear from ships all the time. No one would miss one nosy governess.'

In the brief interval during which Flora plucked up the nerve to turn around, the group had disappeared through the doors in a burst of animated chatter, and the lobby stood empty.

She hadn't imagined it? Had she?

Another three couples descended the stairs, their voices raised as they swept past Flora, leaving an enticing waft of expensive perfume in their wake.

Flora smoothed her skirt with shaking fingers, then joined the tail end of the group as they entered the dining room. Warmth and light combined with the clatter of plates comforted her as she eased through the crowded room to her table.

Bunny looked up with a smile and Cynthia relinquished her seat without being asked.

'Are you quite well, Miss Maguire?' Carl Hersch enquired from the other side of the table. 'You look somewhat shaky.'

'Y-yes. I'm fine, thank you.'

Warmth flooded her face and her glance flicked to the empty chairs. Eloise had yet to make an appearance, but not everyone was seated, making it difficult to tell who else was missing.

'Not still nervous about being in company, are you, Flora?' Bunny whispered.

'N-no, I'm quite all right, but outside just now, I–'

'Ah, here's our notorious actress,' Gerald announced, and nudged Bunny, distracting him.

Eloise approached the table, her stride slow and sensuous. She dimpled at a middle-aged ogler and blew a kiss to another, while their female companions glowered like cross twins.

'I don't care if my wife does disapprove,' Gerald murmured. 'I think our pocket Venus is quite lovely.'

'Good evening, everyone.' Eloise's captivating smile encompassed them all. 'Do get me a drink, Mr Harrington.' She blew a kiss at Bunny, and drawled in her sultry accent, 'I'd like a large gin and tonic as an aperitif.'

Miss Ames exchanged a scandalized look with Monica, who uttered the word, 'Actresses.'

'Sorry, Flora, you were about to say something,' Bunny said, once the waiter had left.

Flora hesitated. The safe, warm atmosphere of the crowded room with its clink of glass and low laughter made the incident in the lobby seem unreal. As if it had happened to someone else.

'It's nothing. I'm fine.'

Eloise sipped her drink, flirting in equal measure with Gerald on one side and Max on the other, seemingly unaware of the hostility emanating from their wives.

'Bank clerks, even secretaries travel to Europe unaccompanied these days,' Mrs Penry-Jones responded to a remark Flora missed. 'I always say, if one cannot afford to employ a maid, one should not be permitted to purchase a ticket.'

'Why shouldn't single, independent ladies enjoy foreign travel simply because they are without husbands or male relatives to escort them?' Miss Ames tossed the trailing end of a canary yellow boa carelessly over her shoulder. 'It seems harsh to deny us the same advantage.'

'I agree,' Flora said, recalling Bunny's advice to stand up to the likes of the old lady.

'Hmm...' Mrs Penry-Jones did not trouble herself to answer, but stared at Flora down her long, pointy nose. 'One cannot be too careful. A woman came out of Lady Radley's suite this morning and struck up a conversation with me. It wasn't until tea-time I discovered I'd been prowling the decks with her maid. Everyone saw us talking too.'

'How distressing, what *did* you do?' Cynthia asked, her face a picture of false outrage.

'When she approached just now, I cut her, naturally.'

By the time the entrées arrived, nerves had robbed Flora of her appetite. Despite her determination to forget it, the man's warning in the lobby kept repeating in her head and wouldn't go away. Even if he didn't actually hurt her, what if he turned his attention on Eddy? A thirteen-year-old boy was an easy target.

She considered excusing herself to see that Eddy was all right, then remembered he would be at his musical evening with the other boys. He was safe there for the time being, and besides, what excuse would she give for dragging him away?

Consumed by worry, Flora only caught the tail end of a question Miss Ames had directed at Eloise, just as the mains were placed around the table.

'...recovered from the death of your travelling companion?'

'We weren't friends!' Eloise waved her fork in the air. 'Ours was purely a business arrangement.' Beside her, Gus Crowe shifted sideways in order to avoid a chunk of beef landing in his lap. 'Someone has since told me I'm talented enough not to need him.' She aimed a wink at Flora.

'That's somewhat callous.' Miss Ames puckered

her thin lips. 'The poor man's been dead less than a day.'

'It was an accident,' Eloise said on a sigh. 'Tragic maybe, but an accident – nothing more.'

Draining her glass, she held it out for a refill from a passing waiter. When she turned clumsily back to the table, her elbow swung perilously close to a crystal rose bowl, whisked away in time by Gerald. Mrs Penry-Jones tutted loudly, while Hester glared at Eloise with disapproval mixed with disgust.

A waiter approached, a wide tray expertly balanced on one shoulder from which he distributed dishes of chocolate mousse among the diners at a nearby table.

Without warning, Eloise rose suddenly from her chair, and unbalanced, staggered backwards, her arm flung out behind her in an effort to stay upright.

Flora brought a hand to her mouth, aware of what was about to happen but helpless to prevent it. Dismayed, she could only watch as Eloise's hand sent a tray of glass dishes flying from the man's hands.

Chairs were hurriedly scraped back. A man at the next table issued an expulsion of rage, his evening shirt sporting a large smear of whipped cream.

Eloise surveyed the damage dispassionately, offering a garbled but incoherent apology.

A steward led the cream-splattered man away, while a stiff-lipped waiter gathered pieces of broken glass with repeated apologies.

'I feel quite woozy.' Eloise raised a hand dramatically to her forehead. 'Would you be a darling and take me back to my suite, Mr Harrington?' she asked, ignoring a respectable offer to do exactly that from Gerald.

'Sit down, Gerald,' Monica snapped. Reluctantly, he resumed his seat.

'We're happy to oblige,' Bunny rose, hauling Flora to her feet.

'What?' Flora gaped. 'Why me?'

'I insist,' Bunny whispered. 'I have no desire to be trapped in a stateroom alone with an inebriated woman.'

'I never took you for a coward,' Flora said mischievously. Then the thought she was about to leave the safety of the crowded dining room brought back the earlier incident. 'I'll come, provided you promise to look in on Eddy for me. He said he would be back by 9.30.'

Her request seemed to take Bunny by surprise, who blinked. 'I'll pour his cocoa for him if you like.'

'You don't have to be sarcastic. He isn't a baby. I-I simply want to make sure he's safe.' Flora trailed after him and an unsteady Eloise, aware of the interested stares turned their way.

She wondered which of her audience had threatened her outside earlier.

By the time Flora had retrieved Eloise's key from her bag, she clung to Bunny like a rag doll, leaving him with no option but to hoist her into his arms and carry her inside. Lowering her limp figure onto the bed, he barely paused to see if she was likely to fall off again before backing away.

'There. My chivalrous deed is done for the night.' He held both hands up in surrender. 'I'll order some coffee for her, but I'll leave the rest to you.'

'Don't forget to stop in on Eddy,' Flora reminded him as he left. He gave an airy backwards wave of one hand without looking back.

Bemused, Flora watched him go before turning her attention to Eloise.

'Black coffee is what you need, Miss Lane, or you'll be fit for nothing in the morning.' She plucked the coverlet from the foot of the bed and spread it over her.

Eloise moaned, but barely stirred, her face in repose and her cloud of messy black curls in stark contrast to the snow white pillow.

The detritus of Eloise's chaotic life lay strewn over every surface in the one-room stateroom; an oyster silk negligee discarded on a chair, open pots of cosmetics scattered on the dresser. A feather puff in a layer of flesh-coloured grains, a string of agate beads looped over the corner of the mirror.

The bulkhead that separated the stateroom from Flora's bedroom bore no trace of whatever had struck it the previous night.

A light knock came at the door and Flora let in the steward, who lowered a tray onto the table in the sitting area where he began arranging the cups.

'I'll manage that, thank you.' Flora ushered him out.

'Is that coffee I smell?'

Flora turned from closing the door and swung round to where Eloise sat with her arms wrapped round the hump formed by her raised knees, regarding her with eyes as clear as glass.

'Excellent! Good thinking, Miss Maguire.' Eloise patted her curls into place with one hand. 'That should convince everyone.'

'I-I thought–' Flora broke off in mute confusion.

'I know what you thought, which was entirely the impression I wished to give.' She heaved the bed cover onto the floor, grimacing at her rumpled skirt before advancing on the coffee tray.

'Why did you want everyone to believe you were drunk?' Flora demanded, her governess instincts rising to the surface.

'Because I intend to take a look in Frank's stateroom.' Her attempt to smooth out the more obvious creases had no effect, and she gave up with a flap of her hand.

'Break in, do you mean?' Flora gaped as she handed her a cup of the hot, fragrant brew from the tray.

'I quite understand if you want nothing to do with it.' Eloise's smile dissolved and she gave a resigned sigh. 'In which case, feel free to go to bed with your cocoa like a good little governess.'

Flora bridled. 'If they find out, won't you be the first one they'll suspect? You're the only one on board who knew him.'

'Perhaps.' Her eyes sparkled with mischief. 'However, I couldn't possibly have done such a thing. After all, I was so inebriated, that nice Mr Harrington and the governess had to put me to bed.'

'I wish you'd stop calling me "the governess".'

Flora took a mouthful of coffee to give herself time to think, but regretted it, the brew was too strong and quite bitter.

'Ooh, I'm impressed,' Eloise said. 'I expected you to go screaming for the captain. I admit, I didn't bargain on you as my nursemaid, but you're here now, so do you want to help me or not?'

'You haven't yet told me what it is you expect to find.' Flora's heartbeat quickened, but she kept her face impassive.

'Money, my dear girl. And don't glare at me like that. It's my money. I gave it to Frank last night. He said he needed it to pay our expenses in London.'

So that was what they had argued about? The dead man's character slipped markedly in Flora's estimation in that he had expected her to pay the bills.

'How much did you give him?' Flora added more milk to her cup to dilute the coffee.

'Three thousand dollars.'

Flora almost choked on her next sip.

'Frank won't need it now, will he?' Eloise's steady gaze challenged Flora to contradict her. 'I still have to pay my hotel bill when I reach London. So I want it back.'

'What if we get caught?' Flora's head filled with unwelcome images of her being escorted off the ship in London in chains by two burly policemen, watched by a distraught Eddy and a calm, but resigned Bunny.

Eloise drained her cup and returned it to the tray. 'You don't have to help me, but it will be quicker with the two of us. Are you game, or not?'

Without waiting for an answer, she made for the door.

Quietly seething, Flora followed. Which, she decided, was what Eloise counted on. Don't give your press-ganged accomplice time to reconsider. She would never admit it, especially to Eloise, but the thought of finding something to prove she was right about Parnell's death to shove beneath Bunny's nose was tempting.

Then her father's stern 'I'm disappointed in you' look floated into her head but she pushed it away on the short walk across the deserted deck to Parnell's stateroom.

'Warn me if anyone comes,' Eloise instructed, inserting what looked like a double hatpin bent at right angles into the lock.

'Have you done this before?' Flora whispered. At Eloise's slow sideways look she added, 'Never mind, it's best I don't know.'

Flora scanned the deck on both sides, but the boards gleamed empty in the moonlight. The passengers must still be at dinner, or had de-camped to the saloon, neither of which was reassuring. She began to wish she hadn't come. What possible explanation could she give if discovered outside a dead man's cabin? Or worse, inside it?

Seconds stretched, then Eloise straightened, throwing her a brief, dazzling smile. 'We're in!' Grabbing Flora by the elbow, she yanked her inside, closed the door and twisted the latch. 'Let down the blinds!'

When the second one fell to the ledge with a dull thump, Eloise flicked the light switch, flooding the room with a sulphurous yellow glow.

A mirror image of Eloise's, Parnell's stateroom was bereft of any signs of human habitation, which, Flora reminded herself, was hardly a surprise.

'You try the bureau,' Eloise ordered as she advanced on the wardrobe, dropped into a crouch and slid open the drawers at the bottom.

Flora felt a stirring of excitement as the top drawer slid open on silent runners, but lay empty except for a few sheets of blank notepaper which bore the Atlantic Transport Line logo. What did $3,000 look like anyway?

'Anything?' Eloise whispered from her kneeling position in front of the wardrobe, replacing an obviously empty valise.

'Not yet.' Flora rifled through immaculate folded white shirts, and a pile of card collars rolled together with some silk ties.

Eloise dislodged a row of shoes in the bottom of the wardrobe that fell in a series of soft thumps onto the floor. One bounced and came to rest beside Flora. She handed it back, noting the upper was highly polished but the sole looked thin and worn. A pile of crisp laundered shirts sat in the drawer, a pristine overcoat on a padded hanger above her head. The contrast appeared incongruous, as if the late Mr Parnell was all front and no substance.

'I'll take a look in the bathroom,' Eloise said. 'You stay here.'

Flora gave a silent nod, then looked down as a paste-board folder dropped to the floor, open to reveal a sepia-coloured photograph. A darkly handsome man stood beside a delicate, pretty blonde who wore a wide smile of uninhibited happiness. Apart from her hair colour and lack of make-up, she resembled Eloise. A relative, maybe?

Retrieving the photograph, a folded sheet of newsprint slid onto the floor.

A loud rattle of the doorknob froze Flora in place. Panicked, she thrust the photograph into the bottom of the drawer and dumped the pile of shirts on top.

Eloise's head appeared around the bathroom door, one finger pressed to her lips.

Flora slid the drawer closed, then spotted the square of paper on the floor. Scooping it up, she shoved it into her pocket, every nerve on edge.

'Darling,' a high-pitched female voice came from outside. 'That's not our cabin. We're three doors farther down.'

A muttered curse followed the release of the doorknob. A brace of footsteps moved away, accompanied by soft feminine laughter.

Eloise tiptoed to the door, pulled back the side of the blind with two fingers and peered onto the deck. Turning to Flora she mouthed, 'They've gone.'

Flora released a held breath, a hand pressed to her chest beneath which her heart thumped uncomfortably.

'We'd better go,' Eloise whispered. 'Did you find anything?'

Flora shook her head. 'There's no money here, not even small change.'

'Damn!' Eloise flicked off the light. 'What a waste of time.' Easing open the door, she checked both ways before beckoning Flora to follow.

Back in Eloise's cabin, they collapsed onto the rumpled bed, in fits of giggles like hysterical schoolgirls.

'I've never done anything like that before.' Flora hugged a pillow to her chest.

'What a dreary life you lead.' Eloise wiggled backwards onto the mattress.

'Possibly,' Flora bridled. 'However, yours will be somewhat less dramatic with your money out of reach. Where does that leave you now?'

'I'm not broke exactly, but honestly, I could kill Frank, I–' She broke off and flushed prettily. 'I mean, if he hadn't fallen down that companionway.' She wrapped her arms around her bent legs, her chin resting on top of her knees. 'Don't mention I said this to anyone, will you, Flora, but something doesn't seem right about Frank's accident.'

Flora stiffened. 'What doesn't seem right?'

'I don't know.' Eloise chewed her bottom lip. 'Falling down staircases wasn't Frank's style. Pushing people down them, now that's more like him.' She stretched her arms luxuriously, yawning. 'Anyway, thanks for your help, Flora. I'm sorry we didn't find anything.'

'Which must strike you as odd.'

Eloise blinked. 'Odd, in what way?'

'Bun – Mr Harrington told me Mr Parnell won a considerable amount of money at cards last night.'

'He did?' A frown appeared between her perfectly plucked eyebrows. 'What do you call a considerable amount?'

'Over $2,000, maybe more.'

'No!' Eloise's head jerked up. 'The sneaky bas–' Words appeared to fail her, and sighing, she dropped her chin back onto her knees.

'The reason I mention it,' Flora went on, 'is because that money wasn't in his stateroom, either. If he died soon after the card game, he didn't have a chance to lodge it in the ship's safe. The purser's office was closed.'

Eloise gave a dismissive 'tsk' through her lips. 'Frank didn't trust banks.' Her head jerked up again, pinning Flora with a hard stare. 'You think he was killed for the money?'

'I couldn't say, but it's beginning to make sense.'

Eloise shook her head. 'I can't imagine anyone on board taking such a risk. It's small change to most of them.'

'Not necessarily. An ocean liner is a great leveller. Once on board we can be whomever we wish.' Flora recalled the state of Parnell's shoes. 'After all, did you know I was a governess when we first met?'

'I didn't, no. Not until Mrs Penry-Jones said – well never mind what she said. Besides, she didn't speak directly to me, more in my presence. Women like her don't talk to actresses. I counted myself lucky she asked me to pass the mustard at dinner.'

'Exactly what I meant. Anyone can buy a first class ticket, everything else can be invented to suit their purpose.' Her thoughts went back to Parnell's worn shoes and undergarments.

Eloise slid off the bed, her arms crossed at her waist. 'Look, Miss Governess, I don't know what you're implying, but I haven't invented anything or killed–'

'I wish you'd stop being so defensive,' Flora cut across her. 'I wasn't referring to you.' Unless her judgement was faulty, Eloise wasn't a killer. 'You said you aren't happy with the manner of Mr Parnell's death, well nor am I. I believe someone killed him.'

'Killed?' Panic entered Eloise's eyes. 'I don't know anything about that. I want to get back what is rightfully mine, nothing else. If you spread talk like that, before you know it, I'll be the one accused.'

'But surely–'

'No, I mean it.' She dragged Flora to her feet by one arm in a surprisingly firm grip for someone with such a slight frame. 'Thank you for helping me tonight, but I'm not being accused of murder.' She propelled Flora out onto the deck where a cool wind tugged at her skirt.

Before the door closed, she heard Eloise whisper, 'Not again.'

Chapter 8

Day Three – Monday

After a surprisingly restful night, Flora was up and dressed, pouring hot tea from the pot brought by the stewardess, when Eddy stumbled into the sitting room.

'You look tired, didn't you sleep well?' Flora picked up the trailing cord of his dressing gown and handed it to him.

'I had a strange dream, about Meely.' His voice softened. 'I was six again, and she took the ladder away from my tree house when I was still inside.' He rubbed his eyes with both hands. 'I dreamed she left me there for days, not just until supper-time.'

'How ungenerous of her.' Flora recalled the incident well. 'I take it you forgave her?' Flora knew all about strange dreams, but this one didn't sound too disturbing. 'Have you and Ozzy any plans for the day?'

'Not really.' Eddy flopped into a chair. 'We've played all the deck games and seen as much of the ship as the crew will let us. We tried to sneak into the engine room but some burly chap in an overall ordered us out.'

'So I should think. I hope you won't try that again. It's dangerous down there.'

'Jolly hot too.' Eddy scratched his head, yawning. 'The other boys are all talking about Mr Parnell's murder. Have they got any ideas as to who did it?'

'Don't joke about such things.' Flora's cup rattled as she handed it to him. 'Besides, who says it was murder?'

'Well, suspicions then. I overheard Giggles tell the second officer he thought Mr Parnell's death wasn't an accident.'

'Who's Giggles?'

'That's what the passengers call Captain Gates, because he laughs all the time.'

'I trust you always address him as Captain

Gates, and nothing else.' She hid a smile at this portrayal of the good captain. He had the most sparkling eyes and a mouth permanently upturned in an amiable smile. Flora had also been witness to the fact he could issue orders from the bridge to the boat deck without the use of a megaphone. 'What exactly did the captain say about the accident?'

'Not much.' Eddy draped one leg over the arm of the chair and swiped a biscuit from the tray. 'We were in one of the lifeboats. "The matter warrants further investigation," were his exact words.'

'To whom did he say that?' Eddy took another biscuit, at which Flora moved the plate out of his reach. 'And what exactly were you doing in a lifeboat?'

'Playing pirates.' His grimace indicated her question was unreasonable. 'He was with that American chap with the grey moustache.' He examined his wristwatch. 'Blimey, it's nearly time for breakfast, and I'm not even dressed.' He slurped half his tea in one gulp, then headed for his room.

'Eddy! Since when do you use words like that?'

He turned back at the door and shrugged. 'Ozzy says it sometimes.'

'It's a profanity, which I'm certain would be frowned upon at Marlborough.'

Eddy murmured something unintelligible before closing his door with a bang, but Flora chose not to ask him to repeat it.

Perhaps it was a good thing he was off to boarding school.

Bunny was seated alone at their table when Flora entered the dining room. She gave her order to the waiter and drummed her fingers on the table until he left.

'Well,' she asked Bunny when the man was out of earshot. 'Aren't you going to ask me about Eloise?'

'What's to ask?' He swallowed a mouthful of coffee, setting the cup back into its saucer with a click. 'She was semi-conscious when I left. I assume you settled her in bed and left her to sleep it off.'

'Not quite, she—' Flora broke off as the waiter returned with a gleaming, silver coffee pot, fidgeting as he fussed with the crockery and enquired if they desired anything further.

'You seem edgy,' Bunny said when they were alone again, a tiny crease between his brows. 'Did something happen after I left last night?'

Flora told him.

'Are you serious?' His voice rose, then dropped again to an angry whisper. 'How could you have been so reckless?'

She shushed him when several heads turned in their direction. 'It all happened so quickly, I didn't have time to argue. Eloise practically dragged me along.'

'I'm not the one to whom you'll have to make your excuses if you are found out.' He spread a piece of toast with butter, adding after a pause. 'There was nothing there, you say?'

'No money, but there was this photograph in amongst his shirts. I didn't have time to study it closely, because we were interrupted, but—'

'You were discovered?' His toast froze halfway to his mouth.

She waved him away, impatient. 'A couple came to the wrong stateroom, but went away again. No one saw us.'

He exhaled slowly through pursed lips and relaxed back in his chair. The relief on his face made her want to wrap her arms around him to reassure him he had no reason to worry on her account. It was a strange sensation, similar to the protectiveness she felt towards Eddy, but somehow different.

'Do you have the photograph?' he asked.

'What?' She slanted a look at him beneath her lashes. 'And add theft to my litany of crime?'

'No, of course not, I simply–' He dropped the toast back onto his plate untouched. 'Can you be sure it wasn't a picture of Eloise and Parnell? They might have been closer than she admitted.'

'I'm positive.' She hunched closer. 'He was taller and far more handsome. And he had a moustache.'

'Like roughly a third of the male population,' Bunny murmured.

'Here's another question then. Why does Eloise dye her hair an unflattering black? It dulls her vibrant looks, which is the opposite of what she would want.'

'I expect actresses do it all the time to suit their roles.' He took a bite of his toast and chewed.

Flora fiddled with her napkin, mainly to give her something to do with her hands to stop her slapping him. Why did he have to contradict everything she said?

97

'Flora?' he said, slowly after a moment. 'You realize that had Eloise taken money from the cabin, and been caught, you would have been an accessory to theft?'

'The money was Eloise's, so that's not like–' she broke off. 'Oh. I couldn't prove that, could I?'

'Exactly. And it worries me that you took her word for it.'

He was right. That was exactly what she had done, believed every word Eloise had told her.

'It didn't sound like a lie at the time.' Aware her excuse sounded feeble, Flora fell silent as the waiter slid a plate of yellow smoked haddock that glistened beneath a layer of melted butter in front of her. A glistening, perfectly round poached egg on top.

'She couldn't have known he was going to die.' Flora trickled vinegar onto her fish, then caught Bunny's expression of horror and frowned. 'What?'

'Are you actually going to eat that now?' He wrinkled his nose and peered at her plate.

'I certainly am.' Dipping her fork into the white flesh, she brought it to her lips, trying not to moan with pleasure as she swallowed the first mouthful. 'Eloise isn't convinced Parnell's death was an accident, either.'

'Why do you care if it was murder or not?' Bunny lowered his voice as passengers filed into the dining room. 'You didn't even know the man.'

'Maybe not.' Flora twirled her fork, pensive. 'I simply hate being told what to do by men who think they have all the answers.' Officer Martin's dismissive sneer loomed into her head. She stabbed the poached egg with her knife, breaking the yolk.

'Governess one minute, emancipated woman the next.' Bunny regarded her over the rim of his coffee cup. 'You're something of an enigma, Miss Maguire.'

A warm glow spread upwards from her stomach, dissolving when it occurred to her that he couldn't be interested in her, not really. He was merely amusing himself.

'What about the cash Parnell won at cards?' Flora said, composed again. 'Eloise didn't know about that. The money should have been in his stateroom, but there was no sign of it.' She was about to dip a piece of bread roll into the runny egg yolk on her plate, but thought better of it.

'His winnings could have been on his body.' Bunny chewed a piece of bacon thoughtfully. 'If so, Captain Gates would have lodged it in the ship's safe.'

'I suppose that's possible.' Flora sighed as her carefully thought out theory began to fall apart.

'So where does this take us?' Bunny asked, when she remained silent. 'Perhaps Eloise thought he would lose her money at the card table and refused to give it to him. They argued and he ended up at the bottom of those steps?'

'But he didn't lose,' Flora said. 'He won.'

'The other night he did, but gamblers always think they'll win. That's why they're gamblers.'

'I don't believe Eloise is either a thief or a killer,' Flora insisted. 'She's a young woman alone who has to make the best of her life because she has no one else to do it for her.'

'How do you know she's alone in the world? Is that what she told you?'

'Well, not in so many words. It was an impression I got.' Flora stirred milk into her coffee, marshalling her thoughts. 'Bunny,' she began, 'something very odd happened last night, I–'

'I know it did. You became a burglar.'

'No, not that, someone–' She gasped, and clamped a hand to her mouth as creeping dread crept into her chest. 'I've just remembered! We didn't lock Parnell's door after we left.'

Bunny groaned. 'Tell me you're joking.'

She shook her head, wincing. 'Do you think anyone will notice?'

'Probably, but there's nothing you can do about it now.' His gaze slid past her shoulder, and he cleared his throat in warning.

Flora turned her head just as Cynthia approached, looking stunning in yellow silk.

'Aren't you two the early birds,' she cooed in a fair imitation of one herself. 'Here I thought I was the first.'

'The sea air makes me hungry.' Bunny stood while Cynthia took her seat.

Flora reached for her coffee, annoyed with herself at having failed again to tell him about the threat. Now Bunny would think she was keeping secrets from him.

The dining room began to fill, putting an end to their conversation. Gerald and Monica squabbled their way from the door. On reaching their places, their sour expressions transformed into

100

identical smiles, as if a switch had been pressed.

Most of the time the Gilmores seemed incapable of being more than a handclasp away from each other, but at others appeared positively hostile.

'Probably sleeping it off,' Gerald said when he caught Flora staring at Eloise's chair.

'I suppose so.' She gave him a weak smile. It wasn't the condition of Eloise's head that concerned her. For the tenth time that morning, Flora wished she had kept the photograph from Parnell's cabin.

Miss Ames arrived on Mr Hersch's arm attired in a combination of lime green and salmon pink, which reminded Flora of a parakeet.

The German wished everyone a breezy 'Good morning' before launching into an animated conversation with Cynthia and the writer. His ability to pay attention to a beautiful woman and a plain one with equal charm was a skill Flora could never have guessed at, but couldn't help admiring.

His penetrating eyes beneath thick, arched silver brows viewed the world with wry amusement, and as with all genuinely clever men, he made no attempt to demonstrate his intellect. He gave a considered response and a warm smile to their every remark, no matter how banal.

'Do you happen to be acquainted with Mrs Moreland's school in Bath, Miss Maguire?' Monica asked, distracting Flora. 'We hope to send our girls there in the autumn.'

'Really, Monica,' her husband said with barely concealed irritation. 'Flora doesn't have an intimate knowledge of every educational establishment in the county.'

'I haven't, I'm afraid,' Flora said gently, softening Gerald's response. 'Cleeve Abbey is at least fifty miles from Bath. Though I may know someone who might. I'd be happy to write and ask them for you.'

'That's most kind of you, my dear.' Monica's gracious smile transformed into a frosty glare she directed at her husband.

'Yesterday must have been something of an ordeal for you, dear lady,' Hersch said to Mrs Penry-Jones casually, though his intense stare told Flora he waited with interest for her answer.

'Ordeal?' The lady's voice rose. 'Why should you think so?'

'I meant the death of Mr Parnell,' Hersch persisted, watching from half-closed lids. 'Violent death is hardly a daily occurrence.'

Mrs Penry-Jones inhaled, narrowing her already thin nostrils. 'Members of the lower classes come to grief all the time. Why should this particular one have affected me?'

'And if that's not a *Pooterism*, I don't know what is.' Gerald snorted.

'Interesting,' Flora murmured, and wondered if that was deliberate self-effacement on Gerald's part, or a genuine lack of vanity?

'Sorry, what did you say?' Bunny broke off his conversation and asked.

'It means someone who takes themselves grotesquely seriously.'

'From the novel, *The Diary of a Nobody*,' Bunny said. 'I've read it.'

'Apparently Gerald has too, and yet he always

looks bored when Monica and Miss Ames talk literature, it surprised me, that's all.'

'Oh, look out.' Bunny nodded to where Mrs Penry-Jones had slapped her companion's hand away from her cup with an angry tut.

'Hester! You know I don't like sugar in my coffee.'

'I'm sorry, Mrs Penry-Jones, I quite forgot.' Flushing, Hester summoned the waiter, who replaced her employer's cup with a fresh one.

Flora's sympathy for Miss Smith rose to the surface, and she wondered if anyone had asked Hester how she felt about Parnell's death.

'What about you, Miss Smith?' Mr Hersch's amiable smile expertly diffused the awkward moment. 'Are you equally unmoved by the death of a fellow passenger?' His question voiced Flora's thoughts so closely, she stared at him, but he was not looking her way.

'I-I think it was a dreadful thing to happen.' Hester pushed her fried egg into mush with her fork, her gaze on her plate. 'I can have no feelings one way or the other. I wasn't acquainted with the gentleman.'

'He wasn't a gentleman!' Mrs Penry-Jones snorted. 'He was a weak, vacillating man with no ambition. Bound to come to a bad end.'

'That seems a very harsh judgement on so short an acquaintance,' Flora said.

'Still looking for villains, Flora?' Bunny whispered, giving her a playful nudge.

Flora was about to deliver a suitably pointed retort when Hester fumbled the glass lid of a jam pot, leaving a smear of apricot conserve on the white tablecloth.

Mrs Penry-Jones fastidiously removed the dish from Hester's reach with a long-suffering sigh.

'It's quite obvious!' The old lady sniffed. 'I was there when he persuaded a room full of strangers to gamble for such high stakes on first meeting. Vulgar man.'

Flora groaned inwardly. So much for her hopes of an actual motive.

'Are you sure you didn't know him, Mrs Penry-Jones?' Gerald spread a bread roll with butter as he talked. 'I could have sworn I saw Parnell being admitted to your suite the night he died.'

'Don't be ridiculous!' The old lady's eyes narrowed with outrage. 'You must have been mistaken.'

'My stateroom adjoins Mrs Penry-Jones's suite,' Hester said. 'Had anyone knocked at her door, I would certainly have heard it.'

Mrs Penry-Jones gave Hersch a look of triumph, though Hester's support went unacknowledged.

'Possibly.' Gerald wiped his fingers on his napkin. 'It's difficult to tell whose stateroom is whose. All the doors look the same.'

'If that is what you saw, Mr Gilmore,' Mr Hersch fixed Gerald with a hard stare, 'why did you not inform the captain?'

Gerald steadily returned the man's gaze. 'What makes you think I didn't?'

Hersch appeared to have no answer to this, though he was saved from further questioning by the arrival of Max.

'Couldn't find my cuff links,' he explained, when Cynthia scolded him for lateness. 'Looked everywhere but they aren't in the suite.'

'Not the ones I gave you for a wedding present?' Cynthia's eyes narrowed.

Max flicked up the back of his jacket and sat. 'No, not those. The emerald ones.' He held up one sleeve, which sported a flat, gold oval. 'Had to wear these instead.'

'You probably packed them in one of the trunks that have been put in the hold. I'm sure they'll turn up.' Cynthia waved him away.

'I had them last night in the smoking room. I went to wash my hands so the cards wouldn't stick, and had to roll up my sleeves, so–' He broke off and pasted on a smile. 'You're probably right, my love. They'll turn up.'

'Is the meal not to your liking, Miss Smith?' Mr Hersch indicated Hester's loaded plate. 'You've hardly touched your breakfast.'

Hester pushed her plate away with a tiny grimace of distaste. 'The eggs are undercooked.'

'My head is pounding this morning.' Mrs Penry-Jones rose from table, pausing theatrically until all eyes were on her. 'I'll return to my suite and lie down. No, Hester, don't get up. Finish your breakfast.'

The gentlemen's chairs scraped back, while a steward scrambled to hold open the door, as she limped past him with the hesitant gait of someone with arthritis.

'It appears your employer is more upset about a death on board than she would have us believe, Miss Smith,' Mr Hersch observed as the gentlemen resumed their seats.

Hester returned his benign look steadily. 'Not

at all. She's notoriously unsentimental.'

Colour returned to her cheeks and her cat-like eyes sparkled. Her features relaxed and she looked, if not pretty, then more animated.

'Does Mrs Penry-Jones have family?' Monica asked, apparently eager to take advantage of the lady's absence.

'Her husband was a lawyer in upstate New York,' Hester replied without hesitation. 'He died years ago. I believe she was married before, but they lived in Baltimore then.' She paused in her monologue to summon the waiter with more confidence than she had exhibited thus far, demanding her congealed eggs be replaced.

'She claims acquaintance with everyone,' Hester continued when the waiter withdrew. 'She talks about Ward McAllister as if she expects him to call. I wonder that someone doesn't tell her the man's been dead these five years.'

Cynthia choked off a cough, her butter knife gripped so hard, her knuckles showed white.

'Wasn't he the chap who collapsed into his roast venison at the Union Club?' Gerald said, then jerked, possibly from a swift kick to his shin delivered by Monica beneath the table.

Flora bit her lip to prevent a smile. It appeared the demise of the disgraced socialite was not suitable breakfast table conversation.

'As for what you saw, Mr Gilmore.' Hester turned a coy look on him. 'I could have been wrong about Mr Parnell. I sleep heavily, so he might very well have called on Mrs Penry-Jones.'

Cynthia's fork clattered nosily onto her plate. 'Excuse me, but I've just remembered there's something important I must do.' She threw her napkin onto the table with the force of someone issuing a challenge to a duel, pushed herself to her feet and marched out.

Rising more slowly, Max sighed. 'I should go and see if she's all right.'

'Honeymooners, eh?' Gerald chuckled when the pair were out of sight. 'Never know what's likely to upset 'em.'

'How would you know, Gerald?' Monica sniffed.

'Wonder what Max said to upset Cynthia?' Bunny whispered. 'Her face was like thunder.'

'Unfortunately, we'll probably never know.' Flora frowned, her gaze drifting to Eloise's empty chair.

Chapter 9

That afternoon, Flora watched Eddy partner Ozzy in an enthusiastic game of chalking the pig's eye on the boat deck.

The sound of her name being called brought her head up to where Bunny waved from the promenade deck. He pointed with a finger at his own chest, then down at her in a gesture inviting himself to join her.

At Flora's nod, he performed a 'thumbs up' gesture, pushed back through the crowd, and emerging again on the boat deck. She watched him with possessive affection as he made his way towards her, offering polite greetings and sheepish smiles to fellow passengers as he passed.

'How is Eddy getting on?' he asked on reaching her.

'He appears to have a remarkable aptitude for guessing where he should enter his mark.' Flora indicated the blackboard which bore a roughly drawn shape of a pig in white chalk. 'Look, he's done it again! That's his third high score.'

The pressure of Bunny's upper arm against her shoulder robbed her briefly of all rational thought.

'Hmmm...' His sceptical tone brought her head round to look at him. 'That could be because his blindfold is thinner than Ozzy's.'

'I hadn't noticed that actually.' Flora narrowed her eyes. Bunny was right. Eddy's blindfold was a thin strip of navy blue chiffon, too thin to obscure his sight. 'I'll have a word with him later on the subject of fair play.'

'Best not to let on you know, and besides, the game is over now.' He nodded to where the board was being manhandled off the deck by two sailors. 'I was about to pay a call on Matilda, would you care to join me?' His tone intimated he granted himself a treat.

Flora hesitated, her desire to spend time with Bunny vying with her responsibility towards her charge. Since the whispered threat the night before she wanted to keep Eddy close. 'That's kind of you, but I need to ensure Eddy is suitably occupied.'

'Don't you think you're suffocating the lad somewhat?' he said with thinly disguised impatience. 'You've barely left his side since breakfast.'

'Maybe you're right, but that's because—'

She broke off as she spotted Eddy approach at a run with Ozzy, while Monica trailed a little way behind, bestowing coy waves to those she passed.

'Because what?' Bunny asked.

'Nothing.' Flora frowned. The longer she left telling Bunny about the man outside the dining room, the harder it became.

'May I listen to Mr Gilmore's gramophone?' Eddy pleaded. 'It's one of the new ones that plays disks, not cylinders. Do say I might, Flora!'

'Father has a recording of "When Johnny Comes Marching Home".' Ozzy joined in. 'He bought it in New York before we left. The gramophone, not the record. Though of course he bought that too—'

'That sounds wonderful, Ozzy,' Bunny said. 'I wouldn't mind hearing that myself sometime.'

Flora hesitated, torn between denying Eddy a treat and protecting him.

'Come now, Flora,' Monica chided as she drew level. 'Surely you could relax your watchful eye a little? After all, there's not much chance he'll get lost on the ship.'

'That's exactly what I've been telling her,' Bunny said.

From the corner of her eye, Flora spotted the captain approach the companionway to the Upper Promenade deck, and came to a decision.

'If Mrs Gilmore is agreeable, you may listen to the gramophone, Eddy.' She turned to Bunny. 'I'll come and see Matilda with you another time. However, if you'll both excuse me, there's something I must do.'

Accompanied by a despondent 'as you wish' from one and enthusiastic thanks from the other, Flora headed for the staircase lobby and climbed the stairs. If what Eddy had overheard was true, the captain should hear about the man with the croaky voice. On the landing above, Captain Gates stood talking to Dr Fletcher, where Flora hovered, hoping for a suitable lull in the conversation. She almost left it too late, when, without warning, Captain Gates nodded curtly to the doctor, turned and pushed through the door onto the outside deck.

Flora was about to follow, when Dr Fletcher intercepted her. 'Is there something you wanted, Miss Maguire?'

'Um – I wanted to have a word with the captain.'

Flora bounced on her heels as she watched her target through the window as he disappeared rapidly down along the deck.

'Anything I can do? He's a busy man, you know.' The implication the captain was too exalted to talk to her showed in his world-weary expression.

'Well, all right.' Flora took a deep breath. 'Last evening, a man whispered a warning to me outside the dining room not to ask questions about Mr Parnell's death. But before you ask, no, I didn't see him, nor did I recognize his voice.'

'I see.' Dr Fletcher paused to acknowledge a regal-looking couple who sauntered past.

'I thought the captain should know, bearing in mind a man has been killed.' Flora sensed his attention had drifting away and she wished she hadn't sounded so vague.

'Mr Parnell died as the result of a fall, Miss Maguire.' He regarded her with a mixture of resignation and false sympathy which must have taken him years to perfect. 'I understand you were distraught at finding the body, though perhaps you have allowed yourself to dwell too much on the incident. As for whispered threats, well, they could simply be your fertile imagination.'

Flora counted backwards from ten.

'I wish you wouldn't keep accusing me of being distraught in a tone you might use for "unhinged". I didn't imagine it, Doctor.' She put emphasis on the last word, attracting attention from several people who traversed the lobby.

The doctor smiled at them in an I-have-this-under-control-way, and with a firm grip on her elbow, guided her into a door recess.

'Forgive me, Miss Maguire, but you do appear somewhat agitated. Would a sedative help?'

'No, it would not, and – oh, never mind.' She eased out of his hold. 'I only ask that you relay my message to the captain. He'll understand its importance, even if you don't.'

'Certainly. If that's what you wish.' He clicked his heels, then left through the same door the captain had used.

Flora stared after him, while several uncomplimentary adjectives about officers and men in general lined up in her head.

'Good afternoon, Miss Maguire,' a voice halted her as she was about to insert her key into her suite door.

Flora turned to the amiable smile of Mr Hersch,

his fedora raised an inch above his head. 'Are you quite well today? You look a little harassed, if I may say so?'

'Maybe I'm still distraught,' she said, then regretted her flippancy. Mr Hersch was hardly responsible for the doctor's attitude. 'I tried to tell the captain something, but... Oh, never mind, it's nothing really.'

'I suspect it's a great deal more than nothing, Miss Maguire.' He cocked his head to one side. 'If it's something to do with the late Mr Parnell, I may be able to help.'

Flora doubted it, but the idea was tempting. She returned her key to her bag and approached the rail where he stood. 'May I ask you something first?'

'Of course, what is it?'

'What is your interest, Mr Hersch?'

His gaze met hers and held. 'Let's say I have some experience in these matters.'

He twisted his hat in his hands before placing it slowly back on his head.

'Has the captain changed his mind about what happened? About it being an accident?'

'He thinks the situation warrants further investigation.' He repeated Eddy's words almost exactly. 'Why? Has something new emerged?'

Flora exhaled in a rush. If he had the captain's confidence, what harm could it do to tell him? After all, she had told the doctor and she respected him less than this thoughtful German.

'Last night,' she began slowly, 'a man outside the dining room warned me in this odd, choked whisper, that I was to leave well alone.'

'Those were his exact words?'

She nodded, grateful he had not asked the more obvious questions and simply taken her word.

'Did you believe him?'

'Dr Fletcher dismissed it as my imagination, but–'

'No, Miss Maguire. I asked if *you* took this man's threat seriously?'

She nodded. 'He unsettled me enough to believe he might hurt me.'

'Therefore you must have said something in public to make him afraid of you.'

'Afraid?'

'Of course. Or why bother to frighten you into silence?'

'Oh, you mean what I said at luncheon yesterday about the lack of blood throwing suspicion on to the time of his death. Yes, that was silly of me, wasn't it?'

'You weren't to know, then. Who else have you told about this man?'

'Only Dr Fletcher. He agreed to relay the details to the captain, but treated me like an hysterical female with an over-active imagination, so I have my doubts.'

'Fletcher is a difficult man to read, with a somewhat inflated view of his own abilities. The captain, on the other hand, is very experienced. I will mention it to him myself if you wish.'

'Thank you, I appreciate that. I didn't know whom to tell.' She hoped she didn't sound self-pitying.

'You're talking to *me*.'

'Yes, I know, but–'

113

He cut her off with a wave of his hand. 'I suggest that for the time being, it would be wise to make everyone believe you have acceded to this man's wishes.'

A middle-aged couple passed them, heads bowed in acknowledgement. Hersch returned their greeting, waiting until they were out of earshot before continuing.

'Tell me, what did you think about Miss Smith's behaviour at breakfast?'

Flora blinked, disarmed by the unexpected change of subject. 'She doesn't appear to like Mrs Penry-Jones much, which makes me wonder why she remains in her employ.'

'I've seen worse masters and less respectful servants, Miss Maguire.' His sigh conveyed long experience of studying his fellow man. 'Perhaps Miss Smith views a few sharp remarks a fair exchange for a life of material comfort?'

'Possibly,' Flora replied, sceptical.

Whatever advantages Hester enjoyed would never really be hers, merely an illusion of affluence.

'Has anyone else on board engendered your mistrust, Miss Maguire?'

'Not really. Cynthia doesn't like Hester Smith, and she and Max whisper together a lot, but that's hardly surprising for honeymooners.' Flora ran through a list of names in her head. 'Miss Ames asks lots of questions, but that ties in with her being an author. Mr Crowe is arrogant as well as grasping, what my father would call a freeloader. He appears to relish other people's disagreements too. Even encourages them.'

'I've noticed that myself.' He ran a thumb and forefinger down either side of his moustache, a gesture he used when thinking. 'And what does Mr Harrington think of your theory about Mr Parnell?'

'He listens, but he's not convinced.' Flora pushed thoughts of Bunny to the back of her mind. He confused her enough without discussing him with a third party. 'Mr Hersch, if the captain has doubts, why hasn't he instigated a search of Mr Parnell's stateroom?'

'What do you expect him to find?' He held her gaze steadily.

Flora hesitated. 'Something among his belongings which might shed some light on the reason for his death. Documents perhaps, a letter, maybe?' She was about to mention the photograph, but her confidence failed her.

A small smile pulled at his lips without revealing his teeth.

'I would ponder that theory, if I were you, Miss Maguire. You may be required to explain it by someone who will not accept dissembling.'

'I'll bear that in mind.' Flora exhaled slowly, aware her cheeks felt hot. 'If someone did kill Mr Parnell, and I am convinced now they did, how will we find out who it was?'

'That, I do not know. If we wait, I feel sure he will make a mistake and reveal himself.'

'Just that? Wait?'

'Where could a murderer go? We're in the middle of the Atlantic.' He touched two fingers to his hat, inclined his head and strolled off along the deck.

Flora didn't find this at all reassuring, although she found some consolation in the fact she wasn't the only one concerned by the circumstances of Parnell's death.

Chapter 10

In the dining room that evening, enthusiastic greetings and swapping of places to chat went on at the other tables as normal, though few ventured near Flora's; as if those who had shared the victim's last evening had been tainted by Parnell's death.

Flora watched the door, but Eloise didn't put in an appearance. Knocks at her stateroom during the day had gone unanswered, and whenever Flora encountered her on deck, she contrived to be in a group, rendering private conversation impossible.

The meal proved uneventful, marked only by Max's preoccupation with his belongings as the diners prepared to adjourn to the bar for coffee and after-dinner drinks.

Flora was about to excuse herself on the grounds she didn't want to leave Eddy alone, then remembered she had engaged a stewardess to sit with him. On reflection, this struck her as overly cautious, for as time passed, she began to feel Dr Fletcher was right and she had imagined the croaky-voiced man.

'I must have dropped my tie pin somewhere.'

Max rummaged through his pockets as he left the table. 'The catch is loose, so it's probably my own fault.'

'Is it valuable?' Miss Ames asked, the pink bows she had attached to her upswept hair bobbing like butterflies.

'I suppose so, it's set with a rather exquisite diamond.' Max turned to where Gerald scoured the floor around the table. 'It's not there, old boy. Take my word for it. I'll ask the waiters to keep a look out.'

Cynthia slipped her hand through his as they negotiated the staircase to the upper deck.

'Don't fuss so, Max. It's only jewellery. At least, that's what you're always telling me.' She exchanged a knowing look with Monica, who rolled her eyes in silent sympathy.

When Eloise finally made an appearance in the bar, she did so on the arm of Gus Crowe.

'I knew it!' Flora's sharp nudge dislodged Bunny's elbow from his chair. 'She's definitely avoiding me. Why else would she miss dinner, then choose a sleazy fellow like Crowe as an escort?'

'Maybe she's embarrassed about last evening?' Bunny suggested.

'She won't escape me that easily.' Flora sniffed, ignoring his oblique criticism. 'I'm determined to find out more about that photograph.'

'Maybe there isn't any more to find out,' Bunny said, one eyebrow raised.

Flora wasn't convinced.

The lack of seating in the small bar on the upper deck necessitated a reorganization of seating. Chairs were allocated to the ladies, leaving the men to perch on stools. Once settled, Max ordered drinks for everyone, while Gerald's insistence he share the tab was garrulously declined, as was Bunny's offer to cover the next round.

Gus Crowe took that moment to excuse himself for a trip to the men's room, returning in time to receive his brandy without a word of acknowledgement.

He caught Flora looking at him, and inclined his head with a reptilian smile that didn't reach his eyes, his glass held aloft for another drink, despite it being three quarters full. Flora wrinkled her nose in distaste. Thus far, the man had refused nothing; a drink, an extra helping, or a cigarette offered by another passenger, accepting whatever came his way with an oily smile.

She was about to mention this unsociable behaviour to Bunny, but he was deep in conversation with Max about an industrialist who wanted to see his designs.

'He knows Frederick Lanchester, the inventor of the disc brake,' Bunny said, breaking off a conversation briefly. 'He invented the electric starter too.'

Flora adopted a suitably enraptured expression, though he might have been speaking Chinese for all she understood, and instead, listened with half an ear to one of Monica's anecdotes about her daughters, ending with an ostentatious dab at her dry cheeks with a lace handkerchief.

'No waterworks tonight, please.' Gerald grimaced. 'We'll be back with the little harridans within the week. Then you'll complain you never get a moment to yourself, despite having a house full of servants.'

Monica threw him a glare cold enough to freeze lava. 'I don't expect a mere man to understand a woman's maternal feelings.'

'Do you have family, Mrs Penry-Jones?' Miss Ames asked, distracting attention from the Gilmores' burgeoning spat.

The old lady's sharp gaze flicked to her questioner over a pair of rectangular pince-nez. 'I had a son, once.'

Flora waited for more, but no further explanation was forthcoming.

'How sad,' Miss Ames also seemed eager to hear more. 'Though nature tends to soften the blow with time, don't you find?'

'I do not.' Mrs Penry-Jones sniffed. 'Nor should one comment on another's misfortunes unless one knows the circumstances.' She rose unsteadily to her feet, setting the stool behind her into a precarious wobble. 'It's quite stuffy in here. I think I'll retire.'

Hester scrambled to her feet, stopped in her tracks by her employer's long-suffering sigh.

'Really, girl, I wish you wouldn't bob up and down whenever I move. I'm quite capable of returning to the suite alone. I shan't require you until the morning.' Manoeuvring with her stick, she caught an arriving passenger on the shin, and almost tripped the steward who sprang forward to assist her.

'Oh, dear, I seem to have upset her.' Miss Ames dropped two cubes of sugar into her coffee. 'Funny old thing.'

'Mrs Penry-Jones is rather fond of grand exits,

isn't she?' Gerald whispered in Flora's ear, earning him a glare from Monica.

'What a shame about her son,' Flora said, turning an enquiring look on Miss Smith.

Hester shrugged. 'She's never mentioned a son to me.'

'Perhaps she lost him quite recently, and her pain is too raw to speak about.' Cynthia pinned Hester with a look filled with dislike.

Ignoring her, Hester turned a flirtatious look on Mr Crowe. 'You promised to teach me how to play poker. I appear to be free now if you have the time?'

'Ah yes, I believe I did.' Crowe delved into a pocket and withdrew a pack of cards.

'The first rule of gambling for money, Miss Smith, is never trust a man who uses his own cards.'

Hersch's voice brought Flora's head up sharply. She hadn't noticed him arrive. Her gaze slid to a brown envelope in his hand, the kind used to deliver telegrams. He saw her looking at him and tucked it hurriedly into his pocket.

'My advice,' he continued, taking a chair, 'would be to ensure the pack is unsealed in front of you.'

'Are you accusing me of underhand dealings?' Crowe's handsome but sly features suffused with colour.

'Not at all,' Hersch said, unruffled. 'Though I doubt the lady is in your league.'

Crowe rolled back his shoulders, and dropped the cards back into his pocket, brightening again when Gerald, ignoring his wife's resigned sigh, said, 'I'll join you for a hand or two.'

Flora tried to catch Eloise's eye, but she appeared disengaged. Her untouched glass in front of her, she ran her pendant absently through the gold chain round her neck. Then she snatched her bag from the table and rose, shouldering her way through the crowd round the bar.

'Excuse me. I won't be a moment,' Flora whispered to Bunny before hurrying after her.

Flora entered the lobby in time to see the door to the ladies' powder room close on Eloise. Following her inside, she stepped into a subdued haven of pink and gold, where elaborate gilt mirrors graced the walls. A marble-topped counter strewn with bottles containing perfume, lotions and fragrant soaps had been piled into porcelain dishes along with piles of fluffy towels.

Apart from a uniformed attendant in a corner reading a book, Eloise was the only occupant. She stood before a wide mirror, her chin jutted forward as she applied an unnecessary coat of lipstick.

'Hello, Flora.' She shot her a quick look before continuing what she was doing. 'Where have you been hiding?'

'I'm not the one who's been hiding.' Flora slapped her velvet clutch bag onto the counter. 'You've been avoiding me.'

Eloise pouted, the lipstick held in mid-air. 'I thought you and your young man preferred some privacy to get to know one another.' She turned back to the mirror, smoothing her lower lip with a finger.

'He isn't my young man. He's simply been very kind to me since–'

'Kind? You shouldn't be so modest.' Eloise returned her lipstick to her bag, withdrew a tiny sheet of oiled paper and applied it to her lips. 'The pair of you have been inseparable since we left New York.'

Flora's immediate rush of pleasure dissolved as common sense reasserted itself.

'I think he's attentive to any woman he meets. He's been brought up that way.' At the same time the idea of Bunny as her beau appealed more each time she saw him.

'I know infatuation when I see it.' Eloise pouted at her reflection. 'Those delicious glasses are quite appealing, don't you find?'

'Don't change the subject.' Flora pushed away from the wall and stepped closer. 'I came to ask you about your young man, not mine.'

Eloise's eyes darkened for half a second, followed by a decisive shake of her head.

'I don't have one. My career is too important to me. Besides, what man would be willing to traipse round the theatres of the world after his wife?'

'Who said anything about a wife?' Flora said, triumphant when Eloise's face paled.

'Don't you find these electric lights unflattering?' Eloise flicked to the attendant in a silent plea for discretion. 'Too stark for me, but then I suppose it's cleaner than gaslight. All that sticky soot ruins everything.'

The attendant chose that moment to leave her seat and disappeared through a door marked 'Private'.

Eloise flung her bag on the vanity, swivelled sideways and glared at Flora. 'Now, will you kindly tell me what this is all about?'

'All right,' Flora began. 'Last night when we searched Mr Parnell's cabin, I found a photograph in his shirt drawer.'

'Really?' Eloise picked up a glass bottle of perfume on the vanity, removed the stopper and lifted it to her nose. 'What sort of photograph?' Her voice remained casual but the stopper shook slightly in her hand.

'I assumed it to be your wedding portrait.'

'I suppose you think you've been very clever.' Her face drained of expression and she gave an awkward shrug. 'All right. I was married once, what of it?'

'Then you won't mind if I tell Mr Hersch where to find the photograph?'

'Why would you tell *him* anything?' Confusion clouded her features. 'What's that German got to do with it?'

'He's been asking questions about Mr Parnell. He and the captain.' Flora pushed her advantage. 'They aren't happy about how he died.'

'What? Oh!'

The bottle slipped from Eloise's hand, spilling perfume onto the counter. A cloying smell of roses filled the air, and with it a dismayed cry. Eloise's hand lowered the bottle to the vanity with a clunk; miraculously it stayed intact. With her other hand, she scrabbled in her bag, tugging out a handkerchief. As she did so, a circle of gold slid onto the floor, rolled along the carpet and came to rest beside Flora's shoe.

Flora bent and retrieved a thick gold bangle with a safety chain and an inscription on the inside.

'Give that to me!' Eloise plucked the bracelet from Flora's fingers, but too late to prevent her reading what was engraved on the inside.

To E on our Wedding Day, T.

'I'd forgotten about this.' Eloise rolled the bangle in the fingers of one hand. 'I should have thrown the thing overboard when–' she broke off on a ragged breath. 'Do you trust me, Flora?'

'That's a big thing to ask after all the lies you've told me.'

Eloise's bravado drained away, leaving her white and trembling. 'I *am* asking.'

'Then I was right. It *is* you in the photograph with the man who gave you that.' She indicated the bangle. 'Why are you so afraid? Mr Parnell is dead, he can't show it to anyone.'

'That German is asking questions, you say?' At Flora's nod, Eloise's delicate features crumpled. 'It wasn't meant to happen like this. Everything is sliding away from me. If he sees that photograph the game will be up. I have to get it back.' Desperation burned in Eloise's eyes and she opened and shut the bracelet clasp with rapid clicks until Flora's own fingers twitched to snatch it away.

'Why are you so frightened of Mr Hersch?' Flora asked. 'He just wants to know who killed your friend, as do I. There's nothing sinister in his questions.'

'Frank wasn't a friend.' Eloise snorted. 'I hadn't even met him until after Theo died. He turned up

124

at a café across from our apartment block one morning. I was upset and scared, and he was sympathetic. Or he pretended to be. Parnell most probably wasn't his real name.' She jammed the bracelet back into her bag and snapped the metal catch shut.

'Go on,' Flora prompted.

'Theo and I eloped, which shocked everyone as he was quite a bit older than me, but that didn't matter to us.' Her breath hitched. 'We were supposed to be together. Then quite suddenly, he died.'

'Oh, I'm so sorry, that must have been awful for you.'

'It was.' Eloise gave a shudder. 'The worst part was when the gossip began, implying that I had something to do with it.'

'Did the police think you were involved?'

'If they did, they never indicated as much to me.' Eloise twisted the bag in her hands. 'Although I received suspicious looks and murmurings wherever I went. Then the letters started.'

'What letters?'

'I received two letters from a lawyer.' Eloise swallowed. 'The first one saying that Theo's family were challenging his estate. He hadn't made a new will after our wedding, you see, so by law everything came to me. The second one said they were unhappy with the coroner's verdict of death by natural causes and sought a prosecution.' Her face crumpled. 'As if losing Theo wasn't bad enough, they wanted the world to think I had killed him. That's when I panicked. I emptied Theo's safe and booked passage on this ship.'

'Couldn't you reason with his family?'

'I've never met them, and didn't want to once the correspondence began. They wouldn't want to hear what I had to say. They had made up their minds.'

'You told Parnell what you planned?'

Eloise nodded. 'That was my first mistake. He told me he could get me a part in *School for Scandal* in London, and would come to England with me. It was the perfect way out, so I jumped at it.'

'Sounds a bit contrived to me,' Flora said.

'I see that – now.' She braced both hands on the counter, her shoulders hunched. 'He pretended to be my friend, then that first night on board he was so different.' She stared into the mirror as if she didn't recognise herself. Was she imagining what she used to look like?

'What changed?'

'Money, I imagine.' Eloise grabbed a linen square from a pile on the counter and dabbed at each eye, careful not to smudge the heavy make-up. 'Isn't it always? He said he knew what I had done, that if I didn't give him money, he would have me arrested when we reached London.'

'Why would that worry you unless it were true?'

'Of course it wasn't true!' Her head jerked up and held Flora's gaze. 'I would never have hurt Theo. Frank claimed he had evidence I had done it.'

'What sort of evidence?' Flora eyed the door marked 'Private' hoping the attendant wouldn't return too soon.

'He wouldn't say, but promised to destroy it if

I gave him money.'

Flora rolled her eyes. Eloise would never have been free of such a man, no matter how much money she gave him.

'If you don't know Mr Hersch, and I assume you don't, where does he come into all this?'

'I'm not sure, but if he's asking questions, he's either working for the lawyer who sent me those letters, or the police. That photograph is the only thing that can link me to Theo now Frank is dead. I can disappear when I reach London, but whilst I'm on this ship, that German could still cause trouble for me.'

Flora was about to suggest Mr Hersch must already know Eloise's identity, but didn't want to make her more distressed than she was already.

'All right.' Her anger dissolved, replaced by exasperated sympathy. 'But we can't do it now, as everyone will be returning to their staterooms any moment. We'll be seen.'

'Tomorrow then, first thing.' Eloise dried her tears. 'I doubt anyone has noticed we didn't lock Frank's door when we were there last time. It will take me two seconds to get inside, so you stand guard and warn me if someone comes.' She closed the space between them until their faces were inches apart. 'Now, where exactly did you see that photograph?'

Chapter 11

'You've been gone a while,' Bunny observed when they both returned to the bar.

Before Flora could think up an excuse, Eloise interrupted. 'Little accident in the powder room with some perfume. Flora was kind enough to help me.'

'I wondered what that delicious scent was.' Gus Crowe slid between them, his oily smile in place. 'I thought you had abandoned me.'

Eloise pouted, running a finger along his jaw. 'How could I, now would you be a prince and buy me a brandy?'

Crowe's face suffused with a look of raw panic.

'Worry not, Crowe,' Gerald said, evidently having overheard. 'We're Max's guests this evening, all drinks are gratis.'

'In that case.' Crowe rubbed his hands together, whispered something to Eloise which made her giggle, then arm in arm the pair headed for the bar.

'Will Eloise never learn,' Flora murmured, nodding her thanks to the waiter who slid a fresh cup of hot coffee in front of her. She had seen Eloise and Crowe together that morning on the boat deck. It had struck her as an unlikely alliance at the time, but she had decided it was Eloise's way of avoiding her. They seemed friendly enough now. But then, how can anyone know what one person finds attractive in another?

She took her first sip of coffee just as a shadow fell across her lap, and looked up to where Carl Hersch bent over them.

'May I buy you a drink?' He dragged a stool forwards and straddled it.

'Oh, er, most kind of you,' Bunny said. 'But I think Max has–'

'Please, I would rather,' Hersch cut across him and summoned a waiter.

'I'm quite happy with my coffee, thank you,' Flora said.

'I'll have another brandy, provided you make it a small one,' Bunny held out his glass.

'I see you are busy forming interesting alliances, Miss Maguire.' Hersch glanced to where Eloise and Crowe stood and away again. 'Have you learned any more since our discussion?'

'Not really,' Flora lied. She would wait until Eloise had fulfilled her promise before revealing anything else to him.

'*I* have a question for you, sir.' Bunny lowered his voice. 'If no one knew Parnell before this voyage, who could have a reason to kill him?'

Hersch tugged at his left earlobe, before answering. 'I'm confident at least two people knew Mr Parnell before this voyage. Apart from Miss Lane that is.'

Cynthia's name popped into Flora's head, but she remained silent.

'Is one of them Mr Gilmore, by any chance?' Bunny threw Flora an apologetic glance. 'I was reluctant to cast aspersions at the time, but it's been niggling at me.' He pushed his glasses up his

129

nose before continuing. 'It's somewhat indelicate, but may be relevant.'

Just then a loud guffaw sounded from Crowe, followed by Eloise's girlish giggle as they availed themselves of Max's generosity.

'Go on, Mr Harrington,' Hersch prompted, bringing Flora's attention back to their conversation.

'Gilmore mentioned that he saw Parnell being over-familiar with Hester Smith the afternoon before he died.'

'In what way over-familiar?' Mr Hersch asked.

'Not indiscreet, or anything like that.' Bunny's eyes glinted behind his lenses. 'At least, I don't think so. He said Hester appeared annoyed at Parnell.'

'Hester is always annoyed.' Flora glanced to where Hester and Miss Ames sat. Both women sipped delicately at tiny glasses of some brown concoction but didn't address a word to one another. 'Like Cynthia Cavendish was annoyed with Parnell when I saw them together?'

Hersch's eyes narrowed. 'You didn't mention that to me, Miss Maguire.'

Flora groaned inwardly. 'Ah, no, but Cynthia dismissed it when I broached the subject.'

'I see.' Hersch's unflinching gaze made her squirm. He drained his brandy, placing the empty glass on the table in front of him. 'So within hours of boarding, Parnell had angered three ladies of different ages, social classes and marital status?'

'Doesn't sound as if the man was very popular with women, does it?' Bunny said.

'Indeed not,' Hersch mused, thoughtful.

'If Gerald is one, then who is the other person who knew Parnell?' Flora asked.

'I have yet to receive confirmation, so I'll keep that to myself for the time being if you don't mind.' Hersch winked at Flora.

Just then a thought struck her. Of course, the envelope! It was a telegram he had put into his pocket earlier. That must have been where he went after dinner. But from whom? Was Eloise right in that he worked for her late husband's lawyers?

'I'm interested that neither of you has asked where *I* was before breakfast on Sunday morning.' Mr Hersch split a look between them.

'Good point,' Bunny said.

'Bun-ny,' Flora dragged out the word in warning.

'We all need an alibi.' Hersch smiled. 'Mine is that I summoned the purser at six-thirty and requested he lodge some papers in the ship's safe He obliged, though I doubt he was very happy about it.'

'I don't suppose you would reveal what sort of papers?' Flora asked.

'You assume correctly, young lady. I was with the purser in his office when a crewman arrived, saying Parnell had been found dead. That was just after seven o'clock.' He rose from his stool with the economic grace of a man used to a lifetime of physical activity. No groans of effort, nor the easing of stiff joints, though he must have been at least sixty. 'I'll take my leave now, but may I ask that if either of you discover anything else of interest pertaining to this matter, that you will let me know?'

'If you wish.' Flora followed his progress through the double glass doors onto the deck. At the rail he paused, withdrew a cigar from his inside pocket, snipped off the end and lit it.

'Have you noticed he always manages to obtain more information than he gives away?' Bunny said.

Flora opened her mouth to agree when he interrupted. 'Hey, did you see that?' Bunny nodded to where Crowe sat at the bar with Eloise. 'He grabbed a large handful of cigarettes from a box on the bar and rammed them into his pocket.'

'I noticed that unpleasant foible of his earlier.' She twisted in her seat, removing Crowe and Eloise from her line of vision. 'Never mind him. We still have no idea who wanted Parnell dead.'

'There are usually only three reasons for murder.' Bunny swirled the brandy round his glass. 'Money, love, jealousy, or to hide another crime.'

'That's four.' Flora's gaze went back to Hersch, who stood talking to another passenger at the rail, a cloud of smoke hovering between them. 'Why summon a purser so early in the morning? It's a bit unusual, don't you think?'

'Not really.' Bunny appeared to give the matter some thought. 'Hersch strikes me as a man who wouldn't hesitate to drag a minion from his bed to do his bidding.'

'In which case, maybe Parnell did the same and lodged the money Eloise gave him in the safe after all?'

'Only the purser or the captain are in a position to know that, and I doubt they'll tell us. What about Gerald?' He nodded to where Gerald sat with Max and Cynthia. 'Perhaps he had a long-standing grudge against Parnell, and decided to spread malicious gossip about him? We've no proof he was arguing with Hester Smith. Why should he?'

'A grudge that would make him wish to kill him? Even if that were so, it's unlikely Gerald would commit murder on the first night of a voyage where he will be trapped for over a week?' Flora gave a dismissive snort. 'He's cleverer than that.'

Flora liked Gerald. The man obviously adored his son and he had been especially kind to Eddy too. Yet on the other hand, she didn't like the way he talked to his wife. Monica might be abrasive and over-emotional at times, but she didn't deserve the cruel edge of his tongue. Especially not in public.

'I cannot help wondering who our German friend is working for,' Flora said.

'What makes you think he's working for anyone?'

'Something Eloise said, but she's scared and may have twisted things.'

'It seems Hersch has persuaded you that everyone's word is suspect in this affair but his own.'

Flora's coffee cup froze on its way to her mouth. 'Are you saying I'm wrong to trust him?'

'Not that exactly. But it could be what he wants.'

Flora's stomach did a sickening lurch. Had she accepted what Hersch had told her too readily? But then what better way to distract her than appearing to be as eager as she to discover the truth?

Then again, it wasn't Hersch who had growled at her outside the dining room. Or was it?

'Flora,' Bunny spoke her name in the slow, contemplative way he did when putting a thought together, his arm draped across the back of her chair inches from her shoulder. 'Why did Hersch ask us to bring information to him? Why not Captain Gates?'

Flora frowned. 'I don't know, but it's a thought. He told me he had examined the body as well.'

'Really?' Bunny shifted his glasses slightly on his nose. 'Why did he do that? And more interestingly, why did the captain allow it?'

'My thoughts exactly.' She took a sip of her now lukewarm coffee without tasting it.

Leaving the other passengers in party mood at the bar, Bunny escorted Flora back to her suite.

They strolled the deck arm in arm, in no hurry despite Flora's excuse she ought to return to check on Eddy. She imagined that to a casual observer they must look like friends who had known each other for years, or maybe even something more. Then the fact struck her that in little more than a week, they would part company in London and go their separate ways, and never see each other again.

He seemed as reluctant to say goodnight as she and as if by mutual consent, they halted at the rail as a shifting veil of milky white fog obscured the moon. 'Can you tell where we are now?' she asked, sadness dragging her mood.

'I could hazard a guess.' He released her arm and stepped sideways, putting a respectable space between them. 'The Newfoundland coast was still visible this morning, so I expect we'll be coming up to the Grand Banks. That's where the warmer Gulf Stream meets the Labrador Current and causes this fog.'

'The temperature has certainly dropped in the last few hours.' Tendrils of hair at her forehead laced with tiny drops of moisture made her shiver, and she gathered her shawl round her shoulders.

'We'll be in "Iceberg Alley" tomorrow,' Bunny said.

'I hope you don't mean that literally.'

'It's a nickname given by superstitious naval types.' His lips twitched into a lop-sided smile she had begun to look for. 'They break off the arctic floes in the spring and float south. I imagine they're virtually melted before they get here, so we can steer round them.'

'I hope I don't get seasick.' She spoke without looking at him, aware he had eased closer, shielding her from the worst of the wind.

'There's an old English sailors' proverb, that the only cure for seasickness is to sit on the shady side of an old brick church in the country.'

'Sounds sensible to me.' Flora laughed.

'Then again, ginger infused in hot water is good for nausea. It's an antiemetic, and very effective.'

'I'll remember that.' She smiled at his habit of explaining everything scientifically. She slipped her arm through his and drew him away from the rail. 'Incidentally, what do you think about those items Max says have gone missing?' she asked as they set off along the deck again.

'Max is careless with his things, apparently, so

not much. Cynthia mentioned much the same thing to Mrs Penry-Jones earlier.'

'Really?' Flora slowed her pace, pulling him back a step. 'I wouldn't have thought Cynthia and the old lady had much in common.'

'I came across them in the writing room, their heads together, arguing.'

'Arguing?'

'That's what it looked like.' He held a hand out level and waggled it. 'Cynthia left soon after I arrived, or rather, she marched out just as I walked in. I didn't catch the more interesting part of their conversation.'

'Didn't you find out anything at all?'

'How was I supposed to do that if Cynthia had left?'

'Easy, you saunter up to Mrs Penry-Jones and ask if she has any spare notepaper, then you make some remark about Cynthia looking upset. Mrs Penry-Jones might have leapt on the chance to gossip about a passenger who had annoyed her and revealed something interesting.'

'How devious.' His left brow lifted. 'Besides, the writing room is a female domain, and I didn't actually want any notepaper.'

'Do you always take everything so literally?' Flora stared at him.

'I'm a trained solicitor, so the answer to that must be yes. Nor do I possess your penchant for investigation, or burglary, come to that.'

Flora administered a hard nudge with her elbow, at which he pretended to stagger in pain for a few steps. She dared not mention Eloise's plan for a repeat performance.

'If you have a moment,' he said, reaching for her door handle. 'I'd like to ask you something.'

Flora hesitated, but before she could think of an excuse, he had ushered her inside.

The stewardess rose from her chair when she saw them, gathered her magazine and with a knowing sideways glance at Bunny, left.

Flora sighed, anticipating the gossip that would likely circulate among the crew about unchaperoned ladies who entertained men in their suites. She could only hope tales of her sullied reputation did not get back to Lady Vaughn.

'Don't tell me you asked her to sit with Eddy?' Bunny hooked a thumb at the closed door.

'I did, actually,' Flora replied, daring him with her eyes to criticize.

'Eddy's too old for a babysitter. I shouldn't imagine he was too pleased about it, either.'

'He wasn't, but I gave him no choice.'

'That's part of what I want to ask you. Why you've been so jumpy lately where Eddy is concerned? Almost as if you are afraid to leave him on his own. It's not gone unnoticed.'

'I was afraid of that. Monica has made a few remarks about it too.' Flora took a deep breath and related the incident with the husky-voiced man who had accosted her outside the dining room.

Bunny gripped her upper arms firmly in both hands. 'Why-didn't-you-tell-me?' He emphasized each word with a tiny but firm shake.

'I tried, but...' She hunched her shoulders. 'The longer I prevaricated, the more ridiculous it sounded. Almost as if I had imagined it.'

He pulled her closer, rubbing her back with one hand. 'I won't let anything to happen to you, or Eddy. Do you believe that?'

She nodded, inhaling the indefinable maleness of him, combined with the clean smell of starched linen. His touch made her blood sing in her veins and she blinked back gathering tears. She wanted nothing more than to lean into him, feel his arms close round her with her cheek pressed against his chest. Fearful of his rejection, she stood quite still until he released her.

'Have you told anyone about this?' he demanded, all business now.

His sudden withdrawal left her hollow, and lost. Turning, she paced the room, rubbing one arm with the other hand as she walked. 'I tried to tell Dr Fletcher, who didn't listen to me, and Mr Hersch, who did. He thinks there's something odd about Parnell's death too.'

'When was this?' He folded his arms across his chest. 'And do sit down, Flora, you're making me nervous. What exactly did Hersch say?'

She shook her head. 'I think better if I keep moving. He asked my opinion, so I told him what I thought about the lack of blood and everything. He said the captain agreed, and my croaky-voiced man appeared to confirm all our suspicions.'

'It's beginning to make sense,' Bunny mused. 'Did Hersch have any ideas as to who might have been responsible for Parnell's death?'

'Not that he's told me.'

'Maybe it's someone with access to all the suites and staterooms?' Bunny suggested. 'A member of the crew maybe, or a chambermaid?'

'How typical!' Flora halted and turned sharply, facing him. 'The upper classes always assume the servants are the culprits. As if your own kind couldn't possibly be avaricious or violent, even though the reverse is true.'

'Which is a prejudice in itself.' Bunny polished his glasses with a handkerchief then replaced them on his nose. 'A badly treated valet or an abused maid could just as easily seek revenge for some slight or bad treatment. A steward or barman may have seen how much money Parnell won at cards, decided to rob him, killing him in the process. It's not unheard of.'

'In which case, the captain should search the crew's quarters for the missing money.' Flora sighed, dissatisfied. 'Oh, but it's too simplistic. There's more at play here than a straightforward robbery.' What Eloise said about her husband's death and lawyers came back to her.

'I'm inclined to agree. If, as you believe, the body was moved to confuse when he was killed, that smacks of an above average intelligence at work here.'

'Then why the a-servant-did-it theory?' On a sudden impulse, Flora grabbed the brass ashtray from a low table, and swung it in an arc towards his head.

His eyes widened, and his free hand shot out, the fingers closing around her wrist, while he fended her off with the other hand. 'Hey! When did I become the enemy?'

'I wasn't going to hit you. Your reflexes are excellent, by the way.' The thought occurred to her then that maybe Parnell's weren't so good, and his killer had surprised him.

He took the ashtray from her and weighed the object in his hands. 'It's heavy enough. What made you think of it?'

'Mr Hersch did. There's one of those in every stateroom. The maid discovered Parnell's was missing, so the killer must have got rid of if there was blood on it.' She sighed, one hand balanced on her hip. 'A pity, as it's probably somewhere in the Atlantic by now. There's one thing that still puzzles me though.'

'Only one?' Bunny slid the ashtray back onto the table, his eyes dancing with laughter behind the lenses.

'*If* the killer had sense enough to throw the weapon overboard,' she said, refusing to let him goad her. 'Why not the body too?'

'Not as easy as it sounds. He would have had to carry it down to the next deck, where he risked being seen, even at that time in the morning.'

'Difficult, agreed, but not impossible. So why didn't he?' Flora chewed at a thumbnail and continued her pacing.

'I cannot possibly answer that. It's not a dilemma I have ever had to wrestle with.'

Suppressing a yawn, he pushed himself away from the fireplace. 'This is all very interesting, but it's been a long day, and I'm exhausted. As a gentleman, I should also preserve your reputation and be on my way.' He raised his hand level with her shoulder but then used it to push up the bridge of his glasses. 'Well, um. I expect I shall see you tomorrow.'

The firm click of the door left Flora bereft,

stranded in the middle of the room. After the intimacy of their near hug earlier, he hadn't even shaken her hand. Even a brotherly tap on her shoulder was rejected at the last second.

He had even refused to sit while she remained on her feet.

'You are indeed a gentleman, Mr Harrington.' Flora sighed as the door clicked shut. 'Too much of one in some respects.'

Chapter 12

Day Four – Tuesday

After breakfast next morning, Flora emerged onto the boat deck where Gerald was overseeing a noisy game of shuffleboard with several young boys, which included Ozzy and Eddy. Gerald greeted her by raising his hat, though she gently declined his invitation to take a turn.

'Have you seen Mr Harrington this morning?' Flora asked him. 'He wasn't at breakfast.'

'I believe he went to check on his motor car first thing.' Gerald replaced his panama on the back of his head. 'He mentioned the straps had worked loose or something.'

'I see, thank you.'

Ozzy called out something to Gerald from the end of the deck.

'What ho.' Gerald lifted a hand in acknowledgement of his son. 'Looks like my turn again.' He loped away.

Flora watched the game for a while, then a burst of male laughter brought her attention to the upper deck where Bunny strolled beside a young woman. She tilted her chin and kept turning to face him as she walked.

Disappointment conjured a bitter taste in Flora's mouth as she recognized the extremely pretty blonde girl as one who occupied the table next to theirs.

She waited until the pair had moved out of sight, then turned and strode in the opposite direction, muttering a curt 'excuse me' to a couple who barred her way, resulting in their surprised stares as she shouldered past.

Once inside the suite, she threw her jacket onto a chair, slammed the door of her room and sprawled on the bed, one arm flung over her head. After an initial rush of anger, common sense prevailed and she chastised herself for stupidity. What did she expect? Charming young men from good families did not take up with governesses too meek to enter a dining room alone.

The bugle sounded for luncheon, and unwilling to witness Bunny flirt with someone else, Flora stubbornly remained where she was. A shaft of light drew patterns on the ceiling as occasional footsteps and an odd murmured comment came from outside. Footsteps filed past her window, but no light knock came at her door, and eventually the deck fell silent.

Flora woke, disoriented, easing up on an elbow, and groaned. The clock on her bedside stood at after four. Half the afternoon had gone, and having missed luncheon, she was ravenously hungry.

Throwing off the coverlet, she washed her face and hands before swapping her creased skirt and blouse for a pastel, flower-print dress with a high collar and mutton leg sleeves.

In the sitting room, Eddy and Ozzy had come and gone, their occupation evidenced by a half-finished game of snakes-and-ladders, beside an empty packet that once contained garibaldi biscuits.

Out on the boat deck, the line of steamer chairs were filled with dozing or reading passengers, but neither Bunny nor the blonde girl were amongst them.

In search of something to eat to still her growling stomach, she headed up the grand staircase to the library, at the top of which Gus Crowe stood talking to a crewman. Flora paused on the half-landing, conscious their discussion was becoming less a talk and more a lecture, delivered by Crowe and accepted with occasional, subservient nods by a sailor who was little more than a boy.

Finally, Crowe wagged a pointed finger beneath the crewman's nose, and headed toward the door to the deck. Flora was about to follow, when Crowe halted, his gaze fixed on the door that led to the Upper Promenade deck that gently swung closed.

From that angle, she couldn't see what had caught his attention, but Crowe continued to stare for long seconds as if pondering his next action. Then he straightened his shoulders and pushed through it onto the deck.

Flora hitched her skirt and ascended the remaining stairs, but before she reached the door, collided with the same crewman Crowe had been talking to on his way down.

'I'm so sorry, miss.' He pressed his back against the wall to let her pass, his frowning expression altering in an instant to abject apology.

'That's quite all right.' Flora took in a pair of troubled eyes that peered out from beneath close-cut sandy hair before she continued on to the library.

The same steward who had attended her last time greeted her at the door with an eager, 'Would you like tea, miss?'

'Thank you. I'll be over there.' She indicated the sofa she had occupied on her last visit, though she had not quite reached it when Bunny's face appeared round a white-painted pillar.

'Thought it was you,' he said, peering over his spectacles. 'Had the same idea myself. Why don't you join me?' He shifted sideways to make room for her, and waved to the steward. 'Miss Maguire will take her tea here.'

Flora sat, the words 'Is your friend not with you?' sprang to her lips, but she swallowed them unsaid.

'Those cakes look nice.' She debated whether she dared order a plate of her own and devour them all.

Bunny's heart-breaking smile appeared, and her stomach lurched as she imagined him directing that same gaze at the girl she had seen him with earlier; but it hurt too much and she pushed it away.

He poured tea for them both, handing her a full cup, then moved the sugar bowl out of her reach. 'You don't use this, do you?'

She shook her head, unaccountably touched that he had remembered.

'It's a pity about the books not having arrived in time before we sailed,' Flora said, partly for something to break the awkward silence. 'I had hoped to give Eddy some work to do in preparation for school.' She eyed the finger sandwiches hungrily.

'Talking of Eddy. I heard he and the Gilmore boy persuaded the purser to let them see the engine room this afternoon.'

'Really?' Flora peered at him over the rim of her cup. 'Eddy was determined to get there somehow. I've tried to keep a closer eye on him, especially since that incident outside the dining room, but Monica says I fuss over him too much.'

'Er – I meant to tell you before.' The look he shot her over his glasses was sheepish. 'I slipped a few dollars to one of the stewards to keep an eye on him.'

'Why did you do that?' Flora's cup hit the saucer with a clink.

'Because I took that threat you received seriously. I also hate to see you so agitated about Eddy all the time.'

'That's – that's really kind of you,' Flora said, touched. 'I wish I had thought of it myself.'

'My pleasure.' He grinned, looking pleased with himself. 'I take it you've heard no more from our mysterious man?'

'No, nothing.'

'If I find out who the fellow was, he'll regret it.'

145

He stirred sugar into his tea with a minute silver spoon. 'Menacing ladies is not to be tolerated.'

'Brave talk, Mr Harrington.' Flora hid the rush of pleasure this gave her behind a challenge.

'Excuse me, but I was boxing champion at school.' He crossed one ankle over the other, revealing an expanse of sock. 'You missed luncheon, not seasick, I hope?'

'I wasn't hungry,' she lied, as shame stabbed at her for her jealousy earlier.

'Do help yourself.' He nodded to the delicate finger sandwiches.

Needing no second prompting, Flora took one and bit into it, savouring the crisp cucumber with piquant salmon, to which the kitchen had added exactly the right amount of vinegar.

'Could we have some more, please?' Bunny asked a passing waiter, pointing to the nearly empty plate. The man bowed and disappeared.

'I like a girl with a proper appetite.' Bunny watched her finish the sandwich. 'Not like these silly society "gels" who push everything away with distaste. So false.'

'I imagine you know quite a few society girls.' She tried to sound casual but her throat constricted, making her voice high.

'Too many,' he murmured into his cup, so Flora almost missed it.

'Here, have one of these.' He offered her the cakes that had caught her eye on arrival.

Flora took her first bite, of a vanilla slice, relishing the combination of cream, sweet icing and strawberry jam on her tongue. In no time at all the cake was gone, leaving her wondering if she dared take another.

Following her gaze, Bunny lifted the plate and held it out towards her.

Flora hesitated.

'Go on, I know you want one,' he urged, waving the plate slowly from side to side an inch beneath her nose. 'Besides, it will appear greedy if I do, and I hate eating alone.'

'You were alone when I arrived,' Flora reminded him. 'And if I'm not mistaken, about to consume the entire contents of the tray by yourself.' She held her breath, hoping he wasn't going to say he was waiting for someone.

'That's different. Now go on, I can't eat while you watch.'

Flora obeyed.

'Tell me about yourself.' He sat back and folded his slender hands across his midriff.

She licked cream from her fingers, giving her time to construct a suitably fascinating answer, but failed. 'My life is quite ordinary, I'm afraid. I've spent most of it in the schoolroom of a country mansion called Cleeve Abbey, in Gloucestershire.' Somehow the second cream slice did not taste quite as inviting as the first.

Bunny finished his in three mouthfuls, then wiped his fingers theatrically on a napkin. 'What made you become a governess?'

'It wasn't so much a choice, more a transition. My father is Lord Vaughn's head butler, whose daughters were educated by governesses. Lord Vaughn doesn't believe in girls attending school. I was the same age as the youngest, Lady Jocasta, so I joined them in the schoolroom. Lady Vaughn had Eddy late in life and when I was eighteen, it seemed a natural progression for me to become his governess.' She lifted her chin proudly. 'In fact, you could say I've been educated far above my station.'

'It doesn't appear to have done you any harm.'

Flora smiled in agreement. She'd felt privileged at having shared a schoolroom with the earl's children, played games with them in the Capability Brown gardens, and rode ponies across the fields. She didn't mention that when the Vaughn girls dined in a room where painted cherubs graced a ceiling two storeys high above an Adam fireplace, Flora ate with her father in the butler's pantry, a candle between them to lift the gloom of the half-basement.

'When Eddy begins at Marlborough, my duties will be confined to school holidays. I've begun teaching the daughters of gentlemen in the village for extra money. I'm cheaper than boarding school, and anyway, I quite enjoy it. The money is useful. I've saved quite a bit.'

'What are you saving for?'

Flora frowned. No one had ever asked her that before. 'My future I suppose, whatever that is.'

'You don't have something you want to do? Or are you content living in someone else's house and teaching young ladies?'

His words struck her hard, and she returned the rest of her cake to her plate. She had always regarded Cleeve Abbey as her home. And yet – a distant memory lingered in the back of her mind, of a time where home was a room with a black-leaded range and a scrubbed pine table where the door opened into a sunny garden that threw a pool of sunlight onto grey flagstones.

Other sensations intruded, of distress mingled with the coppery smell of blood and the scrape of wool on her hands. Pictures too elusive to put a name to, but before she could make sense of them, a shadow filled her head.

'Are you all right, Flora? You've gone pale.' Bunny plucked her hand from her lap, her fingers sandwiched in his; a touch that was comforting and exciting at the same time.

Embarrassed, she snatched her hand away, then wished she hadn't. 'Too much cake, perhaps,' she said, her voice high and brittle.

'You've mentioned your father before, but not your mother.'

'She died. At least, that's what I've always been told.' She attempted a laugh but it fell flat. 'I mean, I've never seen her grave, and whenever I broach the subject with Father, he cuts me off. He's Ulster Scots and quite, well – private. He can avoid a direct question with such subtlety, you don't even realize until the moment has passed and you cannot ask again.'

'What's Ulster Scots?'

'I'm surprised at you, Mr Harrington.' She tucked in her chin in mock surprise. 'Don't they teach history at Marlborough?'

'They tried, but I dozed off sometime between the Wars of the Roses and the Repeal of the Corn Laws. I was more interested in the sciences.'

'That's a lot of history you missed. Anyway, in the seventeenth century,' she began, in the same way she would deliver one of Eddy's lessons, 'the

Scots Border Reivers were banished to Ulster as punishment for their murdering, cattle stealing and other dastardly deeds. Over the next hundred years or so, one of my ancestors married a Maguire, which makes me a mixture of Scots and Irish.'

'From what little I gleaned from the perpetual drone of my history master, those border raiders had a hard life, with little choice but to steal other people's livestock to survive.'

'A generous view, but not everyone was a victim,' Flora sighed.

'Was your mother never mentioned when you were younger?'

'Once, when I was about twelve, I heard the housekeeper say "that poor Lily Maguire" in a tone that implied something dreadful had happened to her.'

'You never discovered what it was?'

'No. No one would have satisfied a child's curiosity about something whispered in hallways. I have dreams about her though, all the time. Disjointed, frightening dreams where I know she's hurt and I cannot help her.' She turned to face him. 'I've never told that to a soul before. Not even my father.'

'Has it occurred to you,' he began, jiggling his foot, 'that your obsession with Parnell's death could stem from unresolved questions about your mother?'

'It's not an obsess–'

'No, don't interrupt.' He held up a hand. 'Maybe you look for complicated explanations for straightforward things.'

'I thought we agreed Parnell's death *wasn't* an accident. What changed your mind?' Flora bridled at the fact he doubted her – again.

'You're avoiding my suggestion about your mother.'

'I'm sorry,' she murmured, not knowing quite what she was apologizing for. 'I'm accustomed to pretending whatever happened, didn't.'

'Perhaps you need answers so you can make peace with it. With her. Then perhaps those dreams might stop.'

'Maybe.' Flora frowned, recalling her father's anguished, haunted gaze that appeared whenever her mother was mentioned.

She pressed a finger into the crumbs on her plate and carried it to her mouth, uncomfortable with the conversation but unsure as to how to change it. 'I can't really remember her, apart from one scene that repeats in my dreams like a stage play.'

'Then use it. Strip it of the dread, the panic that makes you shy away from that image and remember exactly what you saw.' He leaned closer and picked up the teapot, the view of his exposed neck between his collar and hairline strangely sensuous.

'What, now? This minute?' Flora buried her shaking hands in the folds of her skirt, though not quick enough for Bunny.

'No. Wait until you're alone, and in control.' He poured more tea for both of them. 'What do you intend to do when Eddy no longer needs a governess, even for holidays?'

Flora shrugged. 'I could never see a life beyond

151

Cleeve Abbey.'

'I couldn't imagine leaving Winterbourne, either.' He helped himself to another sandwich. 'I had to face a different sort of life when my father died. Daunting in many ways, yet I'm glad it happened.'

'Glad your father died, or you had to sell the family jewels?'

'The second premise. I took my privileged, sheltered way for granted, living on an income I hadn't earned, but with no real idea of how the world worked. Then I came to realize the society parties, shooting house weekends and the social round I was brought up to think important, didn't matter at all. Besides, I meet some far more interesting people these days.' He lifted the bar of his glasses with one hand and adjusted them on his nose. 'You, for instance. That's worth missing a hunt ball or two.'

Flora stared at her lap as a blush threatened. He had not meant it as a declaration, and for her to read something into it would confuse him, and she had already revealed too much of herself.

'Where did you grow up?'

'In Surrey,' he replied, apparently happy to indulge her. 'A lonely, only child with an absent father who travelled a great deal, and – oh my goodness.' Bunny twisted his wrist, indicating his watch. 'Is that the time? The dinner bugle will go in less than an hour.'

Flora surveyed the array of empty plates on the table in front of them, on which sat smears of cream among a few crumbs. The thought of more food made her feel slightly sick. 'To be honest, I don't think I can face dinner after all this.'

'You could be right,' Bunny said, rising, one hand held out to help her up. 'How about I call at your suite in about an hour? We could take a walk on deck to work off all that whipped cream, then have a coffee in the bar later on.'

'As long as you think your friend won't mind.' The second she had spoken Flora regretted it. Warmth crept into her neck, an apology on her lips, but the only emotion in his face was bewilderment.

'Who?' He guided Flora into the staircase lobby, a frown on his face as if trying to recall whom she meant. Then his face brightened. 'Oh, her. Why on earth should she?'

'No reason.' Flora shrugged.

'She asked to see Matilda, but it soon became obvious she wasn't interested in engines. Halfway through an explanation on horsepower and suspension, she asked if we could sit together inside. I told her she wouldn't be able to see the engine from there, but–'

'You're teasing me!' she said, accusing, but unable to stop the broad smile that crept into her face.

'A little.'

'What did you do with ... um?' She couldn't bring herself to ask the girl's name in case it made her too real.

'Oh, I prattled on about the engine until she got bored and gave up. She stormed off actually. Called me a boorish, insensitive ninny.'

'Instead of which, you are actually a calculating ninny.'

153

He hunched both shoulders in a deprecating shrug.

Flora clamped her lips together, trying not to laugh. 'I'll be ready in an hour.'

On her way back to her suite, Flora scolded herself for having almost spoiled their lovely afternoon with her stupid jealousy.

Chapter 13

Flora kept Bunny waiting for a full minute before opening the suite door to his ring, gratified to see his start of admiring surprise when he took in her appearance. After a slow walk round the deck, they climbed to the tiny bar on the Upper Promenade deck, where he held out a chair and bade her sit. His gaze lingered on the rhinestone ornament in her hair, though he made no comment.

Conscious of how her neckline dipped in front, Flora adjusted her shawl around her shoulders while giving the room a surreptitious glance.

'Have you given any more thought as to what I said earlier about those nightmares you have about your mother?' Bunny lowered himself into the chair beside her.

'I wasn't aware I had discussed my dreams with you in any detail, much less referred to them as nightmares,' she said, bemused by the way he re-started conversations they had left off hours before or switched subjects. Though she enjoyed the challenge of having to think fast to keep up with him.

'That's true. But I'm a good listener, and I'm observant.' He slanted a sideways look at her too quick for her to read the emotion behind it. 'Did I exaggerate?'

'No, you didn't.' She glanced away, still uneasy. 'Thus, because I cannot solve the mystery of my own mother's death, you think I turn my attentions to those of strangers?'

'Something like that.' He offered her a plate of almond biscuits, laughing when she feigned horror. 'I have an amateur interest in the work of Sigmund Freud, have you heard of him?'

'The Austrian doctor who hypothesizes the existence of libido?' Flora stifled a giggle when he slopped coffee into the saucer while pouring. 'I do know what the word means.'

'Oh, er, of course, I would never suggest otherwise.' He eased his collar away from his throat with one hand. 'Actually, I was referring to his theory on the unconscious mind and the mechanism of repression.'

'In that dialogue helps us exorcise bad past experiences?'

'Psychoanalysis, yes.' Bunny stared at her in admiration. 'What a surprising young woman you are, Miss Maguire.'

'Thank you.' Flora accepted his compliment along with her coffee cup. 'My father bought a copy of *The Interpretation of Dreams*, when it came out last year. However, after reading it, he said Freud's ideas are thin excuses for unhealthy sexual practices amongst relatives.'

'Your father discussed Freud with you?' Bunny's

eyebrows appeared to have taken up permanent residence halfway up his forehead.

'Of course. He's quite a reactionary. Though I haven't yet convinced him to approve of my joining a suffragette club.'

'And um – what do you think?' Bunny cleared his throat nosily. 'About Freud, not the women's suffrage movement.'

'I'm not convinced.' She decided to stop teasing him, though his discomfort delighted her. 'He ascribes most female ailments to hysteria, no matter what the symptoms. I doubt his male patients receive such casual dismissal.'

'Talking through your dreams may help you.'

'My mother's death isn't a problem, only the circumstances. I believe she was attacked by someone.'

'Your father is probably the one person who knows what really happened. You must ask him, or risk never being at peace with the past.'

'He won't give me a straight answer. He'll prevaricate until I give up.'

'Give him some credit, Flora. You're an adult now. Maybe he's been waiting for you to ask. It makes a sort of logical sense.'

'Possibly.' Still uncomfortable, she turned her attention to the appearance of the other passengers replete from their evening meal. The first to arrive were Gerald and Monica, followed closely by Max and Eloise, then Mrs Penry-Jones, who accepted a chair from Carl Hersch with a condescension that would have shamed Lady Catherine de Bourgh.

Max's head bent close to Eloise as they talked,

her hand straying occasionally to caress his arm. Mrs Penry-Jones glared at them with eagle-like intensity from her chair opposite, matched only by Hester's sulky glare.

Max glanced up and caught the old lady's eye, gave a self-conscious start, and slid his arm from beneath Eloise's grasp. He cleared his throat noisily and leaned backwards, putting another foot of space between them.

'What did I say about honeymooners?' Bunny nodded at a disconcerted Max. 'Poor chap cannot make a move without everyone passing judgement.' He tapped Flora's arm. 'Here's the blushing bride now. Let's see if she notices.'

Cynthia paused on the threshold, her gaze roaming the room until it alighted on Max, then switched to Eloise with such malice, Flora could almost feel the heat.

'Ah yes, I think she has,' Bunny coughed and looked away.

As far as Flora could see, Max was simply being charming, but Eloise certainly came in for more than her fair share of dislike.

Max muttered something to his companion, then rose to greet his wife, leaving Eloise isolated but undaunted at her table until Gus Crowe took the vacated seat.

Day Five – Wednesday

Flora's ablutions took longer than usual the next morning, hampered by the pitch of the ship in heavy seas. She braced a foot against the basin to

157

steady herself as bottles on the shelf above the sink slid to one side, then without warning, changed direction and threatened to topple onto the floor.

Four days of unsteady floors had made her long for the familiar smells of grass, earth, even manure. The clop of horses' hooves and the swish of tree branches in the wind were preferable to the stark loneliness in the creak of bulwarks, or the wind's mournful howl as it sang through the winch lines.

Struggling into her corset, it occurred to her that if she ate any more cream cakes, she would be pounds heavier by the time they reached England. However, the thought of breakfast made her mouth water, so she decided abstemiousness could wait.

In the sitting room, a fully-dressed Eddy greeted her with raised eyebrows and an exaggerated study of his wristwatch.

'I know I'm late, but I didn't sleep particularly well.' Images of being caught in Parnell's cabin had plagued her sleep, making her night less than restful.

'I like it.' Eddy giggled as the deck tipped sideways, sloshing his tea onto the carpet. 'Maybe we're in for a real storm.'

'I do hope not.' Her gaze went to the tray at his elbow. 'You'll have no room for breakfast if you eat all those biscuits.'

'Can't help it.' He grinned. 'This sea air makes me ravenous. I'd better not be late either, or Ozzy will snaffle all the sausages.' He snatched his jacket from a chair by the door and raced out.

Almost immediately, a muffled knock announced the arrival of Eloise.

'I thought that boy would never leave.' She declined Flora's invitation to enter, her head turning back and forth as she raked the deck. 'Ready?'

'I suppose so,' Flora muttered, fighting the stiff wind that threatened to pull the door from her grasp.

Flora's second foray into burglary proved a lot less stressful than her first, in that all she was required to do was to pace the covered deck outside Parnell's stateroom while Eloise made her search.

Guilt made her feel conspicuous, but those who passed by ventured no more than a polite, 'Good morning,' or a casually delivered, 'Blustery weather, isn't it?' from the more adventurous passengers.

'Did you find it?' Flora asked when Eloise finally emerged again.

Her black curls bounced as she shook her head. 'No.'

'You must have!' Flora hissed. 'I didn't lie to you. It was there the last time we searched.'

'Did I say you had?' Eloise snapped. 'Frank's stateroom has been completely emptied since we were last there. His clothes are all gone.'

'What about the bureau by the–' she broke off at Eloise's hard look. 'Sorry, of course you looked there.'

'I can only hope the job was done by some clueless steward who doesn't know how important that is.'

'What are you going to do?' Flora asked.

'There's nothing I can do but hope no one challenges me before we reach London.' She glanced past Flora's shoulder. 'Now hush.'

Flora suppressed a groan as she caught sight of Bunny striding towards them.

Eloise peered up at him through her mascaraed lashes. 'My, you look handsome today, Mr Harrington.'

'Good morning, Eloise, Flora.' He pushed his glasses further up his nose with a middle finger. Had he not flushed a deep red and made a feeble attempt to shy away from Eloise's grasp, Flora might have been jealous. How had such an attractive man not learned to handle compliments with grace, even contrived ones?

'I came to see if you were up to breakfast in this rough weather.' Bunny aimed his remark at Flora.

As if on cue, a gentleman rushed past them, a handkerchief clutched to his mouth.

Eloise backed away. 'I don't mind the wind, but the food on this ship is too rich for my girlish figure, so I'll make do with coffee in my stateroom.'

'Eloise!' Flora aimed a pointed glare in her direction, but with a brief wave through the gap in her door, she closed it on Flora's protests.

'Did I interrupt something?' Bunny asked.

'It doesn't matter,' Flora said through gritted teeth, slipped her arm through his and drew him in the direction of the dining room. 'I'll catch up with her later.'

'Are you sure you want to sit out here?' Flora asked Bunny for the third time since he had suggested the idea over breakfast.

With a firm hand in the small of her back, he guided her onto the boat deck, where passengers scurried past them, their backs to the bulwarks to avoid being showering with salt spray from an angry sea.

'Why not? Look, the Gilmores are game.' He nodded to where Monica and Gerald occupied steamer chairs set in the shelter of the main superstructure. 'Hersch and Gus Crowe are here too. C'mon, Flora, you can't back out now.'

'All right,' Flora muttered, grabbing onto a winch line, the metal slick and sharply cold beneath her fingers. 'I warn you though, if it gets too bad, I'm going back in.' She took her chair with bad grace, wishing she had remained in her suite.

A door banged behind them, announcing the arrival of Max and Cynthia, the latter a few steps behind.

'How did I let you talk me into this, Max?' Cynthia tottered across the slick deck, wrapped from head to toe in a beige fur coat with a matching hat that could never have been mistaken for anything but real fur.

'Rubbish!' Max wrapped his overcoat tighter round himself. 'It's no worse than a walk on Brighton beach in November. Character building.'

Cynthia didn't look convinced, her cheekbones highlighted with angry colour as she took the chair Max had dragged into line for her.

Miss Ames bustled to join them, arms splayed

161

to keep her balance in a calf-length mink coat which might have conceivably survived the early half of the last century. At the end of the row, Mr Hersch resembled an amiable polar bear in his white fur coat that reached to the floor, a matching hat pulled down over his ears.

Ignoring the steamer chairs, Eloise leaned against the rail, her head thrown back and her long jacket flaps spread behind her like wings. She didn't appear at all worried, in stark contrast to earlier when she was frantic the German might see that picture. Had she lied about finding it, after all and didn't want Flora to know? Or had someone already been into the cabin and taken it? If so, who? Mr Hersch? A crewman, or the killer?

She shook her ungracious thoughts away, reluctant to believe Eloise would deceive her – again.

'This Atlantic air is certainly exhilarating,' Gus Crowe said, shivering in his raincoat and thin trousers.

Taking pity on him, Flora handed him the spare blanket from beneath her chair.

'Thanks, awfully.' Like a small boy offered a treat, he grabbed it to his chest as if it were a lifebelt. 'Ankles getting a bit chilled, what?'

A steward staggered along the line, a tureen of hot bouillon balanced precariously on a tray. He paused in front of Bunny, one foot hooked round the metal support to prevent his slide across the deck as he poured for the flurry of orders thrown his way.

Flora accepted a cup of the savoury-smelling brew with a smile, while huddled into a fox-fur coat, Monica cupped her gloved hands round her steaming mug.

The thought struck Flora as she ran her gaze along the line of chairs that they might have raided a zoo with so much fur on display.

Bunny scraped his chair closer with a screech of wood. 'That's better. Now, why do you keep staring at Eloise like that? The two of you looked friendly enough before breakfast.'

Flora debated explaining about the photograph but thought better of it. 'Eloise told me she had been married once. Her husband died.' She turned to gauge his reaction, which was satisfyingly astonished.

'She just came out with it?'

'I saw a bracelet with an inscription on it.'

'Flora,' he lowered his voice in warning. 'Don't you think you're taking this investigation business too far? We all have something we don't wish to world to know. If all Eloise has to hide is a photograph and a bangle, she's doing better than most.'

'According to Eloise, she hasn't got the photograph. Though she admitted Parnell had blackmailed her into giving him that money.'

'Money that hasn't been found,' Bunny reminded her.

'No, but Parnell claimed to have evidence Eloise had killed her husband.'

'Did she? Kill him, I mean?'

'Parnell or her husband?'

'Both. Either. Goodness, Flora, are you saying Eloise murdered Parnell to stop him revealing she had killed her own husband?'

'I don't know, I–' Her gaze flicked to where Max had joined Eloise at the rail, despite Cynthia's jutted lower lip. The moan of the wind made their conversation silent, so they looked as though they were miming.

'She promised to explain everything, but now she's avoiding me again,' Flora muttered into her bouillon. 'I could help her if she was honest with me. I wouldn't judge her.'

'If you insist on sympathizing with suspects, you'll never be a detective,' Bunny said, his low chuckle making her insides melt.

A raised male voice to her right brought Flora's attention to where Gerald glared angrily at Gus Crowe. 'What exactly do you mean by that?'

'I only said that I believe that Parnell chap was a friend of yours. If I was wrong, I apologise. No need to get tetchy.' Though Crowe's smirk revealed triumph and little apology.

'If you hope to get me into strife with the captain, Crowe, you're out of luck,' Gerald snapped. 'We met once under unfortunate circumstances years ago. I hardly recognized the man and he used a different name.'

'What business did you say you're in, Gilmore?' Gus Crowe's hooded eyes were like slits, as if he knew something no one else did.

'I didn't.' Gerald's mouth curved into a superior sneer. 'Export and import mostly, nothing complicated.' He tossed back the contents of his bouillon cup in one swallow.

'Gerald wasn't always in shipping,' Monica sniffed, as if she disapproved of the way her husband earned his living nowadays. 'He once

164

dealt in property.'

'What made you leave that business then, Gilmore?' Max asked.

'It was all because of that awful scandal,' Monica interrupted. 'When–'

'That's enough, Monica,' Gerald scowled her into silence. 'I'm sure everyone here doesn't want to know our entire history.'

'I was only saying,' Monica sniffed and buried her nose in her glass.

Embarrassed looks were exchanged all along the line, while Flora sipped her bouillon and pretended she hadn't heard.

'Is anyone going to this dance tomorrow evening?' Cynthia addressed the entire row in what Flora assumed was a diplomatic change of subject.

'I haven't quite decided,' Miss Ames replied. 'It seems disrespectful after a death on board.' She tossed the trailing end of her ancient fur stole over her shoulder, releasing a flurry of tiny hairs.

Monica seemed to be considering the question, while Flora remained silent.

'Well, I'm going.' Cynthia waved her bouillon cup in the air. 'I need something to cheer me up. I'm sure most of the other passengers feel the same.'

'I expect Eloise will agree with you.' Monica nodded to the figure at the rail. 'This business has spoiled the voyage for the young people. What about you, Flora? Would a dance be agreeable, do you think?'

'Humph, disrespectful if you ask me.' Mrs Penry-Jones said before Flora could answer, her

165

mouth puckered like a chicken.

'At least the fancy dress theme has been abandoned.' Gerald spoke between mouthfuls. 'Makes the prospect slightly more welcoming. Monica would have me decked out as a harlequin if I let her. Bobble hat and all.'

The vision of Gerald's generous, six-foot frame in a diamond-patterned costume complete with pointed hat, made Flora's mouthful of bouillon go down the wrong way. She took a rasping breath, which ended abruptly when Bunny obligingly slapped her hard between her shoulder blades.

'Gerald!' Monica's tone conveyed hurt. 'You look dashing in that costume.' She turned to Flora. 'Well, dear. Will you be going?'

'Not if she has any regard for the way things ought to be done.' Mrs Penry-Jones raised her voice above the wind. 'In my day, governesses did not attend dances.'

Flora hesitated, torn between acceptance and attracting more censure from the old lady.

'Say you will,' Bunny said, nudging her. 'I was hoping for at least one dance with you.'

'I don't have anything suitable to wear,' Flora said, embarrassed with the truth of this statement as much as the plea in Bunny's voice. Even with Lady Amelia's contributions to her wardrobe, she was hardly equipped for dances.

'That's what every woman says,' Max muttered with some bitterness.

'Come to our suite after lunch, Flora,' Cynthia said. 'I have heaps of dresses, and we are about the same size. I'm sure to have something which will suit you.'

166

'Tha-that's most kind, thank you,' Flora stammered, taken unawares by both the offer and its source. She glanced at Bunny, who delivered a 'who would have thought it' look.

Cynthia gave an elegant little shrug, cast a swift sideways look at Mrs Penry-Jones and winked. 'Can't let the old folks have their way every time, can we?'

'Really!' The old lady gave a pointed sniff before going back to her bouillon.

Chapter 14

The pounding of feet along the deck announced the arrival of Eddy and Ozzy, both similarly dressed for the weather in layers of jumper, overcoats and flying scarves.

'What have you two being doing this morning?' Flora asked.

'Not a lot,' Ozzy answered for them both. 'The deck games have been cancelled due to the high winds.' He hunched his shoulders in dejection and scuffed the sole of one shoe against the deck. 'We don't know what to do now.'

'Have some hot bouillon,' Monica suggested, nodding to the steward who had halted a few feet away to serve another group of hardy passengers.

'Not hungry,' Eddy said, caught Flora's hard look and added, 'thank you, Mrs Gilmore.' He wandered to the rail and joined Eloise, braced one foot against the lower metal rail and his chin on the top one just as a particularly large wave broached the rail further along the deck.

'Do be careful, Ozzy.' Mrs Gilmore's voice was edged with panic, though her son's feet were safely planted on the deck.

'Stop fussing, Monica,' her husband growled.

'Perhaps Mrs Gilmore is right, Eddy,' Flora said. 'You're too close to the rail and it's getting quite rough out there.'

The words had only just left her lips, when a plume of spray leapt the rail and showered both boys, sending them backwards with a combined shriek.

Hands held out to their sides, they laughed at each other's soaked hair and wet faces.

Laughingly unconcerned, Eloise brushed droplets of water from her clothes, while Max shook his head like a sheepdog.

'How about we order some hot chocolate?' Bunny suggested. 'Don't need to be hungry for that, do we, boys?'

This order delivered, he enlisted the youngsters' help in the positioning of two deck chairs.

'I'm glad I did my exercise early before this wind got up.' Eloise flopped into an empty steamer chair without bothering to check the label. 'I need to keep slender for my role. Though this sea air makes banting incredibly difficult.' She lifted her feet onto the footrest, grinning like a schoolgirl. 'Is there any hot chocolate for me?' She simpered at Bunny, who gave a small sigh, pushed his glasses up his nose and waved for the steward.

'What's "banting"?' Flora asked no one in particular.

'No idea.' Mr Gilmore blew into his cupped hands, while Gus Crowe shook his head.

'It's the limitation of refined carbohydrates to promote weight loss,' Bunny said as he returned to his seat. 'Devised by a William Banting in the 1860s.'

'How knowledgeable you are, Mr Harrington.' Eloise giggled. 'I don't know what a carbo-what-ever is, but if I follow the plan, I'll become more slender.'

'My mother uses it sometimes,' Bunny said in answer to Flora's unasked question. 'Besides, Miss Lane,' he inclined his head in Eloise's direction. 'I think you are quite slender enough.'

Eloise saluted him with her cup of chocolate, which Flora imagined must contain enough starch and sugar for the entire day.

'I take herbal tea to suppress my appetite,' Cynthia said. 'When my clothes begin to pinch I swear by it. If you wish, I'll bring some to your cabin later, Eloise.'

Cynthia stumbled slightly on the name, as if she had to pluck up courage to address her, the impression confirmed when Mrs Penry-Jones glared at her in evident horror.

Eloise stammered her thanks, echoing Flora's own surprise at Cynthia's new-found generosity.

'Perhaps Cynthia's had an epiphany as to the equality of all God's creatures,' Bunny whispered. 'She normally ignores Eloise, or shoots daggers at her with those beautiful eyes.'

'She's not exactly been my best friend, either,' Flora murmured, making him smile.

'I hope the crew are keeping a watch for icebergs,' Max said, apparently bored with the conversation.

'Aren't we on the southerly course?' Gerald said with authority. 'No *bergy bits* here, I should think.' He nodded to a woman who hurried past, huddled into her coat with her head down.

'Did you see that?' Monica waggled her head at the woman's retreating back. 'Gerald acknowledged her quite civilly and she completely ignored him! That's happened several times recently. Anyone would think one of us had killed Mr Parnell.'

'Who says he was killed?' Gus Crowe looked up from his bouillon. 'The man fell, didn't he?'

'It's human nature to avoid what we regard as a threat,' Hersch said when no one ventured an answer.

'Perhaps our German friend reads Freud too,' Flora said in an undertone.

Bunny rewarded her with a slow spreading smile, while Gerald laughed at something Ozzy said, ruffling the boy's damp hair.

Ozzy ducked away in mock annoyance, and watching them, Flora's heart twisted at the man's easy affection for his son; one which Eddy would benefit from with his own father.

The frequency of waves high enough to jump the rail increased, covering the deck with icy, salt water that swirled and sucked through the gap below the bottom rail.

The tray of empty bouillon cups slid sideways, caught in time by a sprightly steward.

'I don't envy the captain up on the open bridge,' Gerald said. 'They only have a canvas sheet between them and the weather.'

Flora glanced up to where capped heads bobbed above the canvas sheets, collars pulled up to their ears and hats jammed down.

'This is a real adventure!' Ozzy yelled, blinking spray from his eyes, his hair plastered to his forehead.

An officer paused beside them, a hand clamped onto his cap that glistened with spray. 'The weather is deteriorating, I'm afraid. The captain says we are heading into a nor'easter and everyone should go back inside.'

As he spoke, a squall of rain struck the weather cloths around the open bridge above their heads with a loud hiss.

'How exciting! Is it a real storm?' Eloise's face lit with the anticipation of a child.

'It is, miss.' He offered her his arm. 'As I said, it's best I get you inside.'

Monica looked askance at Eloise's flirtatious acceptance of help, possibly because it was not directed at herself.

'Well, help me up, Gerald,' she snapped, rising with difficulty on the heaving deck.

Sighing, Gerald hauled her to her feet.

'It's a while until luncheon,' he shouted at Flora over the wind. 'How about Eddy comes back to our suite?'

'If you're sure that wouldn't be an inconvenience,' Flora called back, her eyes narrowed against the fine spray that stung her face like needles. She jumped to one side as an empty steamer chair crashed into the one Monica had just left.

'I'll get them to the dining room in time for luncheon.' Gerald threw an arm around each of

171

the boys and they hobbled across the deck like competitors in a three-legged race.

Cynthia struggled to stay upright, encumbered by her heavy coat and several blankets. Max stumbled as he took her arm, the pair locked together as they gained the safety of the interior.

At the door to the lobby, Bunny paused, his gaze strained in the direction of the aft deck.

'Aren't you coming inside?' Flora asked, stepping smartly backwards as a sheet of salt spray landed two feet away.

'I'm going to check on Matilda first. Make sure she's tied down.'

'Couldn't you ask a crew member to do that?' Flora asked, as the deck tipped sharply to one side so she had to focus on staying upright. When she looked again he had gone.

Flora staggered towards the staircase lobby, where Crowe stooped to retrieve a book left on a chair by a gentleman in a caped overcoat. The man's retreating back was still visible on the stairs above, but Crowe made no effort to call out to him, and instead, slid the book into his pocket.

Flora sighed, asking herself again why Eloise spared the odious man any of her time.

Flora made her way to Cynthia's suite, her finger having barely grazed the doorbell before it was flung open.

'There you are!' Cynthia cried, as if she had been lurking in wait, 'I was about to order coffee for us.' Cynthia fluttered to the fireplace where she gave the bell an enthusiastic push.

'That would be very welcome.' Flora dithered

on the threshold, feeling a little like Gretel about to enter the witch's house.

Immaculately tidy, the suite was a mirror image of Flora's own, but with not one personal item in evidence. Had she stumbled in there by herself, she would be hard-pressed to place anyone in these rooms.

'We keep our things in here.' Cynthia answered Flora's unasked question, leading her into the unoccupied second bedroom. The beds had been removed, the space taken up with four steamer trunks stacked on their sides. Their front sections stood open to reveal a bank of drawers on one side and rows of gowns, skirts, blouses, under-garments, shawls, scarves and petticoats on the other that were enough to furnish a dressmaker's showroom.

'See if there's anything here you like,' Cynthia waved her arm in a wide arc. 'This is such fun, just like school.'

Flora almost told her she didn't know what that was like, having never attended one, but changed her mind in case it sounded self-pitying.

'You have some beautiful things here, Cynthia.' Her fingers caressed silk, merino wool, muslin and chiffon in pastel shades of primrose, lilac, cornflower blue and ecru with equal awe. Even the Vaughn girls didn't own so many things, the younger ones not above wearing their sisters' hand-me-downs.

'My trousseau,' Cynthia said. 'I left most of it behind, though I had to buy a heavier coat than I imagined I would need.'

Flora forced her mouth closed and feigned non-

173

chalance. 'Was this your first visit to New York?'

'I was born there, actually.' Cynthia examined the fingernails of one hand. 'Mama divorced my father when I was ten. Or he divorced her, I never did find out the reasons behind it. Not something one talks about with one's parent. Mummy married an Englishman not long after, so I was brought up in London.'

'Is that why you decided on New York for your honeymoon?' Flora kept talking, self-conscious that she trawled through another woman's clothes while the owner watched.

'Something like that. Though I wish Max had not announced the fact we are newlyweds to the shipping line. Since the moment we stepped onto this ship we've been gawped at like specimens under glass.'

'Don't you like being the centre of attention?' Flora discarded an eau-de-nil muslin gown as being pretty, but too insipid for her skin tone.

'It isn't that. New York was spoiled for me by–' she broke off at the rattle of crockery. 'Ah, here are our refreshments.' She poked her head round the door frame and called to the unseen stewardess. 'Just leave it on the table, would you?'

An evocative aroma of fresh, brewed coffee and the chink of cups floated out of the sitting room, followed by the suite door closing again.

'What about this one?' Cynthia unhooked a silk gown the colour of poinsettias from the nearest trunk. She frowned, her lips puckered. 'No, it's not your colour.' She returned it to the rail and leaned her hip against the door and her arms folded.

'I don't suppose you've heard any more about that man who died? What was his name? Parnell?' She hesitated on the last word too long for it to be a convincing memory lapse.

'Why do you ask?' Flora pretended to examine a blue dress, suspecting Cynthia had been working up to this question since she had arrived.

'Oh, just idle curiosity.' Cynthia picked at a cuticle. 'Some of the passengers have been talking, and well, it seems there may have been something odd about it after all.'

'Really?' Flora asked, feeling Bunny would have been proud of her acting ability. 'What sort of thing?'

'That Mr Parnell may not have fallen after all.' The hunted look in Cynthia's eyes intensified. 'Max thinks someone is bound to have informed the newspapers.' Her hand on the doorframe tightened until her knuckles showed white.

'A death on board is bound to be newsworthy,' Flora said. 'Especially if the killer is caught. In which case the police will have to be involved.'

Cynthia's eyes darkened, then with an effort, she composed herself. 'Do you like that one?' She indicated the aquamarine gown in Flora's hands. 'That colour makes me look pasty, but flatters your complexion beautifully. Try it on to make sure it fits.'

Flora obeyed, her questions forgotten as she slipped the gown over her curves and down to the floor, the tight bodice covered with gauzy lace where the silk showed through above a full skirt with a small train.

'It's lovely, Cynthia, thank you.' Flora twisted

175

and turned before a cheval mirror, admiring the way the silk, shot through with silver, caught the light.

'Oh, it's nothing. I'll have it pressed and sent to your suite in time for tomorrow. Get changed now and we'll have that coffee.' She patted Flora's arm, before disappearing into the sitting room.

Flora returned the gown to its hanger and pulled on her skirt, fastening the row of side buttons with clumsy fingers. A crackling noise drew her attention to the pocket, from which she drew a slightly crumpled piece of paper. Frowning, she recognized it as the one that had fallen from Parnell's drawer when she and Eloise searched his stateroom. She had shoved into her pocket when the doorknob rattled and forgotten it.

The New York Times' banner was printed across the top of the sheet of paper, with a headline below that read *Bridegroom Van Elder Is Dead.*

New York Mar. 7 1900

The marriage last Saturday evening of Theodore van Elder of this city and Miss Estelle Montgomery, of New York, which was a great surprise to their friends, was followed this evening by the sudden death of Mr Theodore van Elder from acute gastritis. The fact that he had not been in good health for some time, and that the friends of the couple knew nothing of their engagement, made their marriage all the more surprising.

Mr van Elder was a well-known man about town. Miss Montgomery was his second wife. A child by his first wife is heir to a fortune. Mr van Elder's mother is wealthy. Miss Montgomery was to have been the

176

guest of honour at the theatre party last Saturday evening, but she surprised her friends by dropping in upon them just as they were about to start for the theatre and informing them that she had been married to Mr van Elder.

Since the evening of the marriage, Mr van Elder, on account of sickness, has scarcely been able to leave his apartment. Mr van Elder was over forty years of age and originally from Baltimore, but recently engaged in business in New York. His widow is but twenty-three and a beautiful woman.

Flora?' Cynthia called from the sitting room. 'Your coffee will get cold.'

'Coming.' The gown forgotten, Flora thrust the paper back into her pocket and went to join Cynthia.

Chapter 15

Flora paced the suite and read the newspaper clipping again, staring at the stark print long after she reached the end. Her thoughts whirling, she was vaguely aware of the slap of horizontal rain that lashed the deck outside, accompanied by the scream of the wind. That Eloise had changed her name came as no surprise, though the fact her husband had died less than a week after their secret wedding sent chills through her. No wonder his family were suspicious; anyone would be.

The question remained as to how 'Theo' had died. Was Eloise telling the truth when she claimed to have nothing to do with it? If so, then why was she so worried Mr Hersch might discover who she was? That Parnell kept the clipping gave credence to Eloise's claim he had tried to blackmail her.

She recalled the raised voices on her first night on board and tried to picture Eloise battering Parnell with an ashtray, but dismissed it.

Alerted to the sound of repeated knocking at the suite door, her progress across the room was hampered by the fierce bucking of the ship. Finally, she flung it open to reveal Bunny.

Stepping inside, he smoothed his wet hair back with cupped hands, removed his steamed-up glasses and wiped the lenses with a handkerchief produced from a pocket.

Flora fetched a towel from the bathroom, their hands connecting as he took it. She drew hers back sharply, hoping he did not notice the impeding blush that prickled her skin.

'Is the storm getting worse?' Flora asked, self-conscious. He would think her gauche if she coloured at every innocent contact, though at times she caught a sudden sparkle in his eyes that implied he felt it too.

He nodded. 'Looks like it, though Matilda is secure, thank goodness.' He emerged from under the towel, still giving his scalp a vigorous scrub. 'Everything all right? You seem a bit distracted.'

Silently, she handed him the clipping. 'Read this.'

He handed back the towel without speaking,

and took the page from her.

'The night Eloise and I searched Parnell's cabin–'

'Broke into,' he corrected her.

'Yes, all right then, broke into. That fell on the floor with the photograph.'

Bunny wasn't listening, his gaze scanned the paper swiftly then looked up, his expression unfathomable. The deck lurched and he staggered slightly, a hand on the back of a chair to steady himself, while rain sluiced the window like a hosepipe being aimed at the glass.

'I've never heard the names van Elder or Montgomery before.' He paused and narrowed his eyes. 'Unless...'

'Think, Bunny, you must have made the connection by now.' She twirled her hand in a circular motion as encouragement.

'Oh. I see. Eloise is this Estelle van Elder.'

'Exactly!' Flora took the clipping from him and waved it under his nose. 'I'm going to demand Eloise explain this, and everything else she's been hiding since we came aboard.'

'That might not produce the result you wish for.'

'What do you mean?' Flora lowered herself into the nearest chair, waving him into one opposite.

'If Eloise thinks you're nosing into her affairs.' The deck lurched sharply as he lowered himself into a chair, and he fell the rest of the way. 'Suppose she complains to the captain? It's not as if you have the authority to question people.'

'I doubt it. She's too scared. But you have a point.'

'As I recall, I have quite a number of points, but you always manage to circumvent them.' He flicked the page with a finger. 'It says here van Elder died days after they eloped. No wonder she's keeping you guessing.'

'I know it looks bad, but–'

'But what? How come you've become her champion? You hardly know the woman.'

Flora was about to remind him she didn't know him either, but left the words unspoken. Instead, she said, 'Eloise, or Estelle, or whatever her name is, thinks Mr Hersch is working for the van Elder family.'

'I warned you to be careful of that man.' Bunny threw her an 'I told you so' look. 'He might look like an amiable old uncle, but there's more to him than that.'

'He's not that old.' Nothing about Mr Hersch had made her distrust him thus far, but then she had felt the same about Eloise.

'I don't see what we could do, although...' Bunny paused and stroked his chin.

'What?' Flora urged.

'A friend of mine is a reporter for the *New York Times*. I could ask him to discover what he can about this Theodore van Elder chap, including the circumstances surrounding his death. In the meantime, I suggest we don't say anything to anyone.'

'Even Mr Hersch?'

'Especially him. We have no idea what's he's up to or why.'

Flora chewed her bottom lip, torn between her promise to the German, and her wish to stay in

Bunny's favour. Finally, she nodded. 'All right. I won't say anything.'

'Come on then!' Bunny heaved himself to his feet and made his way to the door.

'You want to go to the telegraph office now? In this?' Flora waved at the darkened window which showed a slate grey lowering sky and an angry sea.

'Why not? Most of the passengers are holed up in their staterooms.'

Flora shrugged into her coat, while Bunny braced the door open with his hip and led the way out onto the promenade deck.

'Who would care if we sent a telegram anyway?' Flora said, as a blast of salt spray stung her cheeks and the stiff wind plastered her skirt to her legs.

'Most people wouldn't,' Bunny shouted above the scream of the wind. 'Though the killer might.' He released the door behind them which slammed into its frame with a deafening bang.

'I hadn't thought of that,' Flora murmured to herself.

Bunny's knock on the wireless room door was answered by a fresh-faced crewman whom Flora thought looked vaguely familiar; his brass name plate identifying him as Seaman Crofts.

'You're lucky to catch me, sir, miss.' He ushered them inside and leaned a shoulder against the door when it threatened to spring open again. 'I was seeing to the bells, and have just this moment got back.'

The cramped room held an oversized wooden desk sat below a rack of tightly packed shelves, the atmosphere permeated with aromas of paper and wet wool.

'What were you doing to the bells?' Flora raised her hand to adjust her disarranged hair but gave up when she saw there was no mirror.

'Muffling them, miss. Bells on board ship are considered bad luck as they signify funerals.'

'I thought they were essential to sound the watches?' Bunny said, frowning.

'Yes, sir, that's true. But if they ring of their own accord, as in a storm, it means somebody is going to die.' His youthful face showed complete acceptance of this superstition. 'The deck bell was clanging away like a good'un in this wind.'

Flora had no time for omens or superstitions. She preferred to rely on practicality combined with a keen sense of her own survival. The look she exchanged with Bunny told her his philosophy ran along similar lines, and he muttered a dismissive 'I see,' before explaining why they were there.

The crewman dragged a pad of paper towards him.

'You say this wire is to go to the *New York Times* office?' His expression changed from eagerness to wary suspicion. 'You're not a reporter are you, sir? Because the captain said I wasn't to send details of the death of that passenger to anyone–'

'No, not at all,' Bunny reassured him. 'This is a personal matter I wish treated with the utmost privacy.'

'As you say, sir.' Crofts gave a curt nod, apparently satisfied as he took down the words Bunny dictated.

'There's no mention here of the gentleman who died,' the sailor said when he had finished. 'So I don't reckon it can do any harm. Pounds or dollars, sir?' He scribbled a few symbols on a scrap of paper before handing it to Bunny.

'Oh, er, pounds if you don't mind,' Bunny replied. 'I don't have any American currency left.'

'Then that's twenty-two words, sir, at eight shillings four pence for ten words. The signature is included, so that will be sixteen shillings eight pence.'

'Can't you put it on my account?' Bunny asked, frantically searching his pockets.

'I'm sorry, sir. All wireless telegraphy charges are strictly pre-paid.'

'Well, I'm not sure I – ah!' Bunny withdrew a pound note from an inside pocket and handed it over.

Flora waited as Seaman Crofts counted out change from a cash box into Bunny's hand, her attention caught by a sheet of notepaper on the desk, with 'Telegraph Request – Urgent' on the top and Carl Hersch's name beneath. The word 'Sent' in sketchy block capitals scrawled across it.

'How does the telegraph machine work?' Flora feigned interest in the contraption on the desk, while taking a closer look at the page.

Seaman Crofts launched into a lively description of the wireless telegraphy machine, with its three cylinders of various sizes joined by cogs and strips of metal above an ivory and black keyboard that resembled a small pianoforte.

Paying cursory attention to the combination of metal, wood and wires, Flora squinted at the

183

words *Montana Land Deal 1890*.

Suddenly, the sailor broke off from his explanation and cleared his throat while he slid his elbow over the page, obscuring its contents.

'Time to go, Flora,' Bunny said from behind her.

Flora was about to obey when she realised when she had seen the sailor before. 'Didn't I see you talking with Mr Crowe yesterday in the upstairs lobby?'

He bent his head to a pile of papers, his cheeks flushed. 'I speak to most of the passengers at one time or another, miss.'

'I'm sure you remember this one. He was being unpleasant, wasn't he?' she asked, drawing an enquiring look from Bunny. 'He does have an unfortunate manner sometimes.'

'Um – well, he was a bit cross.' A sheen of sweat appeared on the sailor's forehead. 'We settled the matter, though, miss. I think you'll find he has no complaints.'

'I'm sure he doesn't. You must have to deal with all sorts of people in your job.'

'I do, miss. Now if you don't mind, I have to get on.' He waved Bunny's telegram in the air.

'Of course, and we must get along to our luncheon.' She grabbed Bunny's arm and hustled him into the lobby.

'What was that all about?' Bunny asked, when the door closed behind them.

'I'm not sure.' Flora tapped her teeth with a fingernail. 'It could be nothing at all. Then again...'

The wind continued to howl as Flora made her

way along the interior corridor, while Bunny lurched from one handrail to another in an effort to remain upright. Flora was grateful for Bunny's steadying arm, as they emerged into the lobby outside the dining room.

Braced against the door that led onto the deck, she paused to allow a stream of unsteady diners through the doors ahead of them.

'What's that chap doing?' Bunny pointed through the window onto a deck barely visible through a wall of spray that crashed over the rail.

'Where?' Flora peered through the mist, where she could just make out the figure of a man in a long overcoat. Bent almost double, he concentrated on planting one foot in front of the other on the steeply angled boards. 'He's making for the aft deck.'

Bunny narrowed his eyes but did not answer.

Flora gripped the handrail as the crest of a running wave lifted the floor beneath her feet, hovered, then plunged the ship downwards again, taking her stomach with it.

The man on deck staggered, just as a wave twice the size of the one before rolled over the rail.

He looked over his shoulder, his face suffusing with terror as the water rushed towards him. At the last second, he made a grab for the ladder to the promenade deck, but his hand closed on thin air and the wall of water crashed over him, obscuring him completely.

'Stay here!' Bunny commanded, flinging open the outside door.

'No! Bunny. It's too dangerous!' Flora called

into the wind, aware he couldn't possibly have heard her.

Cold water slammed into her eyes and her skirt billowed out like a sail, her shawl whipping painfully round her shoulders. Knowing she would be blown off her feet if she stayed there, she was left with no option but to heave the door shut again.

Water dripped from her hair as she stared through the glazed door to where Bunny waded through knee-high seawater, using the fenders on the lifeboats as handholds.

Her gaze jumped forwards to the man, who with nothing to hold on to was being pulled towards the rail in the grip of fast flowing water being sucked back into the sea.

A loud creak sounded from the far side of the deck, and Flora gasped in horror as Bunny's motor car slid inexorably across the boards towards both men, its canvas cover billowing in the wind, the straps trailing behind it like streamers.

The deck tilted to the starboard side, and the metal monster gathered speed. The creak and squeal must have alerted Bunny, for he gave the moving car one hesitant look before he plunged past it, straight for the half-submerged man.

A rush of tender admiration filled Flora's chest at what it must have cost him to ignore his beloved motor car and go to the man's aid. Another wave submerged them both beneath a giant grey hand that threatened to pluck them both from the deck. Together, they rolled sideways, dragged towards the gap below the bottom rung, where nothing stood between them and the ferocious sea.

A small crowd had rapidly gathered behind

Flora in the lobby, issuing murmured gasps of dismay, while a line of sailors, heedless of the storm, clambered down the outside companionway, heads down against the wind and rain.

The deluge swirled and receded from the boards, leaving the two figures huddled against a massive circular winch riveted to the deck.

'He's got him!' someone yelled.

Flora's breath hitched and she mouthed silent bargains with God for Bunny's safe return.

The deck levelled out and Bunny hauled the man upright, then clutched together, they limped towards the lobby door. Behind them, the motor car came to a shuddering rest against a pile of folded steamer chairs jammed tight against a lifeboat.

Crewmen surrounded them six feet from the door and dragged them into the lobby where they collapsed; their sodden clothes forming a wide, wet pool on the floor.

'Be careful with him!' Bunny shouted as a sailor helped him to his feet. He braced an arm against the wall and dragged in laboured breaths, his chest heaving.

His glasses were gone and his hair hung in dark rats' tails on his forehead and neck, his drenched jacket clung to his shoulders, accentuating his muscular build.

Weak with relief, Flora pushed her way through the group who clustered round him and threw her arms round his neck. Freezing moisture leached through the bodice of her blouse, but she clung on, inhaling the male scent of him, her throat clogged with grateful tears.

'Hang on now, Flora. It's all over now. No need for theatrics.' Embarrassed, Bunny disentangled her hands, holding them down at her sides while his gaze swept the row of faces around them.

'Sorry, I–' She stepped back, her possessive pride dissolving like mist. He was right, she had no claim on him. But at least he was alive. 'You've lost your glasses,' was the only thing she could think of to say.

'Drat, those were my favourites too.' He peered out to the storm-ravaged deck with a bemused expression, as if somehow he could detect the lost spectacles.

Gerald Gilmore pounded his back in a loud, wet slap, distracting him, while Gus Crowe murmured, 'Good show, old man.'

Flora tugged her coat round her to cover the damp patch on her skirt, as if she could hold in her mortification at what she had just done. She had hugged him, in public! No wonder he had shied away from her!

She longed to apologize, but his focus was now entirely on the rescued man, who now lay on a stretcher slung between two sailors. A lady bent over him, only partly visible through the throng of people, one of his hands sandwiched in both of hers.

'Darling,' she cried piteously. 'Can you hear me? Please say you can hear me.'

'I doubt it, ma'am,' a crewman answered. 'He's out cold, I'm afraid. We'll get the doctor up here in a trice to see to him. He's a lucky chap, we nearly lost him overboard.'

The woman lifted her head, and Flora released

a shocked gasp. 'Bunny, that's Cynthia! The man you rescued was Max.'

'Really?' Bunny blinked, then with mock seriousness, added, 'I must have been too preoccupied in keeping from falling overboard to notice.'

The sailors lifted the stretcher and moved off toward the doctor's room, with Cynthia tottering awkwardly alongside the stretcher.

'What was Max doing out there in such heavy seas?' Flora asked, as the crowd dispersed around them, leaving herself and Bunny stranded in the middle of the lobby.

'He most probably didn't realize the danger,' Bunny said. 'Not everyone is an experienced sailor.'

'Are you all right, sir?' The concerned face of Officer Martin appeared at Bunny's side. 'Shall I ask the doctor to take a look at you as well?'

Bunny shook his head, casting a myopic glance at the now deserted deck. 'I'm fine. My priority is to make sure my motor car is still in once piece.' Without a glance at Flora, he stepped outside.

A stone settled beneath Flora's breastbone as she watched him stride away across a deck that a few moments before had been tilted at forty degrees and beneath several feet deep in freezing sea water. Bunny may have been right about Max being an inexperienced sailor, but if so, why had he headed for the aft deck when the dining room lay in the opposite direction?

Chapter 16

Only the most stalwart of the passengers turned up for the late luncheon, which consisted of sandwiches and coffee arranged in the dining room. Flora noted that neither Eloise nor Hester had put in an appearance, but had little time to ponder on this, kept occupied by the fact the plates and cutlery skittered across table tops. Eating became a balancing act, the ensuing embarrassment covered by uneasy laughter.

Bunny's bravery and Max's lucky escape became the main topic of conversation, however, Dr Fletcher's pronouncement that his injuries were little more than a wrenched arm and concussion, proved something of an anti-climax.

'Probably didn't realize how powerful a rogue wave could be,' Gerald said when someone posed the question as to what Max was doing outside. He swiped a ham sandwich from a tray, pointing it at the group of animated young boys at the far end of the room. 'The storm doesn't appear to have spoiled their appetites.'

Miss Ames's mouth puckered in distaste at the group of children who darted between the tables.

'There's Ozzy! Yoo-hoo, Ozzy, darling!' Monica's high pitched wail made Flora wince, while red-faced, her son hid behind Eddy.

Flora's gaze shifted to the attentive young steward who stood a few feet away, and gave thanks for

Bunny's thoughtfulness.

A ship's officer called for quiet, and when the general chatter had died down, announced what everyone already knew, that although the wind and rain had dropped, outside activities were still hazardous, although the bridge tournament would go ahead after luncheon as scheduled; this statement was greeted by light clapping and a wave of sighs.

'That's something anyway.' Gus Crowe's face visibly brightened.

'I doubt they'll be playing for money,' Gerald warned.

'Not even a little side bet, my friend?' Crowe gave a knowing wink.

Gerald didn't reply, at which Crowe narrowed his eyes, one finger placed against his nose. 'Ah, I get it, the little woman wouldn't approve, eh?'

Monica scrambled to her feet, carefully avoiding Crowe's gaze. 'Flora, dear, there's a musical recital planned in the saloon this afternoon. I thought it would keep the boys occupied whilst we play bridge. I'll cut along and escort them both there, shall I?'

'That's very kind of you, Monica.' Flora's words were accompanied by a discordant scraping back of chairs as the passengers made their way out to the staircase lobby.

'It's so kind of you to put up with Eddy's company for so long, Mrs Gilmore.' Flora caught up with Monica at the door, intent on putting some space between herself and Bunny. 'I've been a bit distracted lately.' How was she going to face him again after that episode in the lobby? Regret

191

mixed with longing as she recalled the feel of his chest pressed against her bodice, his cold breath on her cheek.

'Think nothing of it,' Monica called over her shoulder as they gained the promenade deck. 'I'm only delighted Ozzy has found such a congenial friend.'

Flora returned to her suite in order to check her appearance, mortified to find her soft bun had lost half its pins and her bodice, though now dry was badly creased. No wonder Bunny had pulled away from her so abruptly. With a dismayed sigh she set to repairing the damage.

In the library, sofas and armchairs had been pushed against the walls, the open space occupied by an arrangement of card tables, each containing four chairs. Flora took the empty chair beside Monica, who was quick to reassure her that Eddy was settled at the recital which was scheduled to last until tea time.

'Anyone care to wager who'll turn up after that gale?' Gerald eased past Monica's chair and hovered beside Flora. 'I saw Dr Fletcher dashing about a while ago, I imagine he's kept busy with seasickness. I'll lay evens on Miss Smith not coming.'

'I'll accept that bet, old man.' Crowe swept two glasses from a tray borne aloft by a passing waiter, one of which he set before Gerald. 'Miss Lane didn't come to luncheon, either. I should imagine she's got her head over a bowl at this very moment.'

'How indelicate of you, Mr Crowe.' Miss Ames

inhaled sharply through narrowed nostrils. 'The poor girl could be suffering.'

'Just a little joke, you know.'

Crowe reddened, and eased his collar away from his neck.

Flora hid a smile, noting how crass Crowe could be with the men, but reverted to an embarrassed schoolboy when chastised by a woman.

There was still no sign of Eloise, who had yet to fulfil her promise to explain everything.

Banting or not, Eloise must have been ravenous by lunchtime.

'I see the weather hasn't affected you, dear lady?' Gerald called out to Mrs Penry-Jones as if she were deaf, though she occupied a table not six feet away.

'I never get seasick.' She sipped from one of the glasses handed to her by a waiter, then peered at it, her nose wrinkled. 'Hester, on the other hand, turned positively green earlier and had to lie down. I expect her presently. She would never miss a game of bridge.' She moved her cane from one side of her chair to the other, catching Crowe sharply on the ankle.

Crowe drew his foot rapidly under the table, apparently too proud to rub it in company, though Flora imagined it must have hurt.

'I hope our young hero is fully recovered without any long-term effects,' Gerald said, taking the empty seat beside Flora.

'Oh yes,' Miss Ames simpered, though she had neither the build nor the face for it. 'That was valiant of him to go after Max like that.'

'Foolhardy if you ask me,' Crowe said, then at

Flora's hard look, qualified it by adding, 'But very brave.'

'Ah, here's our young hero now.' Gerald waved to where the crowd had parted to allow Bunny through.

Flora's stomach did a strange flip that had become a habit when in his company.

He had changed his clothes, his still wet hair slicked back. He worked his way towards her, whilst being subjected to a round of back slapping from those who had not been present at the time, but had heard about his heroic effort.

'I persuaded one of the crewmen to help me get Matilda back under canvas,' Bunny said when he reached Flora. 'Odd how she managed to shake loose from the ropes. I checked them myself earlier. No damage though, thank goodness.' He accepted a glass from a waiter of what looked like fruit punch, but which probably wasn't. 'Has anyone found out how Max is?'

Flora sneaked a sideways look at him and away again, but his expression held no embarrassment.

Gus Crowe recounted Dr Fletcher's diagnosis. 'I imagine he's tucked up in bed with his devoted bride in attendance.' He gave a knowing wink.

'Do you play bridge, Flora?' Monica asked, her nostrils narrowed in distaste at Crowe's insensitivity.

'I'm afraid I don't, though I'm happy to learn.'

'It's not difficult.' Bunny picked up a pack of cards and proceeded to shuffle them. 'Bridge is similar to whist, in that each player takes a turn as dummy, and a trump suit is chosen. The players then bid the number of tricks they expect to achieve, and whether they wish to have a trump suit or no trump.'

'You must follow the suit of the player who starts, but if unable to do so, you can play any card,' Monica added.

'The trick is won by the highest trump, if there are trumps in the trick,' Bunny said, evidently getting into his stride. 'Points are also awarded for honours, and–'

'Enough!' Flora lifted her hands in surrender. 'All these rules are giving me a headache.'

'It will make more sense when Flora is actually playing,' Monica said.

'Or maybe not.' Bunny cast Flora a sideways look she pretended not to see.

Crowe nudged Gerald, their combined gazes on Hester, her wide hips swaying with the motion of the deck as she made her way gingerly towards them. As she squeezed past Flora's chair, she caught a whiff of a spicy scent, whose musk undertones struck her as too heavy for Hester. Had she made a special effort for a man? If so, whom?

'Didn't I say she would never miss a game of bridge?' Mrs Penry-Jones muttered darkly.

Gerald held out a chair for Hester, while his other hand extended behind her back, into which Crowe slid a folded banknote.

Gerald held the note up to the light, squinted at it ostentatiously, then pocketed it.

'Quite a character that Gerald, isn't he?' Bunny said, *sotto voce*. Then before she could respond, his smile dissolved into a frown. 'Look, Flora, about earlier. I didn't mean to–'

'Please don't worry.' She stared at her lap, her

cheeks burning. 'I would sooner forget about it if you don't mind.'

She wanted nothing of the sort, but recoiled at having her indiscretion discussed in company.

'*I* don't want to forget,' he insisted in a fierce whisper. 'What's wrong? You keep staring at the door.'

'Eloise didn't come to luncheon and she's not here now.' Flora voiced the worry that had nagged at her all morning. 'She's avoiding me again.'

'There's not a great deal you can do about it if she's reluctant to explain.'

'We had an agreement.' Rising, Flora skirted the table. 'I'm going to find her. I won't accept any excuses, either.'

'Flora!' Bunny half rose, but she ignored him.

'Never mind her, Mr Harrington.' Mrs Penry-Jones' stentorian voice accompanied the loud drum of her fingers on the table top. 'Are you going no trumps, Monica?'

At the bottom of the stairs leading to the promenade deck, Flora leaned her back against the wall, her eyes closed as she recalled Bunny's stern expression which she took to imply such intimacy between them was never to occur again.

Well, if that was what he wanted, he could have his wish. She would be nothing but coolly polite to Mr Bunny Harrington for the rest of the voyage.

Pushing away from the wall, she set off for Eloise's stateroom, past an elderly matron who blocked the door to the promenade deck, uncaring of the outraged, 'Well!' that sounded from behind her.

The wind still sang through the winch lines, but outside Eloise's stateroom, the rain had reduced to little more than a light drizzle, which failed to penetrate the deck canopy.

Flora gave the door a determined rap with her knuckles, then immediately did it again, but no sound came from inside.

'Open the door, Eloise,' she muttered, then louder, 'You've avoided me for long enough!' She rattled the door handle, but it refused to turn.

She blew air between pursed lips and peered in at the window beside the door, but the blind was pulled down, leaving only a small gap at the bottom where it had snagged on something.

Flora crouched lower, her hands cupped round her eyes to block out her reflection in the glass. 'Eloise!' She called in a harsh whisper through the thick glass.

At first glance, the room looked empty, apart from a shoe that poked out from behind the partition.

A shoe with a foot inside it.

A trickle of dread squeezed her chest. She jumped backwards, glancing both ways in search of help, but the deck remained deserted.

Rhythmic footsteps from the boat deck sent her to the rail where the purser walked across the boards below her.

'Mr Willis,' she called, slightly panicked. 'I need your help.'

He glanced up and back at her, nodded, then changed direction and bounded up the outside companionway.

Flora closed the space between them in a few

strides. 'Mr Willis, do you have a key to these state-rooms?'

He looked down at her from his considerable height, a frown between his brows. 'Is something wrong, miss?'

At his brief nod, and anticipating his caveat about company policy, Flora grasped his arm, pulling him towards Eloise's door. 'There's something terribly wrong with my friend.'

'I-I'm not sure I ought to simply barge in. Perhaps she's sleeping?' He gave the door a tentative knock with his knuckles.

'I've already tried that.' Flora clenched her fists at her sides. 'I wouldn't ask if it wasn't serious. I looked in at the window just now and I – well, I saw something. I'll wait out here if you wish. All I ask is that you take a look.'

He looked about to say something but then changed his mind.

She could see he was weakening. 'Please.'

With a resigned sigh, he rummaged in a pocket, withdrew a key and unlocked the door that gave with a sharp click.

Forgetting her promise, Flora pushed past him and burst inside where she jerked to an abrupt halt at the end of the bed. The cabin tilted and her stomach heaved.

'Hey, miss, I can't just let you in, I have to–' He came up behind her, where he broke off. 'Oh, my.'

Eloise lay on her back on the floor, her arms flung outwards from her sides. The area between her neckline and mid-thigh was a bright scarlet against the cream silk of her dress, becoming a deeper crimson on her bodice. Her unnaturally black hair formed a cloud of curls round her head, her vivid blue eyes open, but seeing nothing; devoid of pain or even surprise.

Flora brought a hand to her mouth, her palm dampened by rapid breaths through her fingers.

'Don't look, miss.' Strong hands pulled her backwards, though his voice seemed to come from underwater.

Her knees crumpled. She hung onto his arm to keep herself upright, her gaze fixed on the wide splash of red that seemed to grow and fill her vision.

This couldn't be happening. It had to be one her dreams and she would wake soon, shivering and tearful.

'Is everything all right, Mr Willis?' a tentative male voice called from behind them, followed by a shocked gasp.

'Thank goodness.' The purser sighed in relief. 'Fetch the doctor, would you, Brady? Be quick, and then inform the captain.'

Heavy footfalls marked the man's retreat. The purser gripped Flora's upper arms and twisted her around to face him. 'Miss Maguire, please come outside. I must lock this door again until the captain arrives.' He hustled her back out onto the deck where the wind tugged at her skirt. 'Shall I send for a stewardess to stay with you?'

'Bunny,' Flora murmured his name as a reflex.

'Who, sorry?'

'Mr Harrington. He's at the bridge tournament.' The deck spun and she grabbed an upright support to steady herself. Bile rose into her throat and despite a salt-tinged wind rushing past her face, she couldn't breathe.

Flora turned and ran until the metal bars of the rail bit into her thighs, halting her. She gripped the polished wood top so hard, her fingers cramped in protest. The pain came as a welcome distraction, though not enough to still the words that echoed in her head. Eloise is dead.

Chapter 17

The angry sea of that morning had settled to a gentle swell beneath a sky filled with the soft blues and pinks of a late spring afternoon. The wake of the ship stretched backwards in a surging white line towards the horizon, while the wind tugged Flora's hair from its pins. She had no idea how long she stood there, her gaze fixed on the frothing water until her breathing slowed and the urge to scream dissolved.

Bunny moved into her line of vision, though she sensed he had been there for some time.

'Are you all right, Flora?' he asked gently.

She didn't respond. How could she be all right?

He moved closer, the whoosh of the silk lining of his jacket strangely loud as he slipped a protective arm round her shoulders. 'You were just staring out to sea, I thought it best to leave you alone.'

'You – you know what has happened?' Her voice came out croaky.

Instead of answering, he tucked a strand of her

hair behind her ear, his fingers brushing her cheek. His touch made her want to bury her face in his neck, but she resisted in case he rejected her again; that would be too much to bear.

'How could anyone do something like that to Eloise?' She squeezed her eyes shut, as if she could banish the images in her head.

'The captain is inside her stateroom with Mr Hersch and Dr Fletcher.' Bunny massaged her shoulder with one hand. 'Their combined efforts should catch whoever did this pretty quickly.'

'Huh!' Her anger surfaced again. 'Faint hope of that. At least this time no one can call it an accident.' This time! What was she saying?

'Dr Fletcher wants you to take this.' He held up a small brown bottle with ridges on the side, twisting it round in his fingers. 'It's a sedative. For the shock, he said.'

'That's the last thing I need now,' she snapped, annoyed with herself for taking her temper out on Bunny.

'It's all right to cry, you know.' He slipped the bottle into his pocket, and leaned his elbows on top of the rail, his shoulders hunched.

'I'm too angry to cry.' She swiped a hand across her cheek, though it came away dry. 'Eloise believed no one could touch her if she kept her identity secret.' She sniffed again, then straightened. 'Did you say Mr Hersch was in her stateroom?'

'Yes. It appears our German friend is a detective.' Bunny adjusted his glasses on his nose with his free hand. 'A Pinkerton's detective, no less.'

'I've never heard of them.' Flora sighed. 'Though I should have guessed something of the sort. All those questions, and his authoritative manner all points that way.'

'The agency is quite famous in America.' Bunny stepped closer. 'You realize we have some ex- plaining to do about the van Elders?'

Flora frowned. 'You were the one who told me to keep the newspaper clipping quiet until after we had heard from your reporter friend in New York.'

'Well, yes, but I had no idea Eloise was dead when we sent that telegram.'

'Was she?' She fell silent as a couple strolling the deck passed by, only to pause in front of Eloise's door, murmuring to each other. 'Dead, I mean. What time did we return from the wireless office and you dragged Max from the deck?'

'Difficult to say, around 12.45, or one o'clock maybe. Then we went into luncheon, after which everyone left for the bridge tournament.'

'That's about right.' Flora paused, thoughtful. 'I went back to my suite for a few moments, and – oh dear, this sounds as if we're trying to get our story straight.' She gave an embarrassed laugh that tailed off into a sob.

'Well, we are in a way. As for the clipping, you waited three days before you showed it to me.'

'I genuinely forgot about it,' Flora hissed. 'Are you implying her death is somehow my fault?'

'The reverse, actually.' His arm drifted to her shoulder and tightened. 'I'm trying to reassure you that nothing either of us did or said would have made any impact on the outcome. Someone wanted Eloise dead for reasons of their own.'

Flora's sense of guilt wouldn't be banished that

easily. 'Parnell must have known Eloise's real identity.' She pressed a clenched fist against her mouth and spoke into her fingers. 'I could have confronted Eloise with the clipping, got her to tell me the whole story.'

'Maybe she had no intention of telling you anything. Have you thought of that?'

'I would have convinced her,' Flora said, not quite believing it herself.

'That obituary still doesn't tell us why someone would want to kill them both.'

'No, no, it doesn't.' Flora chewed her bottom lip, unable to banish the thought that Eloise was right in that Mr Hersch was working for the van Elders. But he wouldn't have killed her, surely?

'Maybe Parnell tried to kill Eloise,' Flora said, trying to make sense of her muddled thoughts. 'She managed to fight him off and he died instead.'

'Then who killed her?'

'I don't know.' Her voice came out as a frustrated whine.

'Exactly.' Bunny brought his free hand down on the rail with a thump. 'We must examine the facts, not fit them to our theories.'

'Now you sound like Mr Hersch.'

'Do I? I've always wondered what it would be like to be a detective.' At her exasperated expression he added, 'Before I discovered motor cars, that is.'

He moved his arm from her shoulders to her waist, easing her away from the rail. 'You need to sit down, preferably with some hot sweet tea for shock.'

'That sounds good – oh!' She brought a hand to her mouth. 'Eddy!'

'He's listening to Beethoven in the salon. Gerald said they couldn't keep this from the boys, so he is going to break it to them together after the recital.'

'Gerald knows about Eloise?'

Bunny nodded. 'He was here when I arrived. Drawn by the commotion, I imagine, which probably means most of the passengers will know by now.'

'It's so kind of him, although I feel terrible absolving my responsibility for Eddy to someone else. I've done it too often lately.'

'Maybe it's best coming from Gerald. You know what little monsters young boys can be. They'll probably demand details, and you're in no state to deal with that. Flora.' He lowered his voice, though there was no one close enough to hear. 'I may have chosen the wrong time to talk about this, but when you hugged me this morning, I–'

'It's perfectly all right.' Flora rolled her shoulder out of his hold, her back stiff. 'I quite understand. It was presumptuous of me and won't happen again.'

Everything had become so complicated, when all she really wanted was to get to know this considerate, attractive man. Now nothing could be normal after this.

She set off towards her suite, leaving Bunny to follow.

At the sight of the guard posted outside Eloise's stateroom, Flora's stomach lurched. She froze in place as the deck seemed to tilt beneath her though the sea was almost calm.

'I can't. Not yet,' she whispered, staring past the sailor to where her own suite stood.

'We could go somewhere else. The library, perhaps?' Bunny suggested. 'The bridge tournament will have broken up by now.'

Flora shook her head. 'It's not that. I'm not going to sit over tea waiting to be summoned by the captain. I need to talk to him now.'

She pushed through the door at the far end of the deck and erupted into the interior lobby, uncaring of the astonished faces that turned in her direction. Ignoring them all, she made for the stairs. Bunny's footsteps sounded behind her, but she didn't stop until she reached the Upper Promenade deck. Halting on the landing, she searched frantically for a clue as to where to go next.

'Where is it?' she cried, panicked.

'Opposite the library, over there.' Bunny led her gently to a door marked 'Captain', giving it a sharp knock.

At a mumbled 'come in' from the other side, Flora entered an 'L' shaped cabin no larger than a stateroom, a double aspect view of the ocean she was too heartsick to appreciate.

Captain Gates occupied a swivel chair at a leather-topped desk, with Mr Hersch and Officer Martin, all of whom leapt to their feet at the sight of her.

'Ah, my dear Miss Maguire. How are you feeling?' The captain adopted a sympathetic expression.

She took a second or two to catch her breath, which came in shallow gasps after her run up the stairs.

How should she be feeling? Eloise was dead. Murdered, in the most horrible way.

'I apologize, Captain,' Bunny said, following her in. 'Flora is still very upset, but determined to speak with you.'

Tempted to tell him she could speak for herself, Flora decided against it. He didn't deserve her harsh tongue.

'How are you holding up, Miss Maguire?' Hersch asked, peering into her face.

'Calmer,' she murmured, unable to bring one single question into her mind. Those she could summon were ridiculous. 'Who killed Eloise?' and, 'What are you doing about it?' being the most prominent. 'Are you really a detective?' was the only think she could think of to say.

'I am, my dear,' he said gently. 'I apologize for not confiding in you. However, the information was not mine to give.'

'What does that mean?' Bunny snapped, his irritation equal to Flora's.

'A thing called client confidentiality,' he replied, making no attempt to explain further. 'Captain Gates and I were about to speak with you, so it's expedient you arrived here together,' adding in a gentler tone, 'which is how you have spent most of this voyage, is it not? Together.'

Flora groaned inwardly. Not only had she shamefully neglected Eddy in her quest to prove she was right about Parnell's death, now the entire ship must be gossiping about her and Bunny.

206

She could hear them now. '*Did you know that little hussy governess has set her cap at that nice Mr Harrington? And two bodies she has found now. If that doesn't tell you something about her, I don't know what does.*'

How could she ever face the other passengers again?

Her cheeks flamed, which made Hersch smile. 'I don't mean to imply anything, my dear, but your mutual attachment has not gone unnoticed.' He directed her to the last empty chair in the cramped room, leaving Bunny to hover in between.

Officer Martin withdrew his ubiquitous notebook from his pocket and resumed his seat, his pen poised over a page. Flora almost laughed aloud, but suppressed it in time. Apart from the location, the scene was so reminiscent of Sunday morning, she might have stepped back several days.

'Here we are again, eh?' Hersch appeared to read her thoughts. 'Before we begin, I would ask that neither you nor Mr Harrington discuss what you saw in Miss Lane's stateroom with the other passengers.'

'That's unlikely, isn't it?' Flora clenched both hands in her lap. 'The entire ship will be buzzing by dinner.'

'Not so. A death might not be concealed easily, though the circumstances can be. The crew have put out word that a maid came upon the body during her duties.'

'I didn't see anything,' Bunny said, defensive. 'The purser told me what had happened.'

'What about Gerald Gilmore?' Flora asked. 'Bunny – I mean, Mr Harrington, said he arrived soon afterwards?'

'He has also agreed to co-operate,' Captain Gates said. 'Mr Hersch is of the opinion the killer may reveal himself if we know more than he does.'

'Like baiting a trap, you mean?' Bunny said, his voice sharp.

'In a way.' The German inclined his head. 'We also need to know where everyone was at the time Miss Lane was killed.'

'Most people were in the library at the bridge tournament.' Bunny's eyes widened as he looked from the German to Flora. 'I imagine you don't think Miss Maguire had anything to do with it?'

Flora gasped at this bizarre suggestion. As if she could do something so brutal to any human being, especially lively, fun-loving Eloise? But then, Hersch didn't know her, did he?

'I think we can assume Miss Maguire is not involved.' Hersch lowered his rear end onto the corner of the desk, his arms crossed over his chest. 'Mr Harrington, perhaps you could give us your version of events from the time you last saw Miss Lane?'

Flora listened with barely restrained patience during Bunny's ponderous account of their visit to the wireless room. He made no mention of the telegram they had sent, his rationale being that Flora wanted to see how a telegraph machine worked.

'An odd time to make a visit, after all, the storm was still quite fierce then,' Hersch observed, splitting a look between them.

'Let me ask *you* a question,' Flora asked in an effort to distract him. 'Did you happen to find a large sum of money, or maybe a photograph in either Mr Parnell's or Eloise's staterooms? I assume you instigated a search of them both?'

Officer Martin's fast-moving pen stilled and Captain Gates cleared his throat.

'Why would you ask such a specific question, Miss Maguire?' Hersch lifted one brow in enquiry.

Flora held her nerve and refused to explain. 'Please answer me. Did you find anything?'

'We came upon a photograph during the removal of Mr Parnell's personal effects, yes.' Hersch didn't meet her eyes, giving her the impression the discovery was not unexpected.

'You've seen it before?'

His hesitation answered her question. Eloise was right. He was working for the van Elders.

'The clipping,' she whispered to Bunny without looking at him. After a pause during which Flora imagined Bunny hunting in his pockets, he placed the sheet of newsprint into her open palm.

'Then you have seen this too.' She handed the piece of newsprint to Hersch.

The detective removed a pair of oval spectacles from his pocket that Flora had never seen him use before and put them on. He scanned the page quickly before giving it to Captain Gates, confirming that this too was not a surprise. 'Where did you get this?' He removed the glasses slowly, swinging them gently by an arm.

'I have an explanation.' Flora attempted a

smile. 'Though not a particularly good one, so if you don't mind, I'll save it for another time. Besides, it's not as if we share total honesty. Is it, Mr Hersch?'

'I suppose I asked for that.' Hersch tapped the arm of his glasses against his bottom lip. 'I won't press you. For the moment.' The threat he would do so later was implied. 'However, I would be interested to know why you think this obituary has something to do with Miss Lane's murder?'

'Eloise told me her husband's name was Theo, and he had died. I didn't see the clipping until this morning.'

'Before she was killed?' Captain Gates asked.

'Well, yes, but I didn't realise its relevance then. I still don't. Then there was the bracelet.'

'What bracelet?' Hersch's eyes sharpened.

Flora looked from the German to Officer Martin and back again. 'Eloise had a gold bracelet with an inscription that said: *To E on our wedding day, T.*'

'We found no bracelet,' Hersch said, flicking a look at the captain.

'You must have.' Restless, Flora half rose, though there was no room to pace with five adults occupying the cramped cabin, so she relaxed back onto the chair again. 'It was in her handbag. A plain, gold band about half an inch thick with a safety chain. I told you about it.' She twisted in her seat to include Bunny, who nodded.

'She did mention it. I can verify that.'

'Did you actually see this bracelet, Mr Harrington?'

'Well, no, I–'

'I didn't imagine it!' Flora snapped. 'Whoever killed Eloise must have taken it.'

Officer Martin resumed scribbling.

Chapter 18

When Flora expressed her intention of ordering dinner for herself and Eddy in their suite, this suggestion had been roundly vetoed by Mr Hersch. 'We would rather you carried on as normal, Miss Maguire. You may hear something in the dining room; a detail that would not be revealed in an interview situation.'

'Am I an integral part of the investigation now?' she had asked, a brow raised in challenge.

'You always have been, my dear,' Captain Gates added in his half-amused way.

'Eddy is fine,' Bunny assured her for the fourth time as they approached the dining room. 'He's much happier being with Ozzy and the other boys, and it beats brooding alone with you.'

'He was quite reserved earlier,' Flora said. 'I'm sure he's more upset than he says. He liked Eloise.'

'He didn't really know her.'

'It seems none of us did,' Flora said under her breath, directing a nod at the steward who bowed them into the crowded room. 'I hope there won't be any unkind gossip about how Eloise's choice of profession decided her fate. I couldn't bear that.'

Bunny squeezed her hand that rested on his

forearm. 'If the conversation gets too gruesome, I'll redirect it.'

'No, don't do that. Mr Hersch is right, we may hear something interesting.'

The other diners had assembled by the time they arrived, all but Mr Hersch, whose chair remained empty.

Conversation was slow to gain momentum, often forced in places. Responses to bad jokes were overly enthusiastic, while an undercurrent ran beneath the smiles and polite requests to pass the water jug or the salt.

Gerald and Monica were unusually quiet and avoided each other's eyes. Miss Ames had abandoned her rainbow hues for a slate grey skirt and white blouse, both of which accentuated her sallow complexion. Gus Crowe lounged carelessly in his chair, but even he looked subdued and barely spoke.

'I'm surprised to see her,' Bunny whispered, nodding to where Cynthia made her way slowly to the table, stopping now and then in response to comments she either returned with a brief word or waved away. Poised and lovely as ever, Flora judged her to be slightly diminished somehow, her eyes red-rimmed beneath a layer of make-up.

She had barely sat down before Miss Ames asked in an almost funereal voice, 'How is your poor husband, my dear?'

'In some pain still, and very tired,' Cynthia replied dully. 'He was asleep when I left.' The waiter slid a salad in front of her but she poked desultorily at it with no apparent appetite.

'Sick rooms can be very wearing, can't they?' Miss Ames folded her hands on the table and addressed them like a public meeting.

'However, we cannot simply sit here and make no reference to what has happened. Miss Lane sat right here with us mere hours ago.'

Mrs Penry-Jones cast a vague gaze at her companion. 'We don't trouble ourselves with the affairs of such people, do we, Hester?'

'No, Mrs Penry-Jones.' Hester's cheeks pinked, but her hands remained steady.

'It's not as if we can even get away.' Monica's voice held slight panic. 'I mean, in a hotel we could simply leave, but here–'

'No, we couldn't,' Gus Crowe said, drawing all eyes toward him. 'In a hotel we would all be under house arrest. The police would insist on it. We're all suspects after all.'

'Did anyone here know that German fella was a detective?' A low murmur of dissent greeted Gerald's enquiry, along with several shaken heads.

'Why will no one tell us what actually happened to poor Eloise?' Miss Ames's voice rose. 'That nice young second officer would only say she had been discovered dead in her stateroom.'

'I heard she was strangled.' Monica pressed a hand to her throat. 'What with Mr Parnell possibly being murdered too, at this rate we'll all be slaughtered in our beds.'

'Don't be melodramatic, woman, Parnell wasn't murdered.' Gerald signalled to the waiter to bring him another drink, though he had barely touched his food. 'If one listens long enough to shipboard gossip, you'll hear she was bludgeoned, poisoned,

213

drowned and had a heart attack.'

Gerald glanced at his wife's plate, sighing. 'Monica, dear,' he dragged out the words in barely restrained annoyance. 'What is the point of picking mushrooms out of a beef stroganoff?'

Monica grimaced, but continued to discard the offending items onto the side of her plate.

Flora picked at her poached salmon with a hand that shook slightly, but said nothing. Her chest had started to hurt. How could they talk about Eloise dying in the same breath as mushrooms? Although maybe Mr Hersch was right and allowing everyone to gossip was a good thing. It could also explain why he wasn't here.

'Racy ladies, these actresses.' Gus Crowe waved his fork in mid-air. 'Perhaps it was an assignation that went wrong.' His gaze swung to meet Flora's, returning her scowl with a slow wink.

Flora ground her teeth in mute anger, but was for the moment trapped. Theatrical exits weren't *de rigeur* for governesses, leaving her to fume silently at the callous way he spoke of a woman he professed to be attracted to. Besides, she owed it to Eloise to stay and discover what she could.

'Somewhat inappropriate, old chap.' Bunny appeared to sense Flora's discomfort and frowned at Crowe across her lap. 'Miss Lane is barely cold.'

'Sorry.' Crowe gave a light-hearted shrug but didn't seem at all apologetic. 'Didn't mean to offend and all that.'

'Mr Crowe could have a point,' Hester said. 'Miss Lane was over-familiar with the officers. Maybe it was one of them?' Her attention focused on the cube of meat she brought slowly to her mouth.

Flora frowned, wondering if this was true. She had never seen Eloise behave with more than friendliness towards everyone, except perhaps Gus Crowe, which was still a mystery. The man was certainly attractive, in an oily, ingratiating way, but he made no attempt to hide an underlying sleaziness.

'My stewardess,' Miss Ames began conspiratorially, 'said Miss Lane was found lying on her bed, quite blue and with her tongue hanging out of her mouth.'

'There, you see, strangled.' Monica turned a triumphant gaze on Gerald, but he wasn't looking in her direction.

Flora's hand tightened on her glass until she was in danger of breaking it, then jumped when Bunny told her she had failed to respond to a request to pass the butter.

At her murmured apology, he passed the dish along for her, then squeezed her hand on the table top.

Flora recalled Hersch's comment that their companionship had not gone unnoticed, so although his touch was comforting, she made an effort not to study Bunny's face when he spoke, or return his brief, concerned smiles with betraying ones of her own.

'Weren't you planning to visit Eloise's cabin this afternoon, Mrs Cavendish?' Hester asked, her voice falsely subservient. 'Something to do with an herbal tea, wasn't it?

Cynthia jerked her fork, smearing mustard

onto the tablecloth. 'I-I did, yes. But there was no answer to my knock. The commotion on the deck below distracted me, and when I realized it was Max down there, I–' She halted as if she had come up against some mental image that was too horrible to bear, and shook her head to dismiss it.

Hester went back to her food, apparently unmoved. Flora couldn't decide if her apathy was a case of a plain woman who could not bring herself to regret the passing of a pretty one, or something else.

'I suppose now he's Gates's best buddy, he's too grand to eat with us anymore.' Crowe nodded to the figure of Mr Hersch as he came through the door. 'Oh no, my mistake, here he comes. Watch what you say, everyone.'

'Apologies for my late arrival.' The German's amiable gaze settled briefly on each face in turn as he took his chair.

'Are you really a Pinkerton's detective?' Miss Ames asked before the German's rear had connected with the seat.

'I am, dear lady.' He cleared his throat before requesting someone pass him the water jug.

'You might have been a bit more forthcoming,' Gerald snapped as he handed it over.

'I agree,' Miss Ames added. 'We would have felt safer had we known you were on board.'

'Don't see how.' Gerald gave a derisive snort. 'We still have two dead bodies and no idea who the murderer is.'

'Everyone on board will be investigated fully in due course.' Mr Hersch nodded to the waiter

216

who had delivered his dinner. 'The perpetrator will be discovered, I assure you.'

'Are you suggesting it was one of us, Mr Hersch?' Mrs Penry-Jones looked up sharply. 'I hope you know most of us here were playing bridge when it happened. Except Cynthia of course, she was with dear Max who was being tended by the doctor.' She turned a burning gaze on Flora. 'Come to think of it, Miss Maguire, you left the library in something of a hurry. Where were you all afternoon?'

Flora frowned, not so much at the old lady's accusatory tone, but her reference to Cynthia's husband as 'dear Max' when she couldn't recall them ever having a conversation.

'I can vouch for Miss Maguire's movements, Mrs Penry-Jones.' Bunny answered for her. The words 'If they are any of your concern' hung in the air.

'I'll wager you can,' Gerald said with a knowing grin.

Miss Ames supressed a chuckle, though not quick enough to conceal the glint of mischief in her eyes.

'Miss Lane was with us on deck before luncheon. Then the storm became quite fierce and the steward warned us to go back inside,' Monica said. 'I don't recall seeing her after that.'

'We all know what Max was doing.' Gerald raised one cynical eyebrow. 'Trying not to drown.' Cynthia winced and Gerald leaned toward her. 'Forgive me, my dear. I meant nothing by it. One needs to keep a sense of humour about these things.'

'I thought I saw Eloise at luncheon.' Crowe gave up his attempt to attract a waiter and filled his wine glass himself. 'But it was a buffet and everyone was moving around a lot, so I might be wrong.'

'I saw her on deck on my way to the bridge tournament,' Hester volunteered, flushing as all eyes turned towards her. 'She was at the rail, just staring out to sea.'

'In that storm?' Gerald snapped. 'A tiny thing like Eloise could have been washed overboard.' He raised an enquiring eyebrow at the detective. 'Ah, but that wasn't what happened, was it?'

Hersch didn't acknowledge his remark, remaining stoically stiff-lipped.

'I-I may have been wrong in that case,' Hester said. 'But I thought it was her at the time.'

'Enough of this murder talk.' Gus Crowe tossed his napkin onto the table beside his plate. 'I'm off to the bar. If anyone is in the mood for poker, feel free to join me.'

The evening mist split like curtains being pulled aside to reveal a sea as dark as oil. Flora stood at the rail beside Bunny and hugged her wrap tightly around her shoulders against the cool air.

She appreciated his ability to sense when she wanted to talk and when she preferred silence; a rare skill and one of the things she liked about him. If only she could forget that impulsive embrace as completely as he had.

A rising moon lit a cloud bank pearly grey, while the wind struck a note in the rigging. The steady whoosh of the sea far below worked magic on her nerves, but a parade of images still marched through her head. The worst ones, like Eloise lying dead, she drove down, while examining the less disturbing more closely; Eloise's smiling face as they sat on her bed after they invaded Parnell's stateroom, the palpable fear in her eyes when Flora had told her about the photograph. She hadn't wanted the German to see it. Why? To keep her marriage to Theodore van Elder a secret? The only reason she could think of for that, was Eloise had, in fact, been involved in her husband's death.

'We didn't learn anything new tonight, did we?' she said, disappointed.

'No, I suppose not.' Bunny nodded to an officer who saluted them as they passed. 'Maybe Hersch spotted something. He's the expert, after all. What are you thinking about?' he added, then caught her expression. 'Sorry. Silly question.'

'I know it doesn't look good, but I still cannot see Eloise as a killer.'

'She left New York in a hurry and in disguise, which some might see as the action of a guilty person.'

'She wasn't guilty, she was frightened. She certainly didn't deserve what happened to her. I cannot stop thinking that while we were compiling telegrams, Eloise was being brutally stabbed.' Flora brought her hand down hard on the rail, sending a sharp pain into her wrist.

'How could you have known someone would kill her?' Bunny's arm brushed her shoulder and sent a rush of warmth through her. His breath fanned her cheek, turning her insides to water. 'I don't want you to feel guilty about Eloise,' he whispered. 'We must trust Hersch to live up to the Pinkerton Detective Agency's reputation.'

'What do you know about Pinkerton's?' At that moment she couldn't care less about some detective agency, it was enough simply to be the entire focus of Bunny's attention. Even in this low light, the sprinkle of freckles across his nose were clearly visible.

'Pinkerton was a Scotsman.' He removed his glasses and gently polished them with a handkerchief, another habit of his she was growing used to. 'In the 1850s, his agency guarded President Lincoln on his way to his inauguration in Baltimore. They even foiled an assassination attempt. For years they were regarded as strike-breaking thugs, employed by businessmen who objected to their employees making demands about their working conditions.'

'That sounds more like muscle for hire,' Flora said. 'What did that have to do with solving crimes?'

'Very little.' He held up the spectacles as an indication he hadn't finished before putting them back on. 'Then in the 1870s, the president of the Philadelphia Railroad feared the activity of the coal mine trade unions would reduce his profits. Pinkerton's agents infiltrated a mining organization called, coincidentally, the Molly Maguires, and as a result, over twenty members were executed.'

'My goodness, that's awful.'

'Perhaps, but the Mollys weren't entirely innocent. They did their share of violence, so it was justice of sorts. After that, employers threatened by the unions paid Pinkerton's to infiltrate and disrupt their meetings. They didn't spare the sap, either. A lot of heads got broken in the process.'

'And Mr Hersch works for them?' At his nod she continued, 'He doesn't strike me as a thug.' Flora jerked her chin back as a thought occurred to her. 'You're trying to distract me with one of your stories, aren't you?'

His gaze met hers and held. 'Is it working?'

She nodded. 'You're a nice man, Mr Harrington.'

'I try. I'm also truly sorry about the way I reacted when you hugged me earlier. No, don't pull away, I know you're embarrassed and I made it worse by my behaviour. I was taken by surprise, but in an agreeable way.'

'B-but I thought–'

'I know what you thought,' he whispered, his arm gently encircling her waist. She made no attempt to pull away, nor did she wish to. 'I really like you, Flora. I had hoped our first embrace wasn't going to take place in public while I was soaked to the skin, and gasping air like a landed fish.'

First. He said first. Flora's stomach did a strange but pleasing lurch, though left her unsure as to what was expected of her now. Too embarrassed to ask, she eased away, preparing to offer polite thanks and a formal goodnight.

Before she could speak, he pulled her back into his arms, brushing his mouth across hers in a featherlight touch that ended before it really began. His arms remained round her and he pulled back his chin, studying her closely while his hold tightened again. This time his mouth pressed on hers was not tentative, but confident, even possessive.

Having never kissed anyone in passion before, Flora had no time to worry whether her reaction was appropriate or not as instinct took over. Her arms moved of their own accord to encircle his neck, her head tilted at just the right angle to meet his. The pressure of his mouth increased under hers, his touch insistent, even fierce. His breathing quickened, and when the tip of his tongue flicked over her bottom lip, her nerves jumped.

She didn't hear any footsteps until Hersch's cheery, 'Goodnight, Mr Harrington, Miss Maguire,' sent them springing apart, though he moved swiftly along the deck without looking back.

'I-I had better–' Flora stammered.

'Um – yes, yes of course.' Bunny retreated a pace, ducked his head, both hands jammed into his pockets. 'Goodnight.' He backed away, smiling.

She searched for an excuse to make him stay longer, but Eddy's grinning face with his nose pressed against the window glass changed her mind.

Chapter 19

Day Six – Thursday

Flora stood with Monica at the rail, watching the boys play an enthusiastic game of shuffleboard on the boat deck below.

'I fail to see how a treasure hunt can be considered frivolous, and thus insulting to the dead, whereas a dance is not,' Monica complained. 'My Ozzy was so looking forward to it.'

'Eddy was too, though the horse racing will go ahead this afternoon,' Flora pointed out.

Monica sniffed in evident disapproval. 'Oh, look, Ozzy has scored a point. He's not on form you know, these deaths have affected him badly. He's such a sensitive boy.'

'Really?' Flora's eyebrow rose as Ozzy proceeded to leap in the air, screaming at the top of his lungs.

'It doesn't count!' Eddy shouted above his friend's delighted cries. 'Anything above fifty is subtracted. Don't you know the rules?'

Despite Flora's incipient worry, Eddy had slept well the night before, followed by a pre-breakfast conversation where she reassured him Mr Hersch had everything in hand.

She took refuge in the knowledge children were resilient; safe in the knowledge that however bad things became, they would be shielded from the worst of life's tragedies by the grown-ups.

'It appears,' Monica leaned closer, lowering her voice, 'the steward had to chastise the boys at dinner last night for exchanging lurid details of poor Eloise's death. All imagination of course. We wouldn't dream of telling him what really happened.'

'Do *you* know what happened?' Flora asked, immediately alert.

'Well, not really, but most murders of pretty girls tend to be throttling, don't they. At least in novels.'

Flora only wished that were true, but chose not to contradict her.

'I'll escort the boys to luncheon myself, one cannot be too careful with dangerous people about.' Monica's glance over Flora's shoulder elicited a knowing smile. 'Not that you will be lonely, my dear, for here comes your beau.'

Flora was about to correct her but Monica was already halfway down the deck.

Bunny withdrew a brown envelope from an inside pocket and handed it to her, his expression grim. 'This was waiting in my cabin when I returned from breakfast.'

Flora took it gingerly, though reading the slip of paper proved a frustrating exercise as the corners kept curling in the wind on a quest to escape her fingers.

'Confirm Theodore van Elder born Baltimore 12th April 1859, died 15th Feb. 1900. Leaves wife, Estelle van Elder and child from previous marriage. Father deceased 1880, mother believed still living. Only other family member known, Marlon van Elder born 1865

– arrest record held by New York Police for various misdemeanours including issuing valueless cheques and minor fraud. Aliases include Joseph Ellerman, Frank Ellerman, Frank Parnell. Whereabouts currently unknown.'

'Not unknown anymore,' Flora murmured as she handed it back to him. 'Marlon van Elder is at this moment lying under a sheet in the doctor's office.'

'That's the conclusion I came to.' Bunny refolded the page.

'What it doesn't tell us, is what his relationship was with Theodore van Elder? Brother? Cousin or something else? And why was he travelling with Eloise?'

'Flora,' Bunny's voice held a warning note. 'You're going to have to consider the possibility that Parnell and Eloise killed Theodore van Elder, and were escaping the country.'

'He was blackmailing her. Why would he do that if they were in it together?'

'Greed? A falling out of villains, maybe?'

'I may have accepted that as late as yesterday, but now I think Eloise was as much a victim as Parnell.' Flora couldn't bring herself to call her Estelle, she would always be Eloise to her.

Bunny replaced the telegram back into its envelope. 'I'll give this to Hersch straight away. We don't want him thinking we're keeping any more secrets now he has an official investigation under way.'

'I wish I had told him everything sooner,' Flora sighed.

'That would have been an interesting conversation.' Bunny cleared his throat, addressing a spot over her head. 'Mr Hersch, about that clipping I stole from the dead man's cabin when I was looking for a large amount of money with the girl who was herself murdered yesterday. I–'

'All right, all right, I get it.' Flora hushed him. 'What do *you* suggest?' She worried the side of a thumbnail with her front teeth.

'Well, I–' he broke off and glanced past Flora's shoulder, gave a low groan and hurriedly tucked the envelope back into his pocket.

Flora turned to where Cynthia strolled the deck in a peacock blue dress with a matching coat that enhanced her grey eyes.

'How is Max coming along?' Flora asked as she came to a leisurely halt beside them.

'Bruised and sore, poor dear.' Cynthia's face relaxed in relief. 'He has no memory of why he was out on deck in that storm, and I shan't badger him.' The implication that no one else should either went unspoken. 'I'm so glad the dance is going ahead tonight. It will give us all a welcome distraction from this awful business.'

She stroked Bunny's forearm with a manicured hand. 'You must promise to dance with me, Bunny, because no one else will. No doubt the other passengers will mutter about me not remaining glued to my husband's bedside.'

'I'll be happy to, Cynthia,' Bunny said. 'What about you, Flora?'

Flora hesitated. 'I haven't made up my mind yet. I'll think about it.' It didn't seem right somehow so soon after Eloise's death.

'Of course you'll be there.' Cynthia levelled her clear gaze on Flora. 'You cannot possibly waste that gown, it looks wonderful on you.' Her pretty face lit at the clear note of the bugle announcing luncheon. 'Oh good, I'm quite famished, though I've done nothing all morning except pour tea and plump Max's pillows. It must be this bracing sea air.' She turned on her heel and tripped across the deck with a backwards wave.

'It's as if Eloise never existed,' Flora said, mildly repulsed.

'They were hardly friends, though I admit, I didn't take her for the callous sort.'

'I know I said we hadn't learned anything last night,' Flora said slowly. 'But didn't Cynthia admit she went to Eloise's stateroom with some tea yesterday afternoon?'

'I seem to recall she did,' he said. 'She said there was no answer.'

'Cynthia has lied before, remember.' She also remembered that Mr Hersch hadn't been at the table when that question was asked.

Flora dragged her feet towards the dining room, thoughts of Cynthia quickly replaced by something about the telegram that niggled at the back of her mind, but she couldn't recall just then what it was.

Flora's post-prandial walk brought her to the rail of the promenade deck, where she paused to watch the foam-topped waves crest and fall in the distance. A sharp pain in her chest reminded her that this was where she had met Eloise on their second day at sea.

'Good afternoon, Miss Maguire,' a slightly accented voice dragged her from her sad musing.

'Hello, Mr Hersch,' she replied without turning her head.

'Oh, my dear, are you still brooding about the unfortunate fate of Miss Lane?' He rested his elbows on the rail beside her.

'Does that surprise you?' Flora resumed her contemplation of the sea.

Ignoring her question he asked, 'Are you not joining the ladies today?'

Flora looked to where Miss Ames and Monica sat talking with Mrs Penry-Jones on steamer chairs on the deck below.

'I could do without having to endure Mrs Penry-Jones's comments about governesses with ideas above their station, or actresses getting their just desserts.'

'People like her belong to the past. You should embrace the modern age, my dear. Mr Harrington, for example, is well-equipped to tackle this new century with that horse-less carriage of his.'

Despite herself, Flora's possessive pride rose in her chest. 'I'm sure he'll succeed in his world.'

'His world? Why not yours too?' At Flora's shrug he went on, 'If you would take my advice, I think your pride is getting in the way of a meaningful friendship with that young man.'

'We move in different worlds.' Flora aimed for pragmatism, but he had unwittingly stirred an elusive hope in her. One she continued to fight. 'He's used to more sophisticated company.'

'How interesting that it's the working classes who cling most tenaciously to the "different worlds" adage.'

Flora squirmed, wishing he would change the subject; grateful when he appeared to sense her unease and fell silent, the only sound between them the whoosh of the sea accompanied by the gentle rise and fall of the ship as it cut through the waves.

'It must have been a dreadful shock, seeing Miss Lane like that?' he said after a moment.

'Indeed it was, although the purser hustled me out before I could take a proper inventory of her stateroom.'

'Is that your way of asking me to tell you what we found?'

'If you feel so inclined.'

His eyes slewed sideways, regarding her with a calculating gaze. 'If I didn't know better, I might imagine I'm being manipulated, Miss Maguire.'

Flora smiled. He always used her full name when he teased her. She quite liked it.

'What I can tell you,' he went on, 'despite the disarray in her stateroom, there was no sign of a struggle, therefore I assume–'

'Eloise knew her attacker and let him in willingly.'

He nodded. 'And therefore was someone she had no reason to suspect.'

'Another member of the crew, perhaps?'

He twisted toward her, as if his next words required a certain gravitas. 'What we do know, is she received three deep stab wounds; two just below her ribcage and one in her right breast. Dr Fletcher says they were inflicted with a thin, straight-bladed knife.'

Flora fought down a wave of nausea as the image of Eloise's body flashed into her head. Three stab wounds. Someone really hated Eloise. Or wanted to make sure she kept quiet. Then something struck her and she turned her head, meeting his gaze. 'The knife wasn't found in the stateroom.'

He frowned. 'What makes you say that?'

'Because you described what might have inflicted her injuries. If you had the weapon, you would know.'

Hersch chuckled. 'If Pinkerton's ever decide to employ women again, I wouldn't hesitate to recommend you.'

'Again?' Flora asked. 'Has there ever been such a thing as a lady detective?'

'Indeed, yes.' Hersch chuckled. 'There was an infamous one during the Civil War by the name of Kate Warne, who was Allan Pinkerton's mistress. Then there was Hatty Lawson and Rose Greenhow. All very effective information gatherers from what I understand.'

'Did they actually uncover any crimes, though?' His use of the term information gatherers implied the women were merely busybodies and gossips, character traits assigned to most women and hardly flattering.

'Absolutely. Kate Warne uncovered an assassination plot on Lincoln before that infamous theatre incident, and Rose moved in illustrious circles, thus was able to pass information about Bull Run to Jefferson Davies. I believe you would make a more than credible lady detective, my dear.'

'There is something I should have mentioned,'

she began, warmed by his flattery. 'Eloise gave Mr Parnell $3,000 the night he died.'

'Really?' His mouth twitched, whether in annoyance or scepticism she couldn't tell. 'That explains why you asked about whether we had found any money in Mr Parnell's stateroom.'

'I should have told you before, but–'

'You felt your observations were being treated as trivial?' His penetrating gaze made her squirm. 'Under what circumstances did Miss Lane reveal that information to you?' She opened her mouth, but he silenced her with an upraised hand. 'Perhaps I don't wish to know, and no, we didn't find it in either stateroom.'

'Was Theodore van Elder murdered?' Flora asked.

Had Flora not been watching for the small start he gave, she would have missed it.

'The coroner's report said he died from a gastric complaint.'

Flora wasn't fooled by his mock innocent expression, and suspected he had his own theory.

'Who hired you, Mr Hersch?' She hardly expected an answer, but it was worth a try.

'Do you really expect me to reveal that? Good day, Miss Maguire.' He stepped away from the rail and set off along the deck at a brisk, confident stride.

Flora's gaze remained on his retreating back. The man was infuriating.

Chapter 20

As Mr Hersch's retreating figure turned the corner, a clatter of footsteps accompanied by a baritone shout of, 'Come back here!' alerted Flora to a commotion on the boat deck below.

Eddy appeared from beneath the super-structure, running at full pelt, followed a second later by Ozzy. Bunny gave chase, but collided with a strolling couple, halted to apologize, and by the time they moved on, the boys had disappeared. He scanned the deck, then dropped both arms to his sides in resignation and turned back in the direction he had come.

Suppressing a weary groan, Flora pushed away from the rail and descended to the deck where the cargo was stored.

Matilda's canvas had been pulled aside, the ropes holding it secure lay like coiled snakes on the deck.

'Young rascals,' Bunny muttered to himself. He had discarded his jacket on the bonnet and was rolling up his shirtsleeves.

'I take it you mean Eddy and Ozzy?' Flora said, reaching him.

He pushed a casual hand through his fair hair. 'I caught them playing inside, so chased them off.'

'I'm so sorry. I warned Eddy not to go near Matilda unless you were with him.'

'Not your fault.' Bunny sighed. 'I suspect Ozzy was the ringleader in this case, and boys, as they say, will be boys.'

She cast a critical eye over the gleaming yellow paintwork, but nothing stood out as a source of Bunny's annoyance, apart from the disarranged cover. 'Have they done any damage?'

'A few footprints on the seats and sticky marks on the steering wheel.' He bent to peer inside. 'I cleaned all this earlier. Now I shall have to do it again.'

A movement from the corner of Flora's eye drew her gaze to where the boys hovered twenty feet away. When they saw her watching, they ducked behind a lifeboat.

'I can see you there!' Flora called in her best governess tone. 'Now come out and apologize to Mr Harrington.'

'We didn't mean any harm.' Eddy shuffled forward, followed by a blushing Ozzy. 'The ropes were undone when we got here.'

'It wasn't us, Miss Maguire,' Ozzy insisted, displaying the indignation of a child unaccustomed to being chastised.

'Even so, you shouldn't have–'

'What do you mean?' Bunny cut across her. 'I checked the canvas before luncheon, everything was secure then.'

'The door was open too.' Eddy's courage returned and he crept closer.

'You're sure about that?' Bunny asked him, frowning. 'The canvas was rolled back like this when you got here?'

'Yes, sir!' both boys chorused.

Flora didn't know Ozzy well enough to judge his character accurately. Eddy, on the other hand was more easily read, and she was sure he was being truthful.

'Well if you didn't unwrap it, who did?' Bunny murmured, mostly to himself.

'Ah, got the old motor out, I see.' Gerald strolled briskly towards them, resplendent in a white blazer, his straw hat tipped back on his head. Oblivious of Bunny's concerned frown, and the boys' subdued faces, he circled the contraption with an appraising eye, peering through the window. 'I think I'll buy myself one of these when I get home. You don't see many in Reigate.'

'Oh, Papa, that would be super!' Ozzy threw Eddy a triumphant look.

'Actually I didn't,' Bunny said, resigned. 'Though it appears someone did.'

Gerald eyed his son knowingly. 'Have you been messing about where you weren't supposed to, son?' His voice took on a mock sternness but his eyes glinted with the amused pride at his son's mischievous initiative.

'I don't suppose you saw anyone loitering about here earlier, Gerald?' Bunny asked.

'I've been with Monica in our suite.' Gerald shook his head. 'I've not been near.'

'Does it really matter?' Flora asked. 'There's no harm done. I'm sure the boys won't do it again.'

'We didn't do anything!' Eddy protested.

'You know what I mean.' Flora silenced him with a glare.

'I'm probably being over-protective.' Bunny adjusted his glasses. 'These machines are rare and jolly expensive. My competitors may try to beat me to the English market by sabotaging this model and ruining my future plans.'

'Oh,' Flora said, dismayed. 'I didn't think of that.' First murderers on board, now saboteurs. How had she imagined this voyage would be uneventful?

Bunny grunted something unintelligible, muffled by the fact he was now bent double with his top half tucked inside the vehicle. He backed out and straightened. 'I had better get her wrapped up again.'

'Now, you two.' Gerald winked at Bunny before addressing the boys. 'Let's go and study the form before the horse racing. Might even win a couple of bob, eh?' With a final backwards wave, he guided the two miscreants away.

Gerald paused further along the deck to engage in a play fight with the boys that elicited frowns from some passengers and indulgent smiles from others. He feigned surrender when Eddy sprang at him, then launched a half-hearted attack with one arm. Ozzy pitched in, brandishing a short wooden stick.

Flora watched them, wistful. Eddy had missed out on such horseplay with his own father. Lord Vaughn was a kindly man, but conscious of his importance. His affection for Eddy took the form of lectures about duty and keeping to society's rules. She couldn't imagine him taking time to play soldiers with his only son.

'Thinking again, Flora?' Bunny studied her as he wiped his grubby hands on a cloth.

'Yes, but it's not important.' She chewed her

bottom lip. 'Speaking of storms. Have you given any thought as to why Max was on deck yesterday?'

'It happened too fast for me to think anything. I simply went to grab him before he was sucked under the rail.'

'Then think about it now. A gale is blowing, waves are breaking over the deck strong enough to knock someone off their feet. The luncheon bugle went five minutes before, but instead of using the interior corridors to get to the dining room, Max is outside, working his way between lifeboats and winch lines in the other direction. Where was he going?'

'Give me a clue.'

'No seriously, Bunny,' she snapped. 'What is of interest on deck other than this?' She nodded at the motor car.

'Matilda?' He shrugged. 'It's possible. But then she's been here under canvas all week. You cannot be sure that's where he was headed.'

'No. Which is why I intend to ask him.'

'How nice of you to come,' Cynthia greeted Flora at the door to the Cavendishes' suite. 'Max is still a bit groggy from the sedative the doctor gave him, but he's more comfortable today.' Her overly cheerful voice continued into their bedroom where Max sat propped against a pile of pillows, garbed in a gaudy bed jacket over striped pyjamas. A wide bandage circled his head, and his left arm was tightly wrapped in a sling. Though his youthful pink plumpness had not yet returned, the deathly pallor which had driven Cynthia into hysterics had disappeared.

'I'm so glad you weren't badly hurt, Max.' Flora took the chair tucked into the narrow space at the side of the bed.

'Thanks to Harrington.' Max attempted a laugh that was cut off by a wince. 'Shoulder's deuced sore, but I'm on the mend.' He reached for a glass of water at his elbow, but before his hand connected with the glass, Cynthia leapt forwards and held it to his mouth.

'C'mon, old girl, I'm not an invalid.' He pushed her hand away with a grimace.

'I keep thinking that you could have been killed!' Cynthia blurted on a sob.

'Well I wasn't, so stop fussing.' He softened his sharp retort with a brief caress of her cheek.

'It's all so awful. I wish this business was over.' She grasped his hand and held it to her face with both of hers.

'What business?' Flora searched her gaze, but Cynthia's eyes showed only anguish.

'I meant this voyage,' she said quickly. 'The honeymoon, everything which sets us apart as a focus of common gossip. I want to get back to being simply Mrs Maximilian Cavendish.' She turned a limpid-eyed look on her husband so intense Flora coughed and looked away, embarrassed.

'It must have been terrifying for you,' Flora said. 'Whatever made you go out in that storm must have been important.'

'Yes, Max.' A tiny crease appeared between Cynthia's perfectly plucked brows. 'You never did tell me what you were doing out there in a gale.'

Max split a look between them, and eased up-right against his pillows. 'Actually, Cyn. I would really love some tea. I'm sure Flora would too. Would you oblige, darling?'

Flora was about to refuse, but his imploring look changed her mind. 'Er – yes, that would be very nice, thank you.'

'Of course, I'll summon a steward.' Cynthia nodded, rising.

'Oh, actually Cyn.' Max halted her at the door. 'Gerald borrowed my copy of *The Invisible Man*. He's an H.G. Wells enthusiast, apparently. Would you slip along to fetch it for me? I could do with something to read.'

Flora waited for the door to close before she asked, 'You didn't answer her question about what you were doing on deck.'

'It was an accident,' he replied, but refused to meet her gaze. 'I went for a stroll and misjudged the severity of the wind.'

'The crew had issued a storm warning, Max, and ordered us all inside. Why did you take such a risk?'

'This voyage has been difficult for everyone, what with two deaths.' He gave a long-suffering sigh. 'But you shouldn't read something into a simple accident.'

'Shouldn't I?' Flora waited. Didn't Max know how open his face was? His eyes were full of angst, displaying his every emotion. Even Eddy was more expert at dissembling than this man.

'Look, Flora.' Max swallowed, fiddling with his sling with his uninjured hand. 'You shouldn't involve yourself in this.'

'I am involved, Max. I found Eloise's body.' The words were out before she could stop them.

'I-I had no idea.' His skin blanched as he finally met her gaze. 'I was told a maid found her.'

'That's what Mr Hersch wants everyone to think.' Flora fidgeted, regretting her impulse now. For all she knew Max could be guilty. Then her gaze strayed to the sling and she changed her mind. 'I've already been threatened to keep my mouth shut, but things have gone too far.' Her stomach tightened as she spoke of something she thought she had suppressed until now.

'Threatened?' His eyes clouded with concern. 'By whom?'

'That's just it, I don't know. Look, I hadn't known Eloise long, but I was fond of her. I'm determined to find out who killed her.'

'I have no idea who killed her.' He slapped the coverlet. 'In fact I wish I didn't know anything at all.'

'What *do* you know? If it's something which would help the investigation, you must tell Mr Hersch.'

'Huh! Hersch. He's still trying to run things, is he? I would have thought he would have given up by now with his target dead.'

'Which target? Parnell or Eloise?'

Max didn't answer so, aware that Cynthia would be back any moment and she had little time, Flora took a gamble. 'Who was Marlon van Elder?'

'Where did you hear that name?' His eyes narrowed and he gripped the coverlet with his free hand, creasing the silk.

This time it was Flora's turn not to answer.

'Did you kill him?'

'What?' His anger turned to derision. 'Of course not. The idiot died falling down those steps. Probably drunk, knowing him.'

'So you did know him?'

'I didn't say that. I knew of him.'

'I'm getting tired of your short answers, Max. What aren't you telling me?' She suspected a lot, but how to make him reveal it before Cynthia came back? 'Did he kill Theo van Elder, Eloise's husband?'

'Elo – you mean Estelle,' he said slowly. A flash of anger entered his eyes, turning them from harmless blue to sinister grey. 'Be careful, Miss Maguire. Your meddling might cause more harm than you imagine.'

The click of the door made Flora jump, while Max sighed as if relieved.

'Here you are, darling.' Cynthia's round vowels cut through the oppressive atmosphere, a tray held aloft. 'I ran into Monica outside. She retrieved your book for me.'

Cynthia poured tea, set one at Flora's elbow before tipping three sugar lumps into Max's cup she propped into his free hand. 'Now drink it while it's hot.'

Flora sipped the hot brew while trying to work out how to get Max talking again.

Cynthia perched on the edge of the bed, hands clasped demurely in her lap. 'Now, what have you two been talking about?'

Flora hid her frustration beneath a wide smile. 'I was just saying to Max how the passengers are all nervous about the fact there's a killer on board.'

'Yes, of course.' Cynthia shuddered theatrically but her gaze sharpened. 'Has that detective found out anything?'

'If he has, he isn't sharing it with me. It's only a matter of time though, don't you think, with two murders?' Flora studied their faces, certain the answers lay in this room.

'Mr Hersch thinks Mr er – Parnell was murdered too?' Cynthia's smile turned stale round the edges.

'He's convinced they are connected, and not necessarily committed by the same person,' Flora blurted, not sure where the thought came from.

Max's hand jerked and hot tea splashed onto his bare arm below his sling. He gave a sharp cry which brought Cynthia to her feet, dabbing at the wet stain with a napkin, and murmuring in distress.

'It's all right, Cyn.' Max waved her away. 'You got most of it.' He massaged his forehead with his free hand. 'I'm sorry to be so unsociable, Flora, but I get tired easily, what with the pain. I could do with some sleep.'

Left with no choice but to leave, Flora rose. 'I hope you'll feel better soon, Max.'

'Of course, darling.' Cynthia fussed. 'Let me get rid of this, then I'll see you out, Flora.' She reloaded the tray and manhandled it into the sitting room.

Max thrust out his hand and grabbed Flora's, bringing her attention back to his face. His eyes were open, clear and intense.

'Take my advice, Flora. Don't get pulled into this. Nothing good will come of it.'

241

'Pulled into what?' Flora whispered urgently, aware she had very little time before Cynthia returned. 'What did you do?'

'I can't explain. If only Cyn had listened to me at the beginning, but she's a loyal girl, you see.' His gaze drifted past her shoulder to where Cynthia had reappeared. Dropping Flora's hand as if it were hot, he relaxed onto his pillows with a sigh.

'Poor dear, he didn't sleep well last night,' Cynthia said.

'How are you bearing up, Cynthia?' Flora asked on her way to the door. She took in the darting eyes and the paleness of her skin beneath a layer of face powder.

'Me?' Cynthia issued a high-pitched laugh tinged with hysteria. 'What could possibly be wrong with me?'

Chapter 21

Flora joined the line of spectators gathered to watch the horse racing on the boat deck below, where hemp ropes had been strung on wooden posts marking the course. Several of the more youthful crew wore caps with matching coloured bands across their shoulders, each of whom straddled broomsticks on which had been attached papier mâché horse's heads.

Flora's gaze skimmed the lines of excited children who hung over the rails on the upper decks, finally settling on Eddy, who perched beside Gerald, Monica and Ozzy on one of the bench seats set out for spectators.

Flora sensed rather than saw Bunny's arrival, confirmed when his upper arm grazed hers. She leaned into him slightly and relaxed into the spirit of the warm afternoon where she didn't have to think about violence and death for a while.

'Bunny, I have something to tell you, but–' She broke off when Eddy spotted her and gave an enthusiastic wave. He said something to Gerald, who nodded, then leapt to his feet and mounted the companionway steps towards her.

'I'll tell you later,' she whispered, as Eddy halted beside her, his straw boater tipped back on his head.

'Tease me, why don't you?' Bunny murmured, half serious.

'I'm backing Arthritis in the Seasick Hurdle.' Eddy waved a slip of paper beneath her nose.

'Placing real bets at your age, surely not?' Bunny blinked in feigned shock though his smile remained in place.

'Only twenty-five cents a time, which is about a shilling.' Eddy pulled a mildly disgusted face. 'And it's only a game, I shan't develop the gambling bug.'

'I should hope not.' Bunny delved into his trouser pocket. 'What do you reckon on Count de Money in the Lowbrow Handicap, or shall I lose my shirt?'

'Lose, I think,' Eddy replied. 'His rider is that paunchy fellow in a yellow cap down there, see?'

243

'Hmm. Perhaps I'll just stick with Steam Hammer. He looks sprightly enough.'

'That's Captain Gates's horse.' Eddy spoke with the calm authority of someone who had researched their subject. 'Each horse is sponsored by an officer or a passenger.'

'How many races are there?' Flora asked.

'Six races with six horses per race.' Bunny handed Eddy a pile of small change. 'Here, put this on for me, would you?'

'Right-o.' Eddy raced away with the coins clutched in his hand.

'Must we watch all six races?' Flora fanned her face with her programme. 'It's getting hot out here and it's already noisy.'

'Where's your sense of fun?' Bunny nudged her. 'At least the atmosphere among the passengers has lifted a little after the gloom of the last few days.'

'It's not over though, is it?' she said sadly, though not wishing to spoil the afternoon, added, 'Besides, I'm an English rose who doesn't much like the harsh sun. It creates freckles.'

'Hmm, you could be right.' He gave a start, both hand held up in surrender. 'I meant about the noise and the heat, not the freckles.'

'Forgiven,' Flora conceded, then with more warmth, 'How about we watch the first race, then go to the library for tea? I doubt Eddy will notice. And besides, I have something–'

'–to tell me, yes, I got that. Look, they're getting ready for the off.'

The loud report of a starting gun was followed by squeals of encouragement as the 'horses' set off. Spectators hollered for their favourite, whilst children screamed in delight as the orderly line rapidly deteriorated into a shoving, closely bunched pile of bodies.

When the first hobby horse fell rather than crossed the line, the deck erupted in an enthusiastic roar from the men and a round of polite clapping from the ladies.

'That was energetic!' Flora laughed, easing through the press of the crowd at the rail at Bunny's side. 'I have to admit I enjoyed it more than I had anticipated.'

Bunny rested his hand over hers on his arm as they strolled toward the lobby. 'That man who threatened you hasn't turned up again, has he? Is that what you wanted to tell me?'

Flora shook her head, having almost forgotten the man with the croaky voice. *Almost.*

The muffled sound of far-off cheers reached them as they stepped into the calm of the deserted library. A steward gave a surprised start, surreptitiously stubbed out a cigarette in a tin plate, and tucked it beneath a pot plant before approaching them with a smile of welcome.

'Quiet day?' Bunny's mock-innocent gaze slid to the pot plant.

'Would you like tea, sir?' the steward covered his embarrassment with a bright enquiry. 'For you and the lady?'

'Thank you, yes. We'll be over there.' Bunny indicated a trio of red, leather chesterfield sofas in an alcove visible from the door where they had sat on their last visit.

'Now, what was it you wanted to tell me?'

245

Bunny asked when the tea tray arrived and occupied the table between them.

'I went to see Max this morning.'

'Really?' Bunny looked up from pouring tea for them both. 'By the look of your face he had something interesting to say. Have you solved both murders and now know everyone's secrets?'

'Don't tease, this is important. Max knew Marlon van Elder was on board. He also knows Mr Hersch was working for the van Elder family.'

'Max told you all that?'

'Not exactly. Eloise told me about Hersch, but Max let something slip which confirmed it. At least I think that's what he meant.' Bunny's expression displayed only scepticism. 'You don't look very interested.'

'No, really. I am. I was just thinking. That means Hersch was right, in that more people knew Parnell, or rather van Elder, was on board. But where does that lead us?'

'Not sure yet, though Max knew what Eloise's real name was.'

'Ah, that's more like it.'

'Exactly, and I would have got more out of him if Cynthia hadn't come back.'

'Cynthia doesn't know all this?'

'Evidently not. Max certainly didn't want her overhearing us talking. But surely, if he knew, then she must as well. Although,' she paused as doubt intruded, 'perhaps she knew, but he didn't want her to know he had told me.'

'That's a bit convoluted for me.' Frowning, Bunny lowered the teapot onto the tray. 'Did you find out what Max was doing out on the deck in the storm?'

'I asked him that, but he avoided the question. However, I was thinking about it while we watched the race and it's the only thing that makes sense.'

'Well, don't keep me in suspense.' Bunny accepted a cup of tea she handed him. 'What was it?'

'Cynthia is the daughter of the late Theodore van Elder.'

'How did you come to that conclusion?' Bunny dropped two lumps of sugar into his cup.

'Do you recall Hester telling us Mrs Penry-Jones had been married twice?'

'I'm not sure, I might have done.'

'Well, she did. The obituary stated Theodore van Elder had a child from a previous marriage who was an heiress to a fortune. Can you think of anyone that might be?'

He waved his spoon in mid-air as an aid to thought, then grinned. 'Cynthia?'

'Exactly. I should have guessed from when I saw all those expensive clothes in her suite. Max knew about Eloise and Mr Hersch. Eloise was convinced he worked for the van Elders. Ergo, he worked for Cynthia.'

'But she's English. And van Elder was an American.' Bunny's frown persisted.

'She was born in New York. Her parents divorced and when her mother remarried, she and her new husband moved to England.'

'Well, goodness, Miss Maguire, you have been busy.' Bunny sat back, one ankle crossed over the other and swinging gently as he stirred his tea.

247

'Where are you going with this?'

'Well, actually not very far. I have a theory though.' She wiggled backwards in her seat and prepared for a detailed discussion. 'Say Cynthia believed Eloise killed her father, so she hires Pinkertons, who send Hersch to get some evidence against her. When Eloise comes aboard, Hersch comes too.'

'Eloise was travelling with Marlon van Elder. What was his role in all this?

'Ah, but she didn't know that. He told her his name was Parnell, but he was in fact another of the van Elders.'

'So Cynthia and Max, together with Marlon van Elder combined to prove Eloise had killed her husband, Theodore van Elder? Hmm, seems a bit heavy handed.'

'I agree, but it makes sense, doesn't it?'

'Then who killed Parnell, I mean Marlon van Elder? Max?'

'I did consider that, but what reason would he have?' She eyed her tea but left it untouched, unwilling to interrupt her train of thought. 'And unless he deliberately tried to drown himself, he couldn't have killed Eloise. I'm not sure yet why, but I think they were killed by two separate people.'

'That makes everything more complicated.' Bunny returned his cup to the saucer. 'Marlon van Elder was hardly a respectable member of the family, judging by the list of aliases and charges listed in that telegram my journalist friend sent me. He could still have been in league with Eloise in the killing of her husband. Maybe he got greedy about the money, so she killed him.'

'Then who killed her? Apart from Max, there's only Mr Hersch and Cynthia.'

'I doubt Cynthia could have done it.' Bunny snorted.

'Why, because she's beautiful?' Flora threw him an oblique look. 'If she thought Eloise had murdered her father–'

He silenced her with an upraised hand and a nod at the glazed door that led onto the lobby. 'Looks like we aren't the only ones seeking refuge from the horse racing. Isn't that Hersch with the captain?'

'Yes, it is.' Flora followed his gaze. 'And that's Gus Crowe with them. What's going on?'

'Not like Crowe not to be running a book on the side when there's gambling to be done.' Bunny returned his cup to the tray, straightening. 'Oh, watch out. They're coming in here, and none of them look particularly happy.'

'Is this absolutely necessary?' Crowe's raised voice echoed to the room. 'I've already answered all your questions.'

'I'm aware of that, Mr Crowe.' Captain Gates's half-amused voice conveyed mild impatience. 'Mr Hersch has a few things he wishes to clarify.'

'Well, make it snappy.' Crowe eased his neck inside his collar. 'I don't intend to waste time repeating myself.'

'This looks as if it might be interesting,' Bunny whispered.

Crowe sidled into the seat Hersch indicated, his gaze darting the room until it halted on Flora and Bunny. With his rear hovering above the seat he halted. 'What are *they* doing here?' he demanded, his frown deepening to suspicion.

'Ah, Mr Harrington, Miss Maguire. I didn't see you there.' Hersch's affable smile betrayed no surprise at their presence. 'Surely you don't object, Crowe. After all, it's simply routine.'

'What?' Crowe started. 'Uh – no, of course not.' He hunched into his chair like a sullen schoolboy.

The steward placed a loaded tray in front of Crowe, while Hersch and the captain ranged themselves in chairs on either side, blocking him in.

Captain Gates stirred the contents of the teapot vigorously with a spoon. 'Weak stuff, this American tea.'

'I thought you were a naturalized citizen?' Hersch ignored Crowe, who drummed his fingers on the chair arm, then fidgeted with his shirt cuff.

'Indeed I am,' the captain gave a short version of his famous laugh. 'There are some things I still miss, and this is one of them. Can't wait to get back to London for a proper brew.' He clicked the lid back on the pot, then poured the steaming liquid into three cups before unhurriedly adding milk.

'Could we get on with it?' Crowe snapped, his nerves clearly on edge. He refused the cup held out to him with an angry shrug.

'Let's return to the first night on board, Mr Crowe,' Hersch began as if he hadn't spoken. 'I believe you lost a sum of money to Mr Parnell at cards?'

'I told you that when you questioned me the first time.' Crowe's jaw hardened. 'I wasn't the only one, either. Parnell cleaned up that night, as you well know. It doesn't bear repeating.'

'Maybe it does, simply for my own purposes, you understand.' The detective stirred sugar into his tea, then offered the bowl to the captain, who politely declined. In turn the captain offered a plate of biscuits round the table, including Flora and Bunny in the gesture.

Bemused by their small theatre, Flora accepted one and was about to comment when Hersch began talking again.

'What did you do when you left the card game, Mr Crowe?' Hersch sipped his tea, grimaced and dropped another sugar lump into the cup.

Crowe eased three fingers between his neck and his collar. 'I-I think I stood at the rail for a while and smoked a cigarette.'

The detective's spoon clicked rhythmically against the china, his steady gaze never leaving Crowe's face. 'You said that you saw Mr Parnell going into Hester Smith's cabin.'

'Look, we've already been through all this.' Crowe pushed a hand through his hair, cutting grooves into the liberally applied pomade. 'It could have been that old biddy's cabin, I cannot say for certain. What difference does it make?' He tugged up his sleeve and ostentatiously peered at his watch. 'I really don't see the point of this, so if you don't mind, I'll be going.' He slapped his palms against the arms of his chair, and pushed himself to his feet, halting mid-rise as the door swung open again.

Officer Martin entered with another crewman Flora recognized as the wireless operator, who strode forwards as if he was on a parade ground. He came to an abrupt halt beside the captain's chair where he performed a curt double step, his gaze on the wall above the man's head, his cap tucked beneath one elbow.

Crowe froze into a half crouch, his lips bloodless.

'A new development,' Bunny whispered. Flora shushed him.

'Seaman Crofts has an interesting story to tell,' Hersch said, a warning in his voice.

'Do you recognize this gentleman, Seaman Crofts?' Captain Gates addressed the young crewman, who had licked his lips three times in the last thirty seconds.

A flicker of fear entered Crowe's eyes. He swallowed, then slumped back into his seat.

The sailor's gaze flicked to Crowe and away again, then went back to studying the wall. 'Yes, sir, he's Mr Augustus Crowe.'

'Now, look here,' Crowe snapped, with a hint of his former bravado. 'Are you going to take the word of a kid against mine?'

'It depends what the kid says.' Hersch gestured for Seaman Crofts to continue.

Flora admired the detective's calm handling of the situation, aware whatever the young sailor had to say would not be a waste of anyone's time. She flicked a glance at an equally fascinated Bunny before settling in her seat to listen.

'Well, sir.' The sailor cleared his throat. 'Mr Crowe asked me to deposit some banknotes in the ship's safe.'

'Was there anything unusual about this request?' Hersch asked with all the confidence of someone who knows the answer.

'No, sir, except–' he paused and swallowed. 'He paid me ten dollars to change the date on the receipt slip to that of the day we sailed.'

'You didn't think that strange?'

'Not at the time, sir, no. I didn't connect it to the man who died. Not then. Everyone believed it was an accident. But when Mr Hersch told me someone had killed Mr Parnell ... well, I couldn't remain silent any longer.'

'Indeed not. And how much did Mr Crowe lodge in the safe?' Captain Gates asked.

Crowe murmured something unintelligible, then shrank further in his seat, massaging his forehead with the fingers of one hand.

'Five thousand dollars, sir,' Seaman Crofts replied. 'Three thousand in large banknotes with the banker's ribbon still on them. The rest was loose, in smaller denominations.'

Flora gasped and Bunny muttered, 'Got him.'

'Quite a coincidence,' Hersch said with menacing calm. 'The amount Mr Parnell was alleged to have in his possession on Saturday evening,'

'You may go, Crofts.' The captain inclined his head in curt dismissal, at which Seaman Crofts almost ran from the room, followed by Officer Martin.

'Oh, all right!' Crowe said as the door closed on the two crewmen. 'But I didn't mean to kill the man!'

Hersch relaxed back in his seat, saying nothing.

253

'Look.' Crowe rubbed both palms repeatedly back and forth along his thighs. 'I was angry I lost so much money to Parnell on the first night. It might have been small change to him, but to me – well, sums like that don't come easily. I followed him back to his cabin, hung about outside and smoked a cigarette. I had no firm plan then, but needed to think.'

'Go on,' Hersch prompted.

'The Gilmores walked by, and that's when Parnell came out and went into that companion woman's room.'

'Hester Smith?' Flora blurted. 'He went inside? Are you sure?'

Hersch held up a hand in warning and Bunny gave a low hiss.

'Sorry,' Flora muttered.

'Actually, no.' Crowe blinked as if confused. 'When Gilmore said the next day he saw Parnell going into the old woman's suite, I assumed I'd got it wrong. Anyway, Parnell came out again, then he went into Miss Lane's cabin. I didn't get that wrong, because she came to the door in her night things.' Crowe snorted. 'Quite pally, they were too.'

'You didn't mention that detail in your original account of that night,' Hersch said.

'I was hardly going to admit I was hanging about outside Parnell's cabin, was I?' Crowe gave another snort. 'I wasn't certain the Gilmores hadn't seen me either, but as it turns out they hadn't.'

'Then what did you do?' Captain Gates asked.

Crowe slid a sly look at Flora and away again.

'I assumed Parnell and Miss Lane would be together for the rest of the night. I waited for a bit, then went into Parnell's cabin.'

'You broke in?' Officer Martin asked.

'It wasn't locked,' Crowe said, as if that made a difference. 'He had stashed a wedge of banknotes in a shoe in the bottom of the wardrobe, so I–' he broke off and ran a shaky hand through his hair making it stick up in greasy spikes.

'What did you do?' the captain asked.

'I took it, didn't I?' Crowe hunched his shoulders in a lazy shrug that conveyed anyone would have done the same thing.

'So what went wrong?' Hersch prompted.

'Parnell came back.' Crowe's eyes dulled like a trapped animal. 'I opened the door to leave and there he was. He looked as shocked as me.'

'What happened?'

'What do you think? I threw a punch, he threw one back. We scuffled, and he hit his head on the washbasin in the bathroom. It was over in seconds.' He gave a short, cynical laugh. 'I'm surprised no one heard the noise. He was stunned, so I left him there.'

'The ashtray,' Flora said. 'Is that what you hit him with?'

'What ashtray?' Crowe's eyes clouded with confusion. 'No, I told you. He hit his head on the washbasin.'

'Then you had to get rid of the body,' Hersch said. 'So you threw him down the companionway.'

'No, that's not what happened!' Crow dropped his chin like a sullen child caught stealing apples, not someone who had just robbed and killed a

255

man. 'He was lying on the stateroom floor when I left.

'The next morning, everyone believed he had died in a fall, so I kept quiet.' His thin lips curled into a sneer, as if congratulating himself on his ingenuity. Then he turned a burning gaze on Flora. 'Everyone except you, Miss Busybody Governess.'

'It was you!' Flora gasped. 'You were the one who threatened me outside the dining room!' That she had spent four wakeful nights due to this insipid little man made her furious.

'I only meant to frighten you off.' Crowe fidgeted in his chair, tension drawing furrows in his brow. 'I robbed the man. I hold my hands up to that, but his death was an accident.'

'Even had Mr Parnell woken later that night and somehow staggered to that companionway in search of assistance, and fallen, that still makes you guilty of manslaughter.' Hersch let the information sink in, before asking, 'Why did you kill Miss Lane?'

'I didn't kill her!' Crowe's gaze darted between the detective and the officer, his eyes frantic. 'Why would I want her dead?'

'Miss Lane's stateroom was next door to Parnell's. Maybe she heard you fighting with him and threatened to reveal your part in his death?' Hersch said. 'Or perhaps,' he went on when Crowe failed to answer, 'you and Miss Lane came to an agreement?'

The blood left Crowe's face until his complexion resembled milk.

'Did she suggest you share the haul with her in

return for keeping quiet?' Hersch let the words fall into the heavy silence.

Flora recalled Crowe's start of fear as he stared through the window in the staircase lobby and instinctively she knew what it meant. 'Eloise saw you,' she said, incredulous. 'She saw you with Seaman Crofts and guessed what you had done.'

'I-um. Well, look here. It wasn't as cold as that.' Crowe fisted his hands and brought them down on his knees.

'Crofts wanted to tell the truth, and you wouldn't let him?' Flora rushed on. 'So Eloise had to die too?'

'No!' Crowe hammered the sofa arm with a fist. 'She said the situation would suit us both. She agreed not to stir things up if I split the money with her when we reached London. Then the next thing I know, she's dead. That shook me, I can tell you.' His pleading gaze met Flora's. 'I swear I didn't kill Miss Lane. I had no reason to.'

'You can tell your story to a judge, Crowe.' Had Hersch's moustache been long and curly, Flora imagined he would have twirled it. 'You'll remain confined to your stateroom until we reach London. There you'll be handed over to the authorities.'

He went and opened the door, beckoning to the sailors who stood sentry outside. The pair marched into the room and arranged themselves on either side of Crowe.

'Aren't you forgetting something?' Crowe rose shakily, but summoned enough defiance to shrug off the sailors' hold. 'I didn't commit any crime in England, we were in international waters.'

257

'On an American-owned ship,' Hersch reminded him. 'I imagine the British will send you straight back to New York to stand trial.'

'Good work, Hersch.' Captain Gates stood and tugged down his jacket. 'I'll see you later at dinner then? Miss Maguire, Mr Harrington.' He replaced his cap, touching the peak in salute on his way out.

'Is that all it was? A fight over money and a man is dead?' Flora asked the detective when the door flapped shut.

'Which, as you may recall, was my first theory,' Bunny said, beaming.

'You don't have to be so smug about it.' Still uneasy, Flora split a look between the detective and Bunny. 'I'm still not convinced Mr Crowe killed Eloise.'

'She was blackmailing him,' Bunny said, as if that explained everything.

'He didn't need to kill her,' Flora insisted. Crowe's comment that the situation suited both their purposes struck her as exactly something Eloise would say. 'He may be an unpleasant thief but he's no murderer.'

'Don't give the man any credit, Flora,' Hersch sighed. 'Killers usually maintain their innocence to the end.'

Flora searched for something that might convince him, then a question came to mind. 'Which cabin did Parnell go into? Mrs Penry-Jones's, Hester's or Eloise's?'

'I don't see that it matters now.' Bunny swept a biscuit from the plate in front of him and bit into it.

'Or it could matter a lot,' Flora murmured. 'We

know Eloise lied about Parnell having argued with her that night.' She tapped her top lip with a finger. 'Who else was lying? Crowe or Gerald Gilmore?'

'My money's on Crowe,' Bunny chewing thoughtfully.

'Maybe neither of them,' Hersch mused. 'It was the first night, so perhaps no one was sure about whose cabin was whose.'

'We need to find out. Look.' Panic lifted Flora's voice an octave. 'We dock at Tilbury in two days, after which everyone will disappear into their own lives and you'll never catch him.' The thought that whoever had done such an awful thing to Eloise might escape justice twisted her stomach.

'This affair has been an ordeal for you, Flora.' Hersch rose and shot his cuffs, apparently pleased with himself. 'I hope you can put it behind you and relax for what remains of the voyage.' He gave her shoulder a fatherly pat before following the captain out.

'Did you notice,' Flora said, when she and Bunny were alone again, 'that at no point did Mr Hersch or the captain reveal that Frank Parnell and Eloise Lane weren't their real names?'

'I didn't, actually. Is that significant?' He took a biscuit from the plate and bit into it. 'Maybe he's simply protecting the identity of his clients?'

'Maybe.' Flora still couldn't see Crowe as a cold-blooded killer, and whoever had murdered Eloise was certainly that.

Chapter 22

The peacock blue silk of Flora's borrowed gown hung in heavy folds to the floor, the lining warm and sensuous against her skin. For once in her life, she felt equal to the company who would be present at this evening's dance.

Bunny arrived exactly two minutes before their agreed time, a broad smile of surprised admiration telling her all her efforts had not been in vain.

The evening was almost warm, so instead of taking the interior corridor, they strolled across the deck towards the dining room, stopping every now and then to admire the sunset from the rail. As he eased close to her side, his arm grazed hers and made her shiver.

'You aren't nervous about this evening, are you?'

'No, of course not – I mean yes, I am rather.' She kneaded the delicate purse in one hand, crushing it. 'Sometimes, I wish Lord Vaughn had sent me home on a different ship, one which had a third class.'

'Mrs Penry-Jones is an old lady with antiquated views that hark back to a less enlightened time,' he said, guessing her thoughts. 'The other passengers think you are perfectly charming.'

'For a governess,' Flora murmured too low for him to hear.

'How did Eddy enjoy the horse racing?' Bunny changed the subject.

'He arrived with a pocket full of coins I chose not to ask about. Not that Lord Vaughn would object if he knew. He's not averse to a day at the races himself.'

'I'm glad you felt confident enough to leave him alone tonight.'

'I didn't.' Flora winced. 'He's in the Gilmores' suite listening to the gramophone with Ozzy and some of the other boys. That steward you hired has agreed to deliver him to the suite later.'

'May as well get my money's worth.' Bunny pushed open the door of the dining room, from which a waft of warm air and music greeted them.

'You look very elegant, my dear,' Monica said, when Flora and Bunny took their seats. 'I wish I had the colouring for dramatic hues, but pastels suit me better.' She indicated her peach-coloured gown with its tight-ruffled bodice.

'I wish you did too.' Gerald's appraising gaze slid up and down Flora's costume. 'I hope you'll allow me a dance after dinner, Flora?'

The room rapidly filled, the atmosphere charged with excited chatter and an air of anticipation now everyone believed the killer was under guard.

'I hope there won't be any of that Vaudeville music this evening.' Mrs Penry-Jones eyed the quintet orchestra with suspicion. 'Too low-class in my opinion.'

'Really?' Bunny pinned her with a challenging stare. 'I thought Americans were free thinkers and didn't believe in the class divide?'

'You know what I mean, young man. I'll thank you not to goad me.' Her evening bag hit the table with a thump, though her pebble eyes twinkled with flirtatious amusement. It seemed no woman was safe from Bunny's charm.

'You don't have to defend me, even though I quite like it,' Flora whispered, then looked away quickly when her gaze met his and held. Each time that happened, a sweet, tingling sensation started somewhere deep in her belly and spread into her chest. Memories of their kiss remained, and though her pragmatic nature rose to smother what she regarded as an impossible longing, hope lingered.

Miss Ames swung a sequin encrusted wrap over one shoulder, missing Flora's face by a half inch. She plucked two glasses of transparent red liquid from a tray and handed one to Mrs Penry-Jones.

'Do try some of this, it's quite delicious.' She giggled and downed half the contents of her own glass.

'It tastes just like damsons,' Mrs Penry-Jones said after her first sip, frowning into the glass before she gulped the rest of the contents. 'Goodness, it's hot in here.' She flapped an ostrich-feather fan rapidly in front of her face, the glass held out to Hester. 'Get me another one of these fruit cups, would you?'

Hester obeyed her employer with an annoyed pout, her hair drawn back in a severe bun which put Flora in mind of a bad-tempered Jane Eyre. 'That isn't fruit cup is it?' Flora whispered to Bunny, who winked.

'Not even close.'

262

Flora mouthed, 'You are wicked,' at him, just as Cynthia made her entrance looking serene in a powder blue gown, her hair drawn up onto her head in loose curls which exposed her swan-like neck. A crewman wheeled a bath chair in which Max sat, still wan-looking and with a square plaster on his forehead replacing the bandage, his sling-wrapped arm supported on a cushion on his lap.

'I love Astrakhan Caviar.' Cynthia read from the menu card that she slid into her evening bag. She caught Flora's gaze and giggled, 'A souvenir of the most dramatic honeymoon ever. Maybe I'll ask the captain to autograph it.'

'Why weren't *we* invited to dine with the captain?' Monica said in a harsh stage whisper, nodding to where Captain Gates held court to a table full of smug-looking passengers. 'We're as important as anyone else on this ship.'

'I don't know why they call him Giggles,' Gerald said in an undertone, making no attempt to answer her complaint. 'Haven't seen the fella laugh for days.'

'Hardly surprising,' Miss Ames chided. 'Two deaths are hardly going to look good on his record.'

A sudden, swift depression engulfed Flora, before a voice in her head whispered that Eloise would have been the first to encourage her to enjoy herself.

'Who would have taken that Crowe chap for a double killer, eh?' Gerald held up his empty champagne glass as a summons to a passing server, who sprang forwards and swapped it for a full one.

'If a man is ruthless enough to bludgeon another to death for money,' Hester said, 'he's hardly likely to baulk at stabbing a woman.'

'Oh, do be quiet!' Cynthia gave an exaggerated shudder. 'I hate the word, bludgeon, it conjures up such horrible images.'

'I never liked him. He always struck me as the sleazy type.' Miss Ames peered into her glass as if disappointed to find it empty.

'I thought Mr Crowe was a charming man.' Monica twirled the ice chips in her glass. 'A little rough around the edges maybe.'

Flora was about to point out that neither fact made him homicidal, but kept her thoughts to herself.

'What happens now the killer has been apprehended?' Miss Ames asked no one in particular.

'The police in London will have questions of their own I imagine,' Gerald replied. 'I doubt any of us will get off this ship before that's done.'

Hester's tapestry bag slipped to the floor with a resounding thump. She bent to retrieve it, but had barely replaced it on her lap again before it fell to the floor again.

'Do stop fidgeting, Hester!' Mrs Penry-Jones glared at her.

'Sorry, Mrs Penry-Jones.' Hester's flush deepened.

The meal progressed and conversation moved by mutual agreement away from murder, until the tables were cleared away and the orchestra opened the dancing with a lively tune Flora didn't recognize.

'Can you dance a quadrille?' Bunny whispered.

'Of course I can.' She lifted her chin in mock offence.

Bunny led her onto the dance floor where they made up the set of four couples in a square. In seconds, the music filled Flora's head as she changed partners and returned to her own pairing with Bunny in the formation again. The need to concentrate dispelled the tensions of the last few days among a swirl of colour, light and noise as the fiddlers worked into a noisy crescendo.

Instead of returning to their table at the end of the dance, Bunny slipped his arm round her waist as the strains of *A Bicycle Made for Two* filled the room.

'Don't you think you're holding me too close?' Flora whispered once they had covered half the floor.

'Possibly, but it's nice, isn't it?'

She snuggled closer. Indeed it was. They fit together so naturally, it was as if they had done the same thing many times. She became keenly aware of Bunny's hand at her waist, and the warmth of his jaw beside her cheek, while the room revolved in a swirl of smiling faces in a kaleidoscope of light that leapt and blurred.

His hand shifted to her back, his head lowered until his temple rested against her cheek. Solid and comforting, her chin grazed his shoulder as they swayed around the dance floor, the weight of unspoken words pulled between them.

The music changed again, and Bunny relinquished her to Gerald with regret in his eyes.

'Not too upset by this murder business, are you, my dear?' he asked, his clumsy steps keeping her focus on her feet to prevent them being trampled. 'Nice girl, I thought,' he went on when she didn't answer, gripping her harder round the waist, though it was a fatherly touch rather than a suggestive one. 'Must make the whole mess difficult for you.'

Flora responded with an uneasy smile, unwilling to explain her own misgivings. The fact Gus Crowe was in custody should have been reassuring, but wasn't.

'Not boring you, am I?' Gerald asked with the confidence of a man who cannot imagine doing any such thing.

'No, not at all,' Flora said truthfully. Far from being a polite interval to be endured, Gerald's company was undemanding.

When the tune ended, she searched the room for Bunny. By the time she located him, the next dance had begun and he was partnering Cynthia, who laughed up into his eyes as he twirled her around the floor.

Max was also watching them, his gaze on his wife with a fierce pride tinged with sadness. Did Max, like her, feel he didn't deserve someone so dazzling? Or was he plagued with thoughts of misdeeds as yet unrevealed? Flora shivered, but didn't have time to brood, as a young man from California requested the next dance.

She had hardly returned to the table before Mr Hersch claimed her, which gave Flora momentary dread, but he danced the two-step with remarkable grace for a big man, handing her back to Bunny with a flourish as if that was where she belonged.

The hard-working quintet made a valiant effort with *After The Ball*, and she leaned into Bunny's embrace, wishing the night didn't have to end.

'I don't know about you,' he whispered into her hair when the last notes had faded away. 'But I could do with a sit down and a drink.'

'Good idea.' Flora slipped her hand into his quite naturally, pulling him gently towards their table, where Cynthia and Max sat with Miss Ames and a very flushed Mrs Penry-Jones.

As Bunny summoned a nearby server and ordered fresh drinks, Flora's gaze flicked to Hester's empty chair.

'Gone to the powder room,' Mrs Penry-Jones answered her silent question. 'Though why such a plain woman needs to spend so much time in front of a mirror escapes me.'

Flora said nothing, but resolved to suggest Bunny ask Hester to dance when she returned.

'Y'know,' Gerald mused, as if he had turned the question over in his head all evening, 'It strikes me as odd that that Crowe chap would murder a gel.'

'He robbed her, didn't he?' Monica resumed her seat, apparently catching the tail end of the conversation. 'Sounds simple enough to me.'

'Maybe too simple,' Max murmured.

'That's what I think.' Flora couldn't help herself. 'I don't believe Crowe killed Eloise.'

'Can't we simply forget about all that for one evening?' Cynthia's hand caught Gerald's glass, sending a spray of amber liquid onto the pristine white tablecloth.

'Sorry.' Gerald gave her a sideways look. 'Been

267

preying on my mind somewhat.' He went back to working his way through a plate of petit fours in the middle of the table.

'I agree with Cynthia.' Bunny brought his hand down hard on the table top, making Flora jump. 'Why cannot you simply accept what everyone else has? Crowe bashed Parnell over the head, then went back to his stateroom and slept like a baby. He was a cold-blooded killer.'

'Maybe, but–'

'Flora.' Bunny's hand gripped hers on the table, a plea in his eyes. 'Let's not ruin this delightful evening by bringing up all this business again. Crowe is in custody. It's over.'

'I didn't bring it up!' Flora bridled. 'Gerald did!' She grabbed her bag from the table. 'Excuse me, but I promised to say goodnight to Eddy before he went to sleep.'

'It's after eleven.' Bunny's impatient sigh accompanied the scrape of her chair as she rose. 'Surely he'll be fast asleep by now?'

Ignoring his plaintive 'Flora!' she strode from the room.

A thick layer of fog on the ocean softened the electric lights to a misty glow and muted the thrum of the engines beneath her feet. The ship's bell rang the hour with a muffled gong just as the moon broke through a bank of cloud in a milky ball, pushing through the grey vapour, only to be swallowed again almost immediately.

Flora's angry thoughts matched her brisk footsteps across the boards. How dare Bunny try to control her into silence? He may have decided the culprit was caught, but he had no right to censor her opinions. If he wasn't prepared to accept she had a mind of her own, they weren't suited at all!

Thus preoccupied, it took her a moment to realize that the door to her suite stood slightly ajar.

'Eddy?' She pushed it wider with one hand, her breath held. Had the stewardess forgotten to fasten it when she brought the cocoa?

Guided by the deck light through the window, she clicked open Eddy's door where a night-light cast a soft yellow glow into the lower half of the room.

The mound beneath the covers rose up and Eddy propped himself on one elbow. 'Flora?' He scratched his head and blinked. 'Is something wrong?'

'I'm sorry. I didn't mean to wake you, but the suite door was open.'

He eased upright and wrapped his arms round his bent knees. 'Did you have a good time?'

'Yes,' Flora relaxed. 'It was a lovely dance, I–' She broke off at the sound of a dull thump that came from the sitting room.

'What's that?' Eddy's chin jerked towards the door. He made to slide from beneath the covers, but Flora held up a hand.

'Stay here!' Flora warned, backing out of the room.

Her hand flicked the switch on the wall, flooding the room with light at the same time a figure enveloped in a long cloak disappeared into the hallway.

A lance of anger sliced through Flora's chest, and without thinking, she launched herself after the intruder.

'Flora!' Eddy's voice, both fearful and exasperated called after her.

Chapter 23

Flora's feet thudded along the boards, propelled by raw anger that someone had dared enter their suite while Eddy slept. The running figure glided through the mist ahead of her, appearing then disappearing in the swirling mist, then disappeared.

She rounded the corner and hurtled onto the port side, where the deck stretched before her, empty but for a line of sulphurous lights on the bulkhead.

Panting, she paused, her nerves alert for footsteps, or the sound of a swinging door, but all that came to her was distant music from the lower deck and the persistent rumble of the ship's engines.

Frustrated, Flora banged her clenched fist against the rail and turned back the way she had come, halting at the top of the companionway. A shiver ran through her, as if a vengeful spirit has passed close, raising the hairs on her neck.

The steps dropped below her feet into a soup-like mist obscuring the bottom. Panic bunched beneath her ribs and she took a step back, her gaze searching the line of blank doors beneath bulkhead lamps dulled by the fog.

Then came a grunt on her left, followed by a rough, painful shove between her shoulder blades that launched her forwards into empty air. She groped for the handrail, but missed, the sensation of falling making her stomach lurch sickeningly. The deck came up to meet her like a black wall, and she slammed against the boards, the air expelled from her lungs in a painful rush.

She tried to take a breath, but her ribs refused her brain's orders to expand. Heart hammering, she lay frozen, terrified that whoever had pushed her, would descend the steps and finish her off. Seconds passed slowly, painfully during which she fought to inhale, but couldn't.

Panic built, until a voice in her head screamed at her to calm down and breathe. Slowly, her chest moved and she took in a gasp of air, then a larger one, until her shallow, rapid breathing settled into a more regular rhythm.

'Miss! Miss!' a youthful male voice made her cringe. 'Are you all right?'

With tentative stretches, Flora moved her toes, then her ankles, until with slow, stiff movements, she was able to push herself up onto an elbow.

A pair of uniformed legs ending in regulation shoes filled her vision. Judging him one of the crew, and hopefully benign, she lifted her head to where his silhouette stood out against scudding clouds and wisps of fog that made her head spin.

'Did you see him?' Supporting herself on her palms, she eased into a crouch.

'See who, miss?' The crewman leaned down,

tucked his shoulder into her armpit and hauled her upright.

'Did you see who pushed me?' Flora tested her weight on the sole of her left foot, regretting it instantly when a nausea-inducing pain shot through her leg. Hopping onto her right foot, she leaned against the sailor, grabbing the rail for support on her other side.

'I saw only you, miss. Took quite a tumble, you did.' The boy-man took in her gown and grinned. 'That party punch carries a bit of a wallop, doesn't it? No wonder you were a bit shaky on those steps.'

Incensed, Flora stiffened but was too shaken to argue. Besides, she had only had one glass, or was it two?

'I was sure you were going to end up like–' he broke off mid-sentence.

'Thank you, but I'm neither drunk nor dead.' Pain and his implied insult made her snap. She leaned both forearms on the rail and bent forwards, fighting dizziness.

'I'll send someone to fetch the doctor, shall I, miss?'

'Would you take me back to my suite first? Then if it isn't too much trouble, fetch Mr Harrington? He's at the dance.' She visualised Bunny drumming his fingers on the table, checking his watch every few seconds. The thought comforted her – a little.

Despite the sailor half-carrying her up the steps to the promenade deck, their hop and pause technique made their progress frustratingly slow, hampered further when the crewman stopped to instruct a colleague to fetch Bunny from the dining room. Finally, they reached the upper deck, where the sailor manhandled her inside the suite, apologizing profusely when her injured foot glanced off the door frame.

'What happened, Flora?' Eddy stood at the open door to his bedroom, his eyes wide and frightened. 'I-I stayed here like you said.'

'Now, young sir.' The crewman clucked like a schoolmaster, though he couldn't have been more than five years Eddy's senior. 'Give the lady a chance to catch her breath. She's had a little fall.'

'I have not had – oh, never mind.' Flora gritted her teeth and cast a longing look at the closed door of her bedroom, but abandoned that plan and lowered herself into the nearest chair.

Why was someone in their suite? Crowe was under lock and key in his stateroom. Everyone must have known she was at the dance, so surely they had not come to hurt Eddy?

Bunny appeared at the door, his breathing fast and shallow as if he had run all the way from the dining room. He pushed past the sailor and crouched beside her, all knees and elbows as he attempted a hug, but withdrew when he realized they were not alone.

'A crewman said there's been an accident!'

'That's what they always say.' Flora cast a dark look at several men in uniform who had crowded the door, none of whom appeared to be doing anything useful.

'I'm sorry you got hurt, Flora.' Eddy, biting his lip, hovered at her shoulder. 'Did the man do it?'

'What man?' Bunny demanded, his stern gaze going from Flora to Eddy and back again.

'I was pushed down the companionway.' Flora spoke slowly, then sighed at his sceptical expression. 'You might suggest a search, though I doubt it would do much good now.'

'We both heard him,' Eddy insisted. 'He was in the sitting room. Flora went after him.'

'Did you see this man, Eddy?' Bunny asked, his gaze flicking to the young sailor, who shook his head.

'No, but Flora–'

'He was real!' Flora slapped her skirt, then winced at the sudden pain that jarred her ankle.

'The doctor is on his way, sir,' Flora's helpmate said at Bunny's shoulder.

'Good. Thank you, but I think I can handle it from here.' He ushered the crewman to the door, where Flora watched him conduct a brief, one-sided conversation with another officer, before returning to her side.

'They'll take a quick look around the decks to see if anyone is still about,' Bunny said. 'But they cannot accuse anyone found admiring the night ocean of having attacked you.'

'It's not as if I could describe him, either.' She sighed, and propped her head in one hand. 'I should imagine several people have long cloaks, which is the only part I saw.' Her initial anger dissipated as she began to see things from a bystander's view. Like the sailor who helped her, everyone would assume she had been at the punch bowl and simply lost her footing.

Dr Fletcher stepped into the minor chaos in his white dress uniform, all brisk efficiency and terse questions about where her foot hurt, the answer to which was everywhere, and where had it spread, which seemed to be everywhere as well.

'I doubt you've broken your ankle, Miss Maguire,' he pronounced on completion of his examination. 'Sprained most like. I'll bind it for you. Keep it elevated until the swelling goes down. And get lots of rest.'

Apart from a sharp gasp when his handling of her foot sent a rush of pain into her leg, Flora remained silent. His examination complete, he delved into his ubiquitous black bag, withdrawing a familiar brown bottle she had last seen Bunny put into his pocket.

Dr Fletcher smiled as if he read her mind, pouring the contents into a tiny glass. 'You refused my ministrations before, but I insist you take this. It will help you with the pain and allow you to sleep.'

Flora eyed the murky brown liquid with distaste, then held her breath and tossed it to the back of her throat, swallowing it in one go. 'Ugh! That's bitter.'

'There's a good girl!' He fastened his bag, hefting it in one hand. 'I'll come back in the morning to check on you. Goodnight, Miss Maguire, Mr Harrington.' The pause between their names held a multitude of speculation, but Flora was too weary to protest.

'He's annoying,' Bunny said when the door closed behind him.

'Papa says it's compulsory for medical men.' Eddy sat draped over the opposite chair, his leg swinging. 'Optimism is their stock-in-trade.'

Flora swallowed repeatedly in an effort to rid

herself of the medicinal taste. She attempted a smile, short circuited as a wave of nausea enveloped her. 'Oh, dear. I think I'm going to be sick–'

Bunny moved incredibly fast for a man who had been in a half-crouch a moment before. In seconds, he shoved the porcelain bowl from her dresser into her hands.

The wave of sickness passed without any visible result. 'It's gone. But thank you anyway.'

'My pleasure.' Bunny removed the bowl, placing it on a nearby table.

'I didn't hear the intruder come in,' Eddy said, apologetic. 'I'm so sorry, Flora.'

'It's not your fault.' Flora patted his hand absently. 'Nothing is, Eddy.' She wished she could reassure him there was nothing further to worry about, but it would be a lie.

'C'mon, old man.' Bunny guided Eddy back to his room. 'It's getting very late. Back to bed and get some sleep.'

Eddy issued a half-hearted protest, but allowed himself to be led away.

'He's trying to be brave, I can tell,' Flora said when Bunny returned.

'It could have been worse.' He perched on the arm of the chair Eddy had vacated. 'He might have come face to face with this chap.'

'I'm so glad he didn't.' Flora shifted in her chair, groaning when pain shot through her hip. 'You accept there was a chap then?'

Concern darkened his eyes, but instead of an answer, he clapped his hands on his thighs and rose, his smile false. 'Someone will have to help you into bed.'

'It isn't going to be you, Mr Bunny Harrington. I'll get the stewardess to do it.'

'I wasn't offering, as it happens.' He pressed the bell beside the mantle, then squatted beside her chair, his face inches from hers. 'I want to apologize for my short temper earlier. I should never have spoken to you like that. It's just that, well we were having such a lovely time at the dance and for a little while I wanted to forget about death and – well, you know.' He gave a light shrug. 'I was enjoying your company. Was that selfish of me?'

'No, I was too.' It occurred to her then that if she hadn't stormed out of the dining room at that very moment, she wouldn't have found the intruder at all. Then what would have happened? 'You're forgiven,' she said, grudgingly.

'You did scare me though. When I heard they had found you at the bottom of the companionway, I thought–'

'That I was lying dead on the deck like Mr–'

'Not a bit like Mr Parnell,' he interrupted. 'That fellow didn't create nearly as much chaos.' He tucked a blanket round her and rose. 'I'll make sure a crewman remains outside this suite tonight. Then to reassure you, I'll report what happened to our detective friend.'

She slumped against a cushion he had placed thoughtfully behind her head, too tired to contradict his implication that he didn't entirely accept her version of events.

'I'm going to be black and blue in the morning,' she said through a yawn. 'I can feel the bruises erupt as I sit here.' Her words came out as a slurred mumble, her tongue thick in her mouth as she could feel the sedative take effect. 'Tell me one thing before you go.'

'What's that?' He ducked his head toward her as if he had trouble hearing her.

'What *is* your name?' Though she suspected it came out slurred and thus unintelligible.

Her eyes flickered closed so she could no longer see his face.

'It's Ptolemy.' The laughter in his voice sent pleasant ripples into her stomach. Though she must have misheard, she didn't have the energy to ask him to repeat it, and when the stewardess arrived to help her out of Cynthia's gown, Bunny had gone.

Chapter 24

Day Seven – Friday

Flora eased her swollen ankle onto the footstool, her bottom lip clenched between her teeth.

'Does it hurt much?' Eddy crouched on the floor at her elbow, his eyes sharp with concern. 'Shall I stay here and keep you company?'

'Yes, to the first question, but as for the second, it's not necessary. All I need is a pot of the stewardesses' best coffee.' She tried to sound lighthearted for Eddy's benefit, but the memory of a hard shove at her back and the sensation of falling brought the previous night back in full force.

Her drug-induced slumber hadn't lasted long and pain had woken her in the early hours. She spent the remainder of the night in a futile attempt to get comfortable, but even the weight of the bedclothes sent a dull ache into her thigh and hip.

When daylight had poked through her blinds, she had given up on sleep and begun the awkward task of dressing.

'I heard you and Mr Harrington talking last night,' Eddy said. 'The sailor said you fell, but the intruder hurt you, didn't he?'

Flora's heart sank. 'I might be wrong about that, it happened so fast. Anyway, he's not about to come back.'

'How do you know?' He dropped his chin onto the arm of her chair and stared up at her, an appeal in his eyes.

'Well, I don't, of course.' Flora hesitated. She didn't want to lie, but why frighten him? 'If either you or Ozzy are worried about anything you see or hear, all you have to do is shout for a crewman.'

Eddy pushed a hand through his wayward hair, reminding her she must make an appointment to get it cut before school started.

The temptation to keep him with her all day was strong, but that was neither fair nor practical. The Gilmores had promised to keep an eye on him until she was mobile again, though it was obvious they didn't feel it was necessary.

'I'm glad Mr Harrington is looking after you.' Eddy picked at his sleeve, self-conscious. 'I – I think you make a lovely couple.'

Flora's hand stilled in the process of smoothing Eddy's hair. 'He's a kind man and a welcome friend for the voyage.'

'That isn't what I meant. You're quite old now, Flora, it's time you had a beau.'

'Indeed?' She slapped his shoulder lightly, torn between laughter and pique. 'Now off you go to breakfast before it's all gone.'

'Flora.' Eddy's teeth worried at his lower lip. 'I have a confession to make.'

'You're an Anglican, Eddy, you don't make confessions.' She realised her attempt to make him smile had failed miserably when his bottom lip quivered.

'Well, I need to this time,' he persisted. 'It could be my fault you got hurt.'

'Why would you think that?' She shifted in search of a more comfortable position, wishing she hadn't when pain flared in her ankle.

'Ozzy and me, well, we found something in Mr Harrington's motor car the other day.'

'What sort of something?' At the same time a vague memory intruded, of the Gilmore father and son walking along the deck, but the image remained indistinct.

'I'll show you.' He disappeared into his room, reappearing again seconds later with a flat stick about a foot long, made of dark wood that he held reverently in both hands. 'We found it stuffed down the back of the seat. Ozzy said we should take turns looking after it. I've had it since last night. Is that why the man came to our room last night?'

'I'm not sure.' She took it from him, the wood

smooth, almost waxy to the touch. 'It looks foreign.' She held it up to the light, where a gold strip of metal cut through the polished wood a third of the way down. 'Oriental maybe. What are these marks carved into it?'

'I didn't notice that.' Eddy peered at it. 'Looks like some sort of cuneiform writing.'

'You should have told me about this before. It could be valuable.'

'We didn't know what it was, not at first,' Eddy's voice rose slightly.

'What do you mean, at first?'

He took the object from her and tugged it gently. The end slid off smoothly, revealing a thin steel blade that tapered into a point at the top.

'It's a knife,' he said unnecessarily.

'So I see. When exactly did you find it?' The possibility that it belonged to Bunny made her heart race. She held her breath, hoping Eddy would disabuse her.

'Yesterday, before dinner.' He hunched his shoulders in the nonchalant shrug employed by boys when they know they have done something they shouldn't, but prefer not to explain. 'It wasn't there on Tuesday.'

'I do wish you'd told me about this. I would never have let you keep it had I known what it was.'

Eddy dropped his chin, suddenly sheepish. 'Am I in trouble?'

'Um – no. I'll deal with this.' She had noticed something she hoped Eddy had not. Where the blade met the hilt was a brown stain that resembled dried blood. It occurred to her then with sharp clarity that this was the weapon used to stab Eloise.

Having reminded Eddy that finders are most definitely not keepers, Flora sent him off to breakfast in the company of a steward, with express instructions to go straight to the Gilmores' suite afterwards.

Alone again, Flora fingered the knife while debating what to do. The longer it remained in her possession, the greater the threat to both herself and Eddy. Her first instinct had been to tell Bunny, but suppose it was his? She shook the thought away as ridiculous. Bunny wasn't a killer.

After a nail-biting few moments, she came to the conclusion that the situation required the logical thought of someone with authority.

A quick glance at the mantle clock told her it was still forty minutes to the breakfast bugle. Tucking the knife under her jacket, she let herself out onto the deck.

Her halting walk to the port side of the promenade deck took a frustratingly long time, and when she finally reached Mr Hersch's stateroom, a dull, persistent throbbing radiated up her thigh.

She leaned against the frame and rang the bell, fretting in case Bunny had chosen to go to breakfast early and saw her. She didn't want to have to explain, and the fewer people who knew about the knife the better. The door swung open, and the German detective filled the door frame, his brows drawn together in a scowl. A tiny fleck of shaving foam clung to his skin below one ear, and his tie was undone.

'Good morning, Flora.' His gaze slid to her tightly-bound ankle and the slipper that was the only footwear she could fit over it. 'Should you be on your feet?'

'I'm sorry to bother you this early, but there's something you should see.' She clamped her arm tight against her jacket, where the knife pressed into her side.

'You'd better come in.' He scanned the empty deck both ways before stepping aside.

Flora made for the nearest chair and lowered herself into it with a relieved sigh.

'Forgive me for failing to put in an appearance last night.' Mr Hersch dabbed the foam from his face with a towel draped over his shoulder, then fastened his collar studs while speaking. 'Officer Martin reported your er – mishap to me last night, but assured me you weren't badly hurt. I assumed questions could wait until this morning.'

'It's quite all right, I didn't expect you to come rushing to my side, but–' She pinned him with a steady gaze. 'Mr Hersch, do you think I'm suffering from delusions? That I simply had one glass of punch too many and imagined someone pushed me down those steps?'

He met her gaze, unflinching for long seconds as if searching for doubt, or confirmation, she couldn't tell which.

He wiped his hands on the towel, discarding it onto a chair before answering. 'No, Flora, I don't.'

Satisfied, she withdrew the knife from inside her jacket and held it out.

He took it from her without speaking, subjecting it to an intense, unhurried study.

'Eddy and the Gilmore boy found it.' Flora filled the silence. 'I thought you should see it. It's a–'

'A Korean ceremonial dagger.' He slid open the two ends as if he had done the same thing a hundred times before. 'A particularly nice piece.' He closed it again with a click.

'You've seen it before?'

'I've seen one like it. This one's quite old. Valuable too, I imagine.' His gaze lifted to meet hers. 'Where did young Eddy get it?'

'In Mr Harrington's motor car.' She let the implication settle in. 'Take a closer look at the blade.'

He flicked her a swift enquiring glance before he obeyed, frowning. Then gave a slow, thoughtful nod. 'Blood. Do I take it you think this is the weapon you think was used to kill Miss Lane?'

'Don't you? Then after killing her, they hid the knife in the motor car. It wasn't Gus Crowe.'

'I suspect you're right, but at this stage I cannot go into details as to why.' He straddled the arm of a chair, the knife held loosely between both hands where it resembled nothing more than a harmless wooden stick.

'I apologize if you thought I did not take you seriously in the library yesterday.' He tapped the knife against the palm of his other hand. 'You were quite right, there is another killer on board. My enquiries are not yet over, but I'm getting close.'

'That's something, I suppose.' Flora shifted in the chair in an effort to get comfortable, releasing a low groan when the ache in her hip flared.

'Are you in pain, Flora?'

'I have some colourful bruises, but the discomfort is easing,' she lied. 'It's a shame so many people have touched that knife, or we may have got a fingerprint from the blade which could prove who used it on Eloise.'

'Fingerprint?' Hersch's brows lifted in amused surprise. 'You know of such things?'

Flora glared at him. 'Sir Francis Galton attended a house party at Cleeve Abbey last year.'

'Galton? The British anthropologist?' Hersch's eyes widened. 'I've heard of him. He's known as a polymath, I believe.'

'Charles Darwin is his cousin.' Flora recalled an enlightening conversation she had had with the gentleman during afternoon tea on the lawn. 'Sir Francis published a book on the subject of fingerprinting a while ago. Did you know that no two people in the entire world share the same fingerprint?'

'As a matter of fact, I did. However, even Pinkerton's has yet to establish them as a reliable method of identification. No court in the land would accept them as evidence.'

'No, I suppose you're right,' Flora said, disappointed. 'We'll have to think of another way.'

'We?' He placed the knife on a table at his elbow and sat back in his chair, the fingers of both hands linked together over his stomach. 'Flora,' he began, his rare use of her given name dragging her gaze to his face. 'If I reveal something, can I trust you to keep it to yourself?'

She nodded, her throat dry in anticipation.

'The van Elder family–'

'Employed you to follow Eloise and find evidence against her.'

He straightened. 'How did you know?'

'Eloise told me. She thought you were going to hand her in to the police.'

He gave a slow, understanding nod. 'As I was saying–'

'Were you?' Flora interrupted him. 'Could you prove she killed her husband?'

He shook his head. 'However I am aware Parnell claimed to have such evidence, which is why she gave him the money she had taken from her husband's safe.'

'Then you were hired by Cynthia Cavendish?' The fact Eloise hadn't lied about everything made Flora feel better.

A flutter of surprise entered his eyes, gone in a second. 'You have been busy, my dear. However, that information is confidential.'

'Why must you be so evasive after everything that has happened? I have a right to know when someone tried to hurt me last night.'

'I'm aware of that, my dear, but you must admit you have put yourself in his way.'

Flora squirmed. That may well be true, but she refused to be treated like an annoyance, or worse, a useless female. 'Why won't you tell me what you really think?'

Hersch tucked a hand beneath Flora's elbow and tugged her gently to her feet. 'I think, that if I don't leave now, I will miss my breakfast.'

'There's something else before you throw me out,' Flora snapped, hopping on her good foot, her arm braced against the door frame. 'I think you should talk to Max Cavendish about why he was on deck that day.'

'Mr Cavendish suffered a concussion which has affected his memory.'

'Really? Well I spoke to him yesterday, and he definitely knows more than he's saying.'

'Can you be more specific?'

Flora hesitated. Max was protecting Cynthia, but from whom or what she didn't know.

'Return to your suite and rest that foot.' Hersch stepped back and closed his door.

By the time Flora reached her sitting room, her ankle throbbed painfully. The van Elder clan could easily have had something to do with Eloise's death, but if Mr Hersch was on their payroll, would he be prepared to expose them?

She released a frustrated groan as she remembered she had left the knife in the German's cabin. She hoped it wouldn't go the same way as the bracelet.

Chapter 25

The stewardess had just set Flora's morning tea in front of her when the doorbell sounded.

'That's most probably the doctor.' The stewardess rubbed both hands down her apron. 'I'll let him in as I leave.'

'How is the ankle this morning?' Dr Fletcher's cheery greeting was in stark contrast to Flora's mood. 'How did you sleep last night? Well, I hope?'

'Your sedative helped, but each time I moved, the pain woke me.' Her early morning jaunt to Mr Hersch's cabin had not helped, but she chose not to mention that.

'I have something which might help.' He set his leather bag on the low table in the middle of the room and rummaged inside. 'Although wouldn't you be better off staying in bed?'

'I'd rather not. I hate lying in bed during the day.' Ignoring his disapproving frown, she submitted meekly to having her temperature taken, followed by another gentle, but painful manipulation of her ankle.

'The swelling isn't as bad as I thought, but you do look peaked this morning. Are you sure you didn't hit your head when you fell?'

'I did not fall,' Flora said through gritted teeth. 'I was pushed. I cannot remember whether I hit my head or not. I had rather a lot to think about at the time.'

'Hmm, any nausea, headache or dizziness?' He held her wrist lightly in his fingers and peered at his watch.

'All three, actually, but I'll get over it. Especially if the person who pushed me is found.' She caught his sceptical look beneath the concerned façade. 'You don't believe me, do you?'

'Well, let me put it this way, young females can be particularly fanciful when not kept busy. And you have been running around this ship making some startling claims during this voyage.' He tipped some of the contents from a small brown bottle into a tiny glass and held it out.

'What claims? I haven't said anything that Mr Hersch hasn't.' She took it from him and downed the cloudy liquid in one swallow, shuddering as the bitter taste hit the back of her throat. 'Besides, I must have discovered something important to unsettle our killer. And I don't mean Mr Crowe, either.'

He released a derisive chuckle as he examined the readings on the thermometer under the light. 'Mr Crowe is most certainly the culprit, and he will face the authorities when we reach England.'

'You've accepted he killed Mr Parnell then?' Flora frowned. 'Didn't your report state he died in a fall?'

'Uh, well, I couldn't do a full post-mortem, so perhaps I was mistaken. Besides, he killed that young lady, didn't he? The actress?'

'Mr Hersch doesn't think it wasn't an accident.' The urge to display her superior knowledge was strong. 'Parnell was a fraudster, or something like that.' The memory of the telegram she had seen on Seaman Croft's desk rose into her head, but she wasn't sure why. 'Something to do with Montana, I think.' Her head spun and the details slipped frustratingly out of reach.

'Ah yes, that German chap. He's a Pinkerton's man, I believe.' His eyes narrowed, making them appear closer together than they already were. 'He's been asking a lot of impertinent questions.'

'Hardly impertinent. He's trying to unearth the truth. Between us we have monopolised that wireless operator's time, and–' she broke off as the dizziness returned.

Had Bunny told the captain of her attack? She

couldn't remember. No, she hadn't seen him yet that morning to ask.

'Dr Fletcher, would you ask Captain Gates to come and see me?'

His dismissive grin made her want to slap him. 'The captain knows all he needs to about this affair. As your doctor, I suggest you concentrate on getting better. I'm still worried about your head. You appear to be rambling somewhat.'

'Do I?' Flora gave this idea consideration. He might be right. She did seem to be chattering away to no purpose. 'All right, I'll stop talking and let you do your job.'

'Now,' he began, all smiles now that she was doing as she was told. 'I want you to take another dose of this in an hour. Could you do that for me?' He placed the brown ridged bottle on the table with a firm click.

Flora grimaced. 'If I must, though it makes me groggy and I can't think straight.'

'That's what potassium bromide solution is supposed to do, young lady.'

Flora dozed, the pain in her hip markedly dulled by the sedative, but the passing of time took on an unreal quality, so she barely registered Bunny's arrival. One moment she was alone, then the next time she opened her eyes, he had placed a tray on the table in front of her.

'I brought your breakfast.'

'I doubt I could eat half that.' Flora surveyed the array of sausage, fried eggs, bacon, fruit compote, toast and marmalade. 'The coffee smells good, though, would you mind pouring me a cup?'

'How are you this morning?' He handed her a steaming hot cup that smelled heavenly.

'Sore, drowsy, definitely not myself.' She took a delicious sip of aromatic coffee and eased back in her chair. 'Did I ruin Cynthia's dress?'

'Not at all. Simply a few dirty marks the laundry are confident they can remove. This is hardly the time to worry about a dress.'

'I'm a woman. Clothes matter, especially when they aren't mine.'

'Dr Fletcher thinks you imagined that push, you know.' Bunny perched on the arm of the chair opposite, his arms folded across his chest. 'He said I was to ensure you don't exert yourself for the next couple of days. He suspects you have a head injury.'

Flora dismissed him with a wave, judging the good doctor must be severely under-employed to create problems where none existed.

'Was anyone missing from the dance last night?' Flora picked desultorily at her food, resenting Bunny's critical eye observing her every bite. At the same time, a tiny voice in her head told her she should appreciate his concern instead of being annoyed by it.

'Not that I noticed. Mrs Penry-Jones got quite voluble on the fruit punch and had to be escorted back to her suite by a crewman.'

'Where was Hester?'

'Oh, she had gone to be sick in the powder room. Returned looking very green. Overdid the punch too, I imagine. Then Cynthia sulked when Max got tired early and insisted on leaving. Poor chap looked quite worn out.'

'What about Gerald and Monica?'

'They stayed until they turned the lights out.' He poured coffee for himself and stirred sugar into it. 'Miss Ames proved to be quite an accomplished dancer. Couldn't get her off the floor.'

'I had this strange dream last night,' Flora began as a memory resurfaced. 'Where you told me you had been named after some ancient Greek.' She peered at him over the rim of her cup.

The rhythmic clink of his spoon halted. Slowly, he set it down gently in the saucer. 'Ah, you did hear me. No dream, I'm afraid. A whim of my father's. Ptolemy was Alexander the Great's boyhood companion at Mieza, you know.'

'No, I don't know. What's Mieza?'

'A sort of boarding school for Macedonian nobles. Alexander studied there under Aristotle.'

Flora cut up her sausage into small pieces, mainly to disguise the fact she hadn't eaten any, while speculating on how such a royal name got abbreviated to that of a small furry creature with oversized ears.

'Many believed that Ptolemy was Alexander's illegitimate half-brother.' Bunny balanced the coffee cup in one hand and plucked a slice of toast from the silver rack with the other. 'I like to think that's true, anyway.'

'Why didn't your parents call you Alexander? That wouldn't have raised any eyebrows.'

'They did actually. That's my second name.' He pointed his toast at her, eyes narrowed. 'I would appreciate it if we dropped the subject now.'

'As you wish.' She paused with her fork held in mid-air, a roundel of sausage clinging to the tines.

'You do believe I was pushed down those steps, don't you?'

'I'll admit I wasn't sure at first. No, take that look off your face. It's not beyond the bounds of possibility that your mind played tricks after everything that has happened. However, I lay awake last night thinking about it.'

'And what conclusion did you come to?' Flora held her breath. If he dismissed her again she hadn't the strength to fight him. Her limbs felt heavy and his voice kept receding, then growing louder again. Even the room seemed to be moving, though she attributed that to the motion of the ship.

'I agree with you. Gus Crowe is a sneak thief, not a violent criminal who would stab a woman for a gold bracelet. Parnell died in a botched robbery.' He took a bite of toast and chewed thoughtfully. 'Incidentally, Hersch told me at breakfast that they had found the murder weapon. The one used on Eloise. He didn't say anything else.'

Aware of an uncomfortable buzzing behind her eyes, Flora decided to explain about the knife later; when her head was clearer.

'Tell me about your plans for your factory in England.' Apart from not wishing to discuss knives, the reason for her question escaped her. It wasn't as if she would be a part of it.

'My main problem is finding an engineering firm to make the parts.' He folded both hands over his flat stomach. 'I'll have to manufacture every piece of the engine and bodywork myself, of course, which will make production very slow. Then there's the travelling needed to show my designs to possible buyers at the show.'

'What show?' Flora asked through a yawn.

'There's an automobile show in Madison Square Garden scheduled for next November.'

'Isn't that where they hold those boxing matches?'

'It is, although other events are staged there too. The exhibition will last an entire week, sponsored by the Automobile Club of America.'

'There is a club for motor cars?' Flora asked, incredulous.

'Your scepticism wounds me, Miss Maguire. Motor travel is no temporary madness, I'm confident it has a long and illustrious future. There will be upwards of sixty exhibitors at the show in New York, all displaying at least thirty new autos.'

'So many? I had no idea.' Flora eased her neck from side to side, but it didn't help. She felt as though she were under water.

'I don't think you're listening to me, are you, Flora?' Bunny slapped the arms of his chair and rose, the sound bringing her eyes open with a snap.

'Dr Fletcher said I was to make sure you took some more medicine.' He walked behind her chair towards the mantle, returning with the bottle, poured the liquid into the glass and handed it to her.

She took it with unsteady fingers, staring at it for a few seconds with dismay.

Bunny skirted her chair and when his back was turned, she tipped the contents into the last inch of coffee in her cup. Licking her lips ostentatiously, she held out the empty glass. 'There, now take it away.'

Chuckling, he hauled her to her feet, then swept her into his arms and carried her into the bedroom. Flora tried to say something about wishing the circumstances were different for such a romantic display, but the words came out as an unintelligible slur. The effort to stay awake became too much, and she barely registered the click of the door before sleep claimed her.

Chapter 26

Flora's troubled sleep was interspersed with vivid dreams of storms at sea, which faded into the kitchen with the black range that had been such a strong image throughout her life. The scene played out as it always did, with herself as a small child on a stone floor, her mother's skirt clutched in her hands. Then something new intruded.

Someone was calling her name, over and over.

With a groan of protest, she rolled her shoulder to rid herself of a disturbing weight that pressed down on her.

'Flora!' The voice came again, louder this time.

She prised her eyelids open, bringing a hand to shield her eyes as stark daylight poked the tender spot behind her forehead. A blur of colour and shadows came into focus and turned into Bunny's worried face, looming inches above hers.

She jerked upright on an elbow, blinking. 'What's happening?'

Bunny sighed, gathering her swiftly in his arms and held on tight, his hands seeking out the contours of her back. He pressed his lips against her forehead and he rocked her gently.

Flora stiffened at first, confused, until his touch sent ripples of pleasure through her spine, so she relaxed and leaned into him. Her lips curved into a smile and she opened her eyes, then froze at the sight of Mr Hersch in the door frame, his hand on Eddy's shoulder.

'How are you feeling?' Hersch asked, unsmiling, his penetrating gaze searching her face.

She wriggled out of Bunny's grasp. 'Fast asleep up until two minutes ago.' She brought a hand to her hair, encountered a mass of tousled curls that were past repairing, and lowered it again. 'Why is everyone in my bedroom?'

She hugged the coverlet up to her neck, forgetting that beneath it she was fully dressed.

'She isn't sweating from what I can tell.' Hersch crept closer, making the tiny space claustrophobic. 'No shivering or tremors. Her pupils look clear and are of normal size.'

'How much of that sedative have you taken?' Bunny wrested the coverlet from between her fingers and took her hand in his. 'No, don't scowl at me like that, Flora, this is important. How many doses did you take apart from the one I gave you this morning?'

'Um, well actually, I threw that one away. Dr Fletcher gave me one last night and another this morning.' She shuddered. 'It tasted bitter and made me feel as if I was floating. I haven't taken any more. Why?'

The intense look in Bunny's eyes dissolved with an exhaled breath. 'Oh, thank God for your contrary nature.'

Flora scooted farther up the bed. 'Will someone please tell me what's happening?'

Bunny dropped a kiss on the back of her hand, tugged the coverlet aside and pulled her gently upright. 'Come into the sitting room, and we'll explain.'

'I'll just settle this young man with Mrs Gilmore.' Hersch patted Eddy's shoulder and guided him out of the room. 'There, you see, Ed, old chap, fuss about nothing.' His soothing voice receded as they left, followed by Eddy's half-hearted protest that he wanted to stay.

Monica Gilmore must have been waiting outside the suite door, for Flora heard her high-pitched greeting to Eddy, followed by enthusiastic plans she had in store for the afternoon, most of which seemed to involve food.

Reassured he would be looked after, Flora concentrated on getting her stiff muscles to move.

Bunny supported her as she limped into the sitting room, where Captain Gates stood with Dr Fletcher. Officer Martin stood by the door, hands clasped behind his back as if on guard.

'To what do I owe the pleasure of this gathering?' Flora asked, her voice brisk with embarrassment at her rumpled, sleep-heavy appearance.

'Don't joke, Flora,' Bunny's grip on her arm tightened as he lowered her into a chair. 'We were genuinely worried about you.'

'And very relieved to see you well, Miss Maguire.' Captain Gates's ever-present smile broadened, while the other two remained grim-faced.

Hersch plucked the brown bottle from the mantle and held it up. 'Is this what the doctor gave you, Flora?'

She nodded, frowning. 'It's bromide, to help me sleep.'

'I don't think so, my dear.' He dropped the bottle into his pocket. 'When we have this analysed in London, I suspect we'll find it's. a strong concentration of laudanum. Well, Dr Fletcher?' He turned to face the doctor. 'How much of this did you intend her to take?'

Without warning, Bunny launched himself at the man, both hands encircling his throat. 'You were asked a question! How much did you give her?'

The doctor's eyes bulged and he tried to unhook Bunny's hands, but to no effect.

'Bunny!' Flora started forwards in her chair. 'What are you doing?' She cast a swift glance at the detective, expecting him to intervene, but he remained standing passively to one side.

Officer Martin looked about to step between them, but Captain Gates shook his head.

'I said, how much?' Bunny repeated, giving Dr Fletcher a rough shake.

'Four grains,' the doctor croaked, his voice distorted. 'Four grains each dose.'

Bunny released him with a snort of disgust, flattened both hands against the doctor's chest and shoved him backwards with such force, he staggered against the bulkhead.

Fletcher righted himself again, a sneer on his mouth, though the hand he pushed through his

298

hair shook.

'I don't even know what that means,' Flora murmured, her head still full of images from her dream.

She stared at Bunny, now red-faced as he fought to settle his breathing. Accustomed to his calm manners and gentle nature, his burst of uncontrolled anger shocked her. The fact it was on her behalf was strangely exciting.

'Six grains is a fatal dose,' Hersch said finally, a brow raised. 'The accumulation of that much laudanum over a twelve-hour period would most likely have killed you, Flora.'

'What?' Flora gaped. 'Why would Dr Fletcher try to kill me?' The remnants the fog cleared from her mind, but she had no reason not to believe them. Had the doctor pushed her down the steps? Is that why he was so keen to intimate she had imagined it?

'Care to enlighten the lady, Fletcher?' Captain Gates spoke for the first time.

'Yes, why don't you do that – Fletcher?' Bunny came to stand beside her chair, one hand caressing her shoulder.

The doctor's eyes flickered with doubt and he stared at the floor.

'Nothing to say, Doctor?' Hersch snorted. 'Then let me do it for you. Nine years ago, Mr Parnell once organized a fraudulent land deal in Montana.'

'Montana,' Flora repeated, sifting through the fog in her head. 'Where have I heard that word before?'

'I sent a telegraph to a contact of mine to un-

299

earth a list of those people who lost money in that venture,' Hersch continued. 'Their response came through this morning. Gerald Gilmore lost money in that deal. He remembered Parnell and called him by another name.'

Flora vaguely recalled Bunny mentioning something like that, then pushed the memory away and concentrated on what Hersch was saying.

'Dr Fletcher lost money in the same enterprise,' he went on. 'A lot of money. He also encouraged some of his patients to invest.'

'I didn't know it was fake!' Dr Fletcher interjected. 'I was swindled too.'

'Unfortunately,' Hersch addressed Flora as if he hadn't spoken, 'the good doctor was hounded out of his practice. He could hardly continue his career in an assumed name, so hiding was his only option. He took a position as ship's doctor to avoid the scandal.'

'You call this a career?' Dr Fletcher gave the suite a slow, contemptuous look. 'Handing out plasters and tonics to rich, spoiled hypochondriacs?'

'You also recognized Frank Parnell on that first night,' Hersch continued.

'I spent years rehearsing what I would say if I ever saw him again. Then there he sat, throwing money around without a care. I lay awake half the night, then rose early and went to his stateroom before I lost my nerve.'

'Why? Did you expect him to apologize?' Bunny demanded.

'I wanted him to know he had ruined my life!' Fletcher's gaze, cold and reptilian, slid towards

300

Flora. He reeked of self-pity, making her wonder how she had ever imagined him attractive, let alone trusted him.

'What happened, Doctor?' Hersch said gently, gesturing to Bunny for silence.

'Parnell came to the door with a towel held to a gash on his head.' Fletcher swallowed before continuing. 'Nothing serious, but it bled quite a bit. He assumed that in a fit of remorse, Crowe had sent me along to see to him. When I told him why I was really there, he laughed; said I was simply an unlucky punter and should have got over it by now.'

'I can see why that would enrage you,' Hersch said. 'However, that doesn't explain how Mr Parnell ended up dead.'

'I don't know what came over me.' Dr Fletcher hunched his shoulders as if the events of that night still confused him. 'I wanted to remove that smug look from his face. I picked up the first thing I laid my hands on, which happened to be an ashtray, and hit him.' His mouth twisted as if the memory gave him a certain satisfaction. 'That gash was a darned sight worse when I had finished, I can tell you.'

He massaged the knuckles of his right hand repeatedly, and having begun, appeared reluctant to stop. 'I cleaned the wound with the same towel, then removed any traces of blood I found from the stateroom. I waited until the crew had finished washing the decks. I was going to throw him overboard. After all, no body, no crime, eh?'

Flora winced, but no one else responded to the doctor's uneasy smile.

301

'I dragged him as far as the companionway, but heard voices, so dumped him down the steps. I went back to his stateroom to collect the bloodied towel and the ashtray, then returned to my cabin, where I waited for a crewman to tell me a body had been found.

'It was simple after that.' He gave a resigned shrug. 'Once he was delivered to my office, I stripped and washed the body to ensure no evidence remained to contradict my report that he had died from a fall.'

'What did you do with the towel and the ashtray?' Bunny asked

'I threw them overboard.' Fletcher's upper lip curled in contempt. 'A task which proved more difficult than it sounds. Whenever I left my cabin, a passenger waylaid me with a minor complaint. You'd be surprised how little free time the crew get aboard this ship.'

'I still don't understand why you tried to kill *me*,' Flora said. 'I never suspected you.'

'When I came to examine you this morning, you mentioned that accursed land deal.' His sullen glare turned to uncertainty. 'I knew it was only a matter of time before you and the detective here discovered I was involved. So I swapped the bromide for laudanum.'

'You weren't supposed to wake up.' The weight of Bunny's stare made Fletcher fidget and turn red. 'Our good doctor had already prepared the ground about a possible head injury.'

'Which I didn't have,' Flora murmured. Tipping the medicine into her coffee was a momentary impulse. She could just as easily have drunk

302

it to keep Bunny happy. Although had it not been for that awful drug, she wouldn't have been so voluble with Fletcher in the first place.

Captain Gates jerked his chin towards Officer Martin as a signal to escort the doctor out. Fletcher shrugged off the man's retraining arm with a harsh, guttural snort, raked the company with a final defiant glare and stomped outside where two crewmen waited.

The captain replaced his cap, tipped the peak at each of them, then followed.

'I cannot believe it was him,' Flora said softly as the door clicked shut. She looked up at Mr Hersch. 'Did you know all along he had been swindled by Parnell, or rather, Marlon van Elder?'

'No,' Hersch replied. 'I told the truth about the list. I only received it this morning. I certainly didn't expect his name to be on it.'

'How did you know about the sedative?' Flora asked.

'Eddy told me. We met on his way back from breakfast. When I asked how you were, he said you were sleeping and the suite smelled like a sweet shop. That's how I knew something wasn't right.'

Flora stared at him. 'What has that got to do with anything?'

'Cinnamon. It's not used in the administration of bromide, but often mixed into laudanum to disguise the bitter taste.'

'Well it didn't work, that stuff tasted horrible.' Flora wrinkled her nose in remembrance.

'I even insisted you take it.' Bunny shook his head, his face white. 'Thank goodness you defied

303

me.' He sniffed ostentatiously. 'Come to think of it, it does smell a bit like a confectioners' emporium in here.'

Flora giggled, but the sound was too close to hysteria for comfort.

'I happened to be in the upper lobby when our intrepid detective pounded on Fletcher's office door and dragged him out,' Bunny said.

'He was quite insistent about tagging along,' Hersch said, amused.

'I wonder if Seaman Crofts is aware his telegraph machine has captured a dangerous criminal?' Flora rubbed her upper arms with both hands to still a shiver that wouldn't go away.

'I doubt the good doctor was dangerous until Parnell goaded him,' Hersch said. 'Then something just snapped. In nine years, rage can embitter a man into desperation. Now.' He rubbed his hands together. 'I'll leave you to recover fully, Flora. I, however, have another killer to apprehend.'

'I had almost forgotten Eloise,' Flora said on a sigh. 'You don't think Dr Fletcher was responsible for her death?'

'That would make everything conveniently simple, wouldn't it? But no, I think not. However, you may rest assured, the net is closing in.' He held up a finger as he backed towards the door.

When he had left, Flora became keenly aware of Bunny's presence. The fact he had been so angry at the doctor's actions thrilled her on the one hand, but a niggling thought scraped incessantly at the edge of her brain.

'Bunny? Do you happen to have an interest in

antique oriental daggers?'

'I beg your pardon?' He stood over her, a frown drawing his brows together. 'Are you sure you didn't take more of that laudanum than you said?' He tucked a strand of her hair behind her ear. 'What was that about daggers?'

'Nothing, just something that occurred to me.' She raised her chin to meet the angle of his gaze, searching for something in his eyes. There was nothing there. No hostility, no anxiety; simply a man who had feared for someone he cared for. She squeezed the hand that he still held against her hair.

Chapter 27

Flora hobbled along the deck at Bunny's side, her coat buttoned to her neck, one arm tucked through his. The *Minneapolis* would dock at Tilbury the next afternoon, and she found herself counting each hour before she would have to say goodbye to him.

'I'm sorry to drag you out into the cold, but I needed some air after being in the cabin most of the day. Taking meals in the suite may sound like an unheard of luxury, but it palls after a while.'

'Cabin fever, I believe they call it.' He pressed her elbow into his side. 'I don't feel at all dragged. Should whoever attacked you reappear, I intend to be on hand to protect you.'

'I take it Dr Fletcher still insists he didn't push

me, or that he killed Eloise?'

'He will only admit to battering Marlon van Elder, who, incidentally, used his real name for that land fraud.'

Flora bit her lip. The thought that whoever tried to hurt her still roamed the ship remained an uncomfortable one.

'That idea of yours for hot and cold compresses on my ankle worked well.' She brushed a strand of hair from her face and huddled into him, determined to relish every moment of their last evening together. 'The pain is little more than a dull ache now.'

Bunny didn't appear to hear her. 'I wonder what's going on over there?'

Flora followed his gaze to where Mr Hersch stood with the captain and two crewmen beside an open door.

'Isn't that Mrs Penry-Jones's suite?' Bunny shifted his hold on her arm, pulling her in the reverse direction. 'Perhaps they wouldn't want us listening to their private conversation. Shall we go back?'

'Not on your life.' Flora carried on walking, though it was more of a hop and stagger. 'I want to know what's going on.'

He capitulated with a sigh, though Flora suspected he was not as reluctant as he pretended.

As they came level, Mr Hersch greeted them with a tilt of his head. 'Good evening, Flora. How nice to see you out and about again.'

'Thank you. We were just getting some air.' She tried to peer round him but his bulk effectively blocked the door. 'Is something wrong?'

306

'Do feel free to make a party of it!' Mrs Penry-Jones' harsh laugh drifted out from the interior room. 'Come in, come in, the governess and her *inamorato* may as well witness my downfall.'

Flora directed an astonished look at Bunny, who blinked behind his glasses.

Mr Hersch stepped to one side, a hand extended as an invitation for them to enter.

Flora risked a glance at Captain Gates, prepared for his dismissal, but he didn't react.

Needing no further urging, Flora pulled Bunny behind her and limped into the suite.

Mrs Penry-Jones dominated the room, her complexion pale but for two spots of red on her sharp cheeks; her back held straight, though her head wobbled on her thin neck. With one hand, she gripped her silver-topped cane propped beside her right knee, the other folded and re-folded a pleat of her skirt.

Max acknowledged Flora from his chair against the wall, the plaster on his forehead reduced to the size of a half crown, his injured arm still strapped to his chest.

Cynthia paced the room, chewing a thumbnail, her dark-blue gown matching her troubled eyes.

'Do sit down, Cynthia,' Max snapped, apparently at the end of his patience.

Cynthia broke off her restless pacing to glare at Flora, but made no attempt to sit. 'Are we a public spectacle now?'

'Where's Miss Smith?' the detective asked, ignoring Cynthia's question.

'I sent her to fetch me some tea to help calm my nerves at this dreadful intrusion,' Mrs Penry-

Jones said, then clamped her lips in a hard line.

'I shan't intrude long,' the detective said archly. 'I merely wished to ask if anyone here has seen this before?' From an inside pocket he withdrew the knife Eddy had found, slid the blade from its wooden sheath and held it up. 'I shall ask Miss Smith the same question when she returns.'

Flora may have imagined it, but though no one spoke, backs stiffened perceptively.

'It belongs to me,' Mrs Penry-Jones said after a moment. 'My first husband brought it back from Korea thirty years ago.'

'I suspect it's considerably older than that.' Hersch returned the blade to its sheath. 'May I ask why you brought it with you on this voyage?'

She gave a mild shrug, her gaze sliding to Cynthia.

'Don't look at *me!*' Cynthia squeaked. 'The last time I saw that – that thing,' she waved her hand in Hersch's direction, 'it was in Grandmamma's vanity case. I swear I never touched it.'

Flora bit her lip to prevent a smile. Cynthia's jutted chin, the superior gaze and the wagging finger were all Mrs Penry-Jones, but in a younger body.

'She's her grandmother?' Bunny whispered beside Flora's ear, though he did not require a response.

'I keep that dagger for protection,' Mrs Penry-Jones continued as if Cynthia hadn't spoken. 'However, I swear to you, I never used it to kill anyone. I didn't even know it was missing.'

'Mrs Cavendish,' Hersch said. 'Is it possible you used the knife to stab Estelle van Elder?'

308

'How could you, Cynthia?' Mrs Penry-Jones released a horrified gasp. 'We agreed! We sought justice, not bloody revenge. Why couldn't you simply wait?'

'Grandmamma! How could you think such a thing?' Cynthia enunciated each word, her furious gaze on the old lady.

'Would someone care to explain?' Captain Gates asked, bemused.

'I wish they would too,' Bunny muttered, evidently confused.

'Of course, it all makes sense now,' Flora said, a finger to her lips when Bunny started to speak. 'I wonder if Mr Hersch is about to blow the family's story apart or give them all alibis?'

'What do you mean, how–?'

Flora shushed him. 'Just listen.'

'It was all *her* idea.' Cynthia cocked her chin at Mrs Penry-Jones. 'No one was supposed to die!'

'We're every bit as responsible, Cyn,' Max began. 'If only we had let the authorities–'

'Shut up, Max!' Mrs Penry-Jones snapped. 'You don't have to say anything. You cannot be compelled to give evidence against her anyway. She's your wife.'

A look of patient sympathy crossed Max's face, before he reverted to silence.

'For the benefit of Miss Maguire and Mr Harrington, allow me to return to the beginning.' Hersch set the knife on the low table in front of him with a sharp click. 'Earlier this year, Mr Theodore van Elder took, as his second wife, Estelle Montgomery, a woman considerably younger than himself.'

The old lady straightened slowly, as if gathering her dignity around her like a cape. 'Theodore van Elder was my son.' She paused for effect, adding, 'That girl was nothing more than a scheming trollop!'

'However,' Hersch drew out the word in warning, 'a week after the wedding, Mr van Elder died.'

'I thought that sounded suspicious when I read the clipping,' Bunny said with a snort.

'Exactly!' Mrs Penry-Jones pinned the detective with a triumphant glare.

The detective shook his head. 'The coroner's report stated he succumbed to a bout of gastro enteritis. There was nothing suspicious about his death.'

'Fiddlesticks!' Mrs Penry-Jones sniffed. 'Theodore was only forty-two. No, Estelle, or Eloise or whatever she called herself, persuaded him into a hole-in-the-wall wedding, only to murder him for his money.'

'That makes no sense,' Flora said. 'They were married, so she already had his money. Why would she kill him?'

'Well, *I* didn't do it,' Cynthia insisted, two spots of red bloomed on her porcelain cheeks.

'No, Mrs Cavendish,' Hersch said. 'I don't believe you did. After the stewardess helped you dress for the bridge tournament that afternoon, you called at Mrs van Elder's cabin with the tea you promised her, but you received no answer because she was already dead.'

'There, you see, Grandmamma!' Cynthia flung in triumph. 'Now do you believe me?'

Mrs Penry-Jones snorted, but did not reply.

'Is that why you all came on board together?' Flora asked. 'To accuse Eloise of murder?'

'And why ever not!' Mrs Penry-Jones narrowed her eyes at Flora. 'I wanted her exposed. That was Marlon's job, but he fluffed it. Marlon was my nephew by marriage, estranged from the family due to some disreputable behaviour I won't go into here.' She closed her eyes briefly as if the embarrassment was too much. 'After Theodore's death, he came crawling to me, asking for a chance to redeem himself. I charged him with befriending Theodore's widow in order to discover how to make her pay for what she had done.'

'Then why engage Pinkerton's?' The term, belt-and-braces, jumped into Flora's head.

'Insurance.' Mrs Penry-Jones glared at her. 'When Marlon told me Eloise had booked passage for England, I couldn't risk her getting away before I could expose her. I had no idea he was working for them.' She waved her stick at Mr Hersch before bringing it down on the floor again with a thump. 'The agency operates beneath a cloud of secrecy.'

'That's quite true,' Hersch said. 'I was engaged to keep Miss Lane, er – Mrs van Elder under surveillance, I had no idea Mrs Penry-Jones or her granddaughter were on board.'

'You weren't meant to know!' Mrs Penry-Jones snapped, then her eyes glinted. 'You also work for me, so I won't tolerate being questioned in this way.'

'The young lady's death ended our agreement, Mrs Penry-Jones.' Hersch's voice brooked no

311

argument. 'At which I offered my services to Captain Gates.'

Mrs Penry-Jones merely grunted, and continued kneading the top of her walking stick with both hands.

'Now if you don't mind, I'll continue,' Hersch said. 'For the benefit of you, Flora, and Mr Harrington, how did you become involved in all this, Mrs Cavendish, when you reside in England?'

Cynthia sighed, as if whatever fight remained drained out of her. 'Max and I were about to leave for Rome on our honeymoon when a telegram arrived saying Daddy had been murdered.' Her eyes filled with tears, making them more vivid. 'I didn't know him that well, but he was still my father. We changed our booking and sailed here instead. Grandmamma told me what she suspected and Max and I agreed to help.'

Max gave a snort but no one took any notice.

'On that first night,' Mrs Penry-Jones took up the story, 'Marlon told me he had obtained the evidence I needed. He was supposed to bring it to me the next morning but he never arrived. When I was told he had been found dead, I thought–'

'That Eloise had killed him to prevent him doing so?' Hersch finished for her.

She nodded stiffly.

'I'm afraid he deceived you, dear lady.' The detective sighed. 'Marlon possessed no such evidence. We cannot know exactly what happened between him and Miss Lane, but we believe,' he said, turning to Flora, 'that he convinced Miss Lane to part with her money in exchange for a

312

pardon from you.'

'Why would Eloise agree to that when she wasn't guilty?' Flora recalled the argument she had heard through the bulkhead on the first night.

'Perhaps she imagined she would never be rid of a family prepared to hound her across the Atlantic.' Hersch turned to glare at the old lady. 'Maybe she was simply desperate?'

'Oh, dear.' Mrs Penry-Jones brought a wrinkled hand to her chest, blinking rapidly.

Max groaned and pressed a thumb and forefinger into the fleshy part above his nose.

'If you believed that your stepmother killed your father, Mrs Cavendish,' Hersch broke the oppressive silence that had descended, 'it's understandable you would wish her dead.'

'I did wish her dead,' Cynthia spat. 'Stepmother, indeed! She was a year younger than me.'

'Are you accusing my wife of murder?' Max's furious gaze raked the detective in challenge.

'I'm quite capable of answering for myself, Max.' Cynthia waved him away and turned on Mrs Penry-Jones. 'How could you think I would do such a thing?' Her breath hitched and close to tears, she dragged her bottom lip through her teeth.

Flora forced down belated sympathy for Eloise, who had found herself caught up in this twisted family. Recently widowed and with no one else to turn to, she had fled for a new life in another country. Then Parnell, a man who had pretended to be a friend, revealed that her husband's vengeful mother was on board issuing threats. Being offered a lifeline in exchange for money must have seemed not only attractive, but her only hope. That she had overheard Crowe's argument with Seaman Crofts and turning it to her advantage was an act borne of desperation.

'And you, Mrs Penry-Jones, could you bring yourself to plunge a dagger into a young woman's chest?' Hersch asked.

'Most assuredly.' The old lady's eyes fluttered closed for a second. 'In my head I did so several times. But no, I didn't kill the girl. I wanted her to suffer for the rest of her life, and for the world to know what she had done. Dead, she provides me with no satisfaction.'

'Then who did kill Eloise?' Flora demanded.

Chapter 28

Hester nudged the suite door open with a hip and manhandled a tray inside that Flora could tell at a glance held a good deal more than a solitary cup of tea.

'I'm sorry I was so long, Mrs Penry-Jones, but the kitchen didn't have any cucumber sandwiches left.'

She took in the now silent room with a slow sweeping glance, then with a dismayed cry, the tray of sandwiches, plate of cakes crockery flew from her hands.

Mrs Penry-Jones let out a horrified shriek as the lid separated from the teapot, spraying her skirt with scalding liquid.

Sandwiches and cakes went in one direction, the milk jug and crockery in another. A slice of smoked salmon splattered onto Cynthia's arm, eliciting a howl of protest, while Bunny backed against the wall, avoiding the trajectory of the hot water jug.

The sugar bowl tipped its contents over the floor, bounced once on the carpet before it rolled to a halt against the fireplace; the scene reminding Flora of a farce in a West End play. Surely Hester didn't need to throw the tray across the room? She could have simply let it fall to the floor.

The mounting laugh which worked its way into Flora's chest was short-lived when she realized the one person who had made no effort to help bring order to the chaos was Hester herself. She had backed away before the tray did its devastating work and disappeared.

Flora rose unsteadily to her feet, and approached Mr Hersch, who was that moment occupied with collecting debris from the floor.

'Mr Hersch,' Flora laid a hand on his shoulder. 'Hester's gone.'

Uttering a curse under his breath, the detective beckoned the captain who was busy wiping cream from his coat and they lunged for the door.

Cynthia picked her way over the scattered sandwiches and squashed cakes that littered the floor, and ran outside.

'Now what?' Max muttered, heaving himself awkwardly from his chair and looked about to follow, when Mrs Penry-Jones caught him on the shin with her stick.

'Where do you think you're going?' she snarled, raising both arms. 'Help me up. I'm coming too.'

Sighing, Max did as he was told, though with one usable arm, the process was seriously protracted.

'I take it you wish to go too?' Bunny looked up from removing chocolate icing from his trouser leg with a linen napkin.

'Absolutely.' Flora limped onto the promenade deck, gazing frantically around to see which direction the captain and Hersch had gone. There was no sign of Hester, but the clatter of heavy shoes on metal steps drew her towards the companionway to the boat deck.

Flora grasped the rail but Bunny gripped her elbow from behind, halting her. 'Oh no, you don't. You'll slip. Let me help you.' He wrapped his arm round her waist, slid the other beneath her knees and swept her into his arms.

'What happened in there exactly?' Bunny asked as he carried her down to the bottom of the companionway.

Behind them, Max struggled with Mrs Penry-Jones, who kept up a constant stream of fractious complaints.

'Hester saw the knife,' Flora said. 'I knew it sounded wrong when I heard her at the dining table. I just didn't put it together until now.'

'Put what together?' He set her gently onto the boat deck.

'She said,' Flora continued, trying to concentrate, '*If a man is ruthless enough to bludgeon another to death with an ashtray, he's hardly likely to baulk at stabbing a woman.* Bunny, no one knew Eloise

316

had been stabbed.'

'Good grief! You mean Hester stabbed Eloise?'

They reached the deck where the detective and the captain had halted.

Hester stood at the aft rail, her features in profile and both elbows hooked over the top, her full skirt billowing in the wind.

Several crewmen held back a group of spectators, forming a wide semi-circle around the woman at the rail.

Max released an anguished, 'Oh, Lord,' as he joined Cynthia, who, white-faced, leaned against his uninjured shoulder.

Hester swivelled her head a quarter turn, raking them all with a dispassionate look, as if she didn't recognize them, or had dismissed them all from her mind as irrelevant.

Then her gaze snagged on Flora and held. 'What's *she* doing here?'

'She's concerned for you, Miss Smith, as we all are.' Hersch eased Flora backwards with an outstretched arm. 'You know that Eloise didn't kill Theodore van Elder, don't you, Hester?' His tone conciliatory, as if persuading a child. 'I may call you Hester, mayn't I?'

'What does it matter? Nothing does.' Hester's low voice competed with the whoosh of the sea beneath the hull, while above them the wind rattled the winch lines.

Hersch took a step closer, but Hester spotted him, stiffened and leaned back, her upper body balanced precariously on the rail. He paused, hands held up in surrender.

'What are you doing, Hester?' Mrs Penry-Jones

demanded, her stick tapping a rhythm on the boards as she drew closer. 'Come away from there at once!'

Hersch frantically signalled her back, but she ignored him.

Hester's head whipped round to face her, eyes narrowed. 'Go away, you awful old dragon. If you hadn't demanded so much of him, he wouldn't have failed.'

'Who wouldn't?' Bunny said at Flora's shoulder.

'I think she means Marlon,' Flora replied.

'Of course I mean Marlon!' Hester shouted. 'He was my husband.'

'You're lying!' Mrs Penry-Jones said, indignant. 'Marlon was never married.'

'Of course,' Flora whispered. 'That would explain it.'

'Not to me, it doesn't,' Bunny said. 'What's she talking about?'

Flora stilled him with a finger to her lips, her head angled into his shoulder. 'Don't you males ever understand affairs of the heart? Listen, I think she'll tell us.'

'We had it all planned,' Hester began, responding to her own inner voice. 'I would take the position as his aunt's companion.' Her world-weary look told Flora that had she known what a trial the exercise would become, she might have chosen to stab the old lady instead. 'Then, once Marlon was accepted back into the family, we would pretend to elope.'

'Ah, now I see,' Bunny said into Flora's hair. 'Parnell was her husband. Sorry, I got him muddled with this Marlon chap.'

'Marlon *was* Parnell. Oh, do listen.' Flora shushed him.

'But Marlon wasn't as clever as you, was he, Hester?' Hersch took half a step towards her, but Hester was sharper than he had anticipated.

'Get away from me!' She scooted backwards until her rear end protruded over the rail, her feet hooked into the metal bars.

'Why don't we discuss this rationally, inside, Hester?' his tone softened.

'No!' Hester screamed. 'You're trying to trick me.'

Captain Gates whispered an instruction to a crewman Flora had to strain to hear. 'Tell the chief engineer to slow all engines.'

The crewman slipped away and Flora looked up at Bunny, who shook his head. 'It won't help if she jumps. We must be doing sixteen knots and it's getting dark.'

Flora winced and swallowed, but kept silent.

'He was weak,' Hester screamed, bringing Flora's attention back to her. 'Eloise convinced him she hadn't killed Theodore. I knew the old woman wouldn't accept that. She would never let him back into the family.'

'What did you do, Hester?' Hersch made no further attempt to close the gap between them, which appeared to reassure her, so she continued to talk.

'I told him that we could at least get the money Eloise took from Theo's safe. It would help us start again back in New York. But I thought she had killed him rather than hand it over.'

319

'Why did you think that?' Hersch asked.

'I hung around Eloise's cabin the morning after he died, and heard that governess say she had heard them arguing.' She cocked her chin in Flora's direction. 'Eloise was the last person to see him alive. I thought she *must* have killed him.'

'Hester.' The detective kept his voice low, almost hypnotic. 'Tell us what happened on Wednesday.'

The ship dipped as a wave ran below the hull, causing Hester to tilt. A collective gasp ran round the small group before Hester regained her balance. She adjusted her grip, though by now the wind had loosened the bun at her neck and her honey-coloured hair streamed behind her.

She looked graceful sitting there, almost calm when she started to speak again.

'When the officer told us all to go inside during the storm, I told Mrs Penry-Jones I was seasick and needed to lie down. Instead, I went to Eloise's stateroom.' A sly smile tugged at her mouth at the memory. 'The silly madam ordered me out. She had no idea who I was and I didn't bother to explain, I just plunged that knife into her chest.' Her gaze clouded, as if she was unsure about the next part of her story. 'I think I did it more than once. She didn't even cry out, just stared at me as she slid to the floor.'

'What did you do then?' Hersch asked.

Hester blinked and shook her head. 'I knew I had to get the knife back to Mrs Penry-Jones jewel case before it was missed, but I could hear her talking to someone through the door. Cynthia probably.

'I could barely stand up in that wind, but I had

320

to get rid of the knife, so I went to the lower deck and hid it in that motor car. I was soaked to the skin by then and couldn't go to the dining room like that or everyone would have noticed. So I went to my cabin and pretended I had been there all the time. When I went back to the motor car for the knife later, those brats were playing in it.' Hester glared at Flora again as if she were solely responsible for her ruined plans. 'I tried to get it from her suite but–'

Flora gasped. 'It was *you* who pushed me down the companionway!'

Hester curled her lip and turned her face away in contempt, but said nothing.

A salt-tinged gust of wind swept the open deck, biting through Flora's coat. She released Bunny's arm and took a hesitant step forwards.

'Flora? What do you think you're doing?' Bunny made a grab for her but missed.

'You can't stay there forever, Hester,' Flora wheedled. 'It's getting dark and you must be cold in that thin dress.'

'Why should you care?' Hester snarled. 'If you hadn't asked all those questions, he–' She bit her lip, inhaling on a choked sob.

'Marlon would still be alive?' Flora finished for her. 'Dr Fletcher killed him, Hester. Not Eloise.'

'I know that – now!' The wind pushed Hester's hair into her face. She took one hand off the rail to brush it back, unbalanced slightly, and for a heart-stopping second, rocked on the rail.

Cynthia gasped and Flora held her breath, but somehow Hester hung on.

'Even if you aren't cold, I am.' Flora held out

her hand, her palm upwards in invitation. 'Now why don't we do what Mr Hersch suggested and talk about this inside?'

Hester's gaze swivelled to meet Flora's, her thin lips quirked into a parody of a smile, like a cat who has spotted a friendly bird. Slowly, her hand lifted so that no more than a foot lay between their outstretched fingers.

Hester's gaze swept the row of spectators before coming to rest on Mrs Penry-Jones.

For a long second, Flora was convinced Hester would take her hand, but then something entered her eyes which made Flora's breath catch. In an instant, she knew what was about to happen, knowing she was helpless to prevent it.

A triumphant smile spread slowly across Hester's face, and without another word, she withdrew her hand, leaned backwards, and floated over the rail.

Mrs Penry-Jones's mouth opened in silent horror.

Hersch groaned in frustration, while Bunny issued a loud curse. Max wrapped his arms around Cynthia, who buried her face in his shoulder.

A low murmur of dismay went up among the watchers, some of whom made sudden, but useless rush towards the rail. A line of crewmen spread out along the deck, bent over the rail and frantically searched the waves below.

Flora's coat flapped around her, buffeted by the rising wind. She stood frozen, her hand dropping nerveless to her side. She swivelled her head to where the captain stood and threw him a pleading look. His brief head shake reiterated what Bunny had already said. They were travelling too fast and it was almost dark. If Hester had managed to survive the fall, there was the shock of the freezing water that would likely stop her heart. By the time the ship manoeuvred around and went back for her, she would most certainly have drowned.

Despite that, Flora hoped they might try.

Chapter 29

At Hersch's instigation, they re-assembled in Mrs Penry-Jones's sitting room; silent and absorbed with their own disturbing thoughts.

The devastation caused by the spilled tea tray had been cleared up; the Korean dagger repositioned on the mantle. A damp area of carpet evidenced a vigorous scrubbing, but otherwise the room looked untouched.

'I saw everything from the upper deck.' Mary Ames bustled into the room and plucked at Flora's sleeve. 'Has the captain ordered we go back to look for Hester?'

'I – I believe so,' Flora stammered, still numb. 'He's ordered a lifeboat lowered, but–' She shook her head, arms wrapped round her midriff as the image of Hester floating away from the rail repeated in her head.

If by some faint chance Hester had survived the fall, did instinct take over? Did she fight to stay afloat, then watch in horror as the stern of the ship sailed steadily away from her?

'Flora?' Bunny's voice came to her as if from a long way off. 'Are you all right?'

She nodded, not trusting herself to speak.

Miss Ames fussed over Mrs Penry-Jones, who ignored her completely. 'At times like this, I feel the tragedies of life can be mitigated by portraying them in art.' She patted her pocket, where the outline of her notebook stood out. 'In this case, literary art.'

'She's going to put Hester's story in a book?' Flora said to Bunny. 'Can you imagine that?'

'It's quite a good plot actually.' Bunny shrugged. 'We all have our own coping strategies.'

'Really? What was Hester's?'

'Maybe she couldn't face the prospect of dying at the end of a rope. It isn't a pleasant way to go.'

'And drowning is?' Flora murmured, not expecting an answer. Her ankle began to ache, which she contemplated using as an excuse to return to her suite. Passengers had been running all over the ship during the last half hour and soon everyone would know what had happened. She didn't want Eddy to find out via shipboard gossip.

'Then this entire fiasco was for nothing?' Mrs Penry-Jones spoke at last. Fat tears carved lines in her face powder, hovered on her upper lip and dropped onto her clasped hands that sat like bundles of bones in her lap. 'Hester deceived me, too.'

'I'm afraid that's true, dear lady.' Hersch spoke with restraint, though Flora imagined he would have liked to say a great deal more had his innate good manners not prevented him.

Max comforted Cynthia, his uninjured arm across her shoulders while he whispered into her hair.

'Max,' Flora asked as something occurred to her. 'Did you see Hester leave Eloise's stateroom after she ... well, you know. Is that why you were on deck in the storm?'

Cynthia lifted her face from his shoulder and stared up into his face. 'Max?'

'I – I saw someone coming out of Eloise's room in a cloak just like the one I bought Cynthia in London.' Max blew air between his pursed lips 'It was obvious they didn't want to be seen, and I thought–'

'That it was me?' Cynthia said, aghast.

'No, I mean maybe I did.' He licked his lips. 'I couldn't be sure. The storm was severe by then and the deck awash. Then the wave hit me, and Mr Harrington dragged me back.'

'You never told me any of this,' Cynthia said.

'How could I? When I woke up in our stateroom an hour later to find out Eloise had been killed, I thought–' He massaged his forehead with his free hand. 'I knew you blamed her for your father's death. My first thought was to protect you. No matter what you had done.'

'Oh, Max.' Cynthia crumpled into his one-armed embrace. 'It *was* my cloak. I lent it to Hester, but I didn't kill Eloise.'

'I know that now,' he whispered. 'I feel terrible for having thought you capable of such a thing. I'm so sorry.'

'Don't be.' Cynthia ran her hand down his jaw. 'I should have insisted you tell me what you were doing outside in that storm, but I didn't want to hear it.'

Max's face paled. 'You thought *I* had done it?'

Cynthia's lips parted, whether to issue a denial or not, Flora couldn't tell. What damage had been done to their marriage with so much doubt she couldn't imagine. They would have to learn to live with it.

'I think we should go,' she whispered to Bunny, who nodded, laced his fingers with hers and drew her to her feet.

Hersch followed them onto the deck, leaving the captain and Officer Martin to do whatever was necessary.

'Well,' Bunny said, when they came to a halt outside Flora's suite. 'That explains how Matilda ended up on the other side of the boat deck. Hester must have undone the straps when she hid the knife.'

'I cannot help feeling that had I linked Dr Fletcher with that land deal earlier, at least two people would still be alive.'

'You cannot be held responsible for that,' Flora said. 'Had Mrs Penry-Jones informed the agency they were all travelling under different names, you would have known what was going on.'

'Instead, she chose to wrap herself in intrigue, convinced she sought justice for her son.'

Flora followed the German's gaze to where small groups of passengers gathered at the rail, necks stretched and talking earnestly among themselves. A knot of sailors clustered round an empty lifeboat support below them on the boat deck.

'Have they found anything?' Flora asked.

'I doubt it,' Bunny sighed. 'But they have to go through the motions.'

'I suppose so.' She bit her lip, sad that two women's lives had been wasted. And for what?

'There's nothing more we can do, so I'll wish you both a good night.' Hersch performed a polite bow and left them, his rhythmic footsteps receding along the deck.

'Well, who would have thought,' Bunny said. 'No one was who they pretended to be. A secret wife, a vengeful mother and a grieving daughter.'

'Everyone can be whom they choose aboard ship. Which is what I said at the beginning.'

'Indeed you did. I shall have to listen to you more closely in future.' He leaned against the door frame, arms folded.

Flora returned his admiring smile and hoped there might be a time in the not too distant future when he could do exactly that.

'In a way it's admirable that Max was prepared to protect his wife to such an extent,' Bunny said.

'I regard it as sinister that Cynthia will always remember her husband believed her capable of murder. With a knife.'

'Hmm. I didn't think of it like that. Is it romantic that Hester's passion for her husband turned her into a killer?'

'I don't think romantic is the right word.' Flora recalled that moment at the top of the companionway, and the vicious shove that had sent her to the bottom. In that second she had felt something inherently evil behind her.

'We arrive in London tomorrow.' Bunny nodded at a pinpoint of light that blinked in the distance. 'That must be the Eddystone Lighthouse.'

'Yes,' Flora sighed, though the prospect of home seemed less attractive than it might have done.

'I expect you're tired, so I'll say goodnight too.' His hand slid down her arm, pausing to squeeze her hand. Something entered his eyes and for a moment she half-expected him to kiss her again, but the moment passed. Instead, he coughed, dropped a light kiss on her cheek and walked away.

Flora watched him go, a hand braced against the doorframe. When he reached the corner, she whispered, 'Goodnight, Ptolemy Harrington.'

'Is that you, Flora?' Eddy's voice sounded from the sitting room.

'Yes, it's me.' She stayed where she was for a moment, staring at the tiny blinking light as the ship carried her closer to home.

Eddy's face appeared round the door jamb. 'C'mon, Flora. This steward they sent to sit with me can't play chess for toffee. I've beaten him three times already. By the way, what was going on down on the boat deck earlier? He wouldn't let me look!'

Day Eight – Saturday

'Have you finished your packing, Eddy?' Flora called to him through his bedroom door.

'I did mine last night.' He wandered into the

sitting room, buckling his belt over a hastily tucked-in shirt. 'Can't wait to see Ozzy this morning. I'll bet he doesn't know about Miss Smith.'

'I imagine his father will have told him. The entire ship must know by now.'

'Oh, bother!' His face fell for a second and then his eyes filled with concern. 'I forgot to ask, how's your ankle?'

'Much better.' She flexed her foot to demonstrate. 'It still aches a little, but that's all. I recovered quicker than I thought.'

'You *are* going to see Mr Harrington again when we get home, aren't you?' He leaned against one of the wicker chairs, fixing her with a speculative stare so like his father's, she looked away, disconcerted. Lord Vaughn was a formidable employer.

'Doesn't that rather depend on what Mr Harrington wants?'

'What about you? What do *you* want?'

Flora paused in the act of transferring her vanity case to the pile of trunks lined up by the door. 'Maybe I should look further than Cleeve Abbey now that you'll be at Marlborough. I could take a position at a school in London, or go to Paris to teach English to French children.' Her heart lifted with new enthusiasm, her voice with it.

'You'll be alone,' Eddy said, despondent. 'Is that what you want?'

'I – I don't know. But whatever I do, I cannot rely on Mr Harrington, or any other man to make my happiness for me.'

'You'll always come home to Cleeve Abbey, though, won't you?'

'Possibly.' A smile tugged at Flora's mouth. Where else could she consider home? 'Now go and say goodbye to Ozzy. We'll be leaving soon.'

A look of abject horror crossed Eddy's face. 'Gosh, yes. I don't even have his address. See you later, then.'

The porter arrived and removed their trunks, after which Flora surveyed the empty suite, bereft now of the items which marked it as having temporarily been hers. Like her hairbrushes on the dresser and her negligee on the end of the bed.

The morning she had found Parnell's body seemed a long time ago now. So much had happened since then. What had Bunny said about stripping the emotion to lessen the impact of the past? She doubted she would be able to do it at Cleeve Abbey; no one at home had ever been willing to discuss Lily Maguire.

What had her mother done that was so reprehensible? Or maybe it was more what had been done to her. Whichever it was, maybe Bunny was right and it was time to find out for once and for all. Too much hurt was caused by secrets, as the Van Elders could attest.

Retrieving her handbag from a chair, Flora stepped onto the promenade deck, where the discordant clamour of mechanical noise combined with the rumble of loaded trolleys across the deck. A line of carriages waited on the quayside for city-bound passengers.

'Someone will be here to meet you, I assume?' Bunny said, coming to her side.

'Lord Vaughn will send a driver, I expect.'

She looked past him to where a group of police officers stood beside a black closed carriage on the quayside beside the gangplank. Bunny followed her gaze to where Gus Crowe and Dr Fletcher emerged from beneath the superstructure, both with shackled hands and flanked by two policemen.

'Mr Crowe has regained his jaunty look,' Bunny said, as a low murmuring went up amongst the crowd waiting to disembark.

'The charges against him have been reduced to theft and assault,' Flora said. 'Oh and they found Max's tie pin and cufflinks hidden in his stateroom as well.'

The doctor kept his head down, his shoulders hunched. Flora could only imagine how he felt now, with the hangman's rope his only future. Did he envy Hester, perhaps, or would he do anything to prolong whatever life he had left?

As the metal door slammed on the windowless Black Maria, she flinched, aware she would never know the answer to that question

'So, what of the future of Flora Maguire, the intrepid detective?' Bunny asked once the carriage had moved off.

'She's retired before reaching her zenith. Too dangerous – and complicated.'

'Hersch told me you were right about that bracelet by the way.'

'Oh?' Flora turned to face him, forcing herself not to flush beneath his steady gaze. 'Did they find it?'

'Amongst Hester's things. Why she took it is a mystery. The inscription would surely only serve as a constant reminder of how it was obtained.'

'I believe there was a more prosaic reason than that. She would most likely have sold it at her first opportunity.'

'You're probably right.'

'Flora!' Eddy called from the end of the deck. 'Papa's carriage is here. They're loading our trunks right now.'

'I'm coming!' Flora replied, her heart doing a small dip of disappointment. She hesitated, studying Bunny from the corner of her eye.

He glanced away and then back again, followed by the straightening of his tie. Was it her imagination, or was he looking for a way to prolong the conversation?

'Goodbye, Bunny Harrington.' She placed her gloved hand in his and shook it firmly. 'If you want any murders solved, I hope I will be the last person you think of.' She tossed her head and with a bright smile, turned on her heel and began to walk away.

Was he going to let her leave just like that? A shipboard friendship destined to shrivel the moment they stepped onto dry land again? In her head she offered a plea to whatever fate organized such things that he would think of a way to stop her.

'Flora!' His voice brought her to a stop. She didn't turn round in case he saw the wide smile that had crept into her face.

He overtook her, then stepped in front of her. 'I cannot let you leave without trying to express a little of what has happened to me during this voyage.'

Flora waited, not daring to hope his feelings may reflect hers, and yet how could she not?

'When I boarded at New York, my every thought was about Matilda, the business I am going to set up in England, and very little else.'

'And now?' Flora's breath caught.

'When you hit your head on the support and were angry, guilty and defensive all at the same time, I haven't been able to think of much else. You've become almost an obsession, Flora.'

'Obsession is a strange word. One most people would prefer to avoid.'

The deck seemed to dip beneath her, but surely not? They were at anchor, weren't they?

'What do you mean?'

'Am I a nice obsession, or do you seek to protect your heart against hurt?' She groaned inwardly. She was gabbling again. Why didn't he stop her?

'Do I possess the ability to hurt your heart, Miss Maguire?' His lop-sided smile appeared slowly. First as a twitch beside his lips and then a full, heart-stopping grin.

He held her gaze and no matter how much she wanted to look away, she could not. 'Yes.'

'In that case, may I call upon you at Cleeve Abbey? I would very much like to see you again. If that's agreeable to you.'

If only he knew how agreeable. She fought down the bubble of excitement that fizzed in her veins. It wouldn't do to appear too eager.

'Will you arrive in your motor car?'

'No. Matilda's engine cannot get much above fifteen miles an hour, whereas a train—' he broke off and coughed again.

She returned his smile, not caring if he arrived by dog cart or had to walk all the way from Surrey. She would meet him halfway if need be. Flora's chest filled with sea air and happiness.

'Although I'm not at all sure about being courted by a man who regards a house with eight bedrooms as a modest residence.'

'You'll get used to it. If I can tolerate a lady with a penchant for investigating murders, it's a small thing to put up with.' He paused and frowned. 'There is of course my mother to consider. She can be an acquired taste.'

'Flora!' Eddy whined. 'We have to go.'

Impulsively, Flora's hand closed on Bunny's upper arm. She pushed herself up on tiptoe and pressed her mouth briefly to his before she turned and ran down the gangplank to where Eddy waited.

She chose not to mention that Ptolemy Harrington would find Riordan Maguire a match for anyone. He could discover that for himself.

The publishers hope that this book has given you enjoyable reading. Large Print Books are especially designed to be as easy to see and hold as possible. If you wish a complete list of our books please ask at your local library or write directly to:

Magna Large Print Books
Magna House, Long Preston,
Skipton, North Yorkshire.
BD23 4ND

This Large Print Book for the partially sighted, who cannot read normal print, is published under the auspices of

THE ULVERSCROFT FOUNDATION